BABY TOOTH AND TANGLED ROOTS

THE TOOTH FAIRY CHRONICLES

BOOK THREE

VICTORIA ROCUS

For Valerie James Rocus, my own little "Peanut." Grammy loves you in any world.

ALSO BY VICTORIA ROCUS

The Tooth Fairy Chronicles

Tooth Decay With A Side Of Fae

Toothaches And Wedding Cakes

Baby Tooth And Tangled Roots

Wisdom Tooth And The Awful Truth

GLOSSARY AND PRONUNCIATION OF ANCIENT OTHERWORLD GAELIC

Am ullmhuchain - (ă oval-hăn) - "preparation time" - morning toiletry/dressing

Athair - (ă-hair) - "father" - when capitalized, used as a formal title

Bairn - (bĕrhn) - "baby"

Beag Tiogair - (Bē-og Tē-găr) - "Little Tiger" - Declan's nickname for Rosie

Cac - (cock) - "shit" – slang word

Cac tarbh - (cock tar-who) - "Bullshit" - slang word

Chabhair - (hŏwt) - "a boon" – ancient Fae custom of awarding a favor or reward

Caladbolg - (Kăl-uv-bŏlg) - an ancient Otherworldly Fae sword with magical powers given to the *"Ridre Dubh"* (Black Knight) of *I Idir* to protect its people and the monarchy; currently in the possession of the reigning Black Knight, Theodore H. Beckett (Myrdynn), the 27th Merlin

Carraig an Bhroin - (kăr-ig ĕn frăwn) - "Rock of Grief" - a treacherous out crop of cliffs overlooking the Gorm Sea;

the land is part of House *Nuada's* holding and is infa-
mously known as being the location of choice for those
Fae wishing to commit a quick suicide

Coinin - (koo-nean) - "rabbit"

Craiceailte - (krŏk-coal-tă) - "crazy"

Crann Bethadh - (Krŏn Bĕ-hĕ) - "Tree of Life" - the royal seat
of The Morrigan, Queen Maeve, built out of a giant, ancient
oak and sometimes referred to as "The Raven's Nest"

Deaglan - (Dĕk-lĕn) - "full of goodness" - the Otherworld
spelling of Declan

Dubnos - (dŏv-nus) - the Fae version of the Underworld

Dun Siorai - (Dune Shear-ē) "Eternal Fortress" - House
Nuada's ancestral home

Eamon - (Ā-mŏ) - "Edward" - the Otherworld spelling and
pronunciation of "Edward"

Fae (Fā) - an ancient Otherworldly fairy folk with
multiple sub-ethnic groups, all whom possess varying
levels of magical skills; most Fae call *I Idir* their home, but
they have been known to live in many kingdoms of the
Otherworld, especially the Avalon and *Asgard,* kingdoms
which share a border with *I Idir*

Fear ceile - (firh kă-lee) - "husband"

Fiodoir Aisling - (fee-a-door ash-ling) - "Dream Weaver" -
a mind-altering, psychoactive plant, similar to the
Mundane world drug marijuana; it produces a relaxed
euphoric state, and is said to aid in the ability to prophe-
size. Banned for general use in *I Idir* and procured only
for spiritual and medical use

Gancanagh - (ghan-kan-ah) - "love talker" - Celtic incubus

Granna - (graw-na) - "ugly"

I Idir - (ē ēdar) "In Between"- the Fae kingdom in the Otherworld ruled by The Morrigan, Queen Maeve, as its monarch.

Lupercalia - (lewper-kā-lee-a) - an ancient Fae festival focused on the fertility cycle

Mac- (mc)- "son of"- a title given to an eldest son and heir of a Ruling House

Mathair - (mă-hair) - "mother" - when capitalized, used as a formal title

Mo Shiorghra - (mō hear-gra) - "My Eternal Love" - a soulmate in magical Fae tradition

Nuada - (new-a-da) - the name of an ancient Celtic king who possessed a silver arm; a major House within I Idir's Ruling Council descended from his bloodline

Pis Talun - (peace tă-lune) - "peanut" - the nickname Rosie and Declan give their unborn baby

Prais - (prās) - an alloy of both copper and zinc, known as brass in the Mundane world; highly toxic to the magical energy and physical well-being of most Fae born individuals

Ros Beag - (rōs bē-og) - "Little Rose" - Declan's love name for Rosie

Seanmhathair - (shin-a-ver) - "grandmother"

Sidhe - (shē) - the term used for the Fae race in Celtic mythology, as well as the forts and mounds they once lived in during ancient times; the *Sidhe* possess higher levels of magical skill, and thus are considered part of Fae higher society

Siobhan - (shiv-awn) - a Celtic female name meaning "gracious gift"; the name of Declan's Mother

Soith - (soyth) - "bitch" - considered a vulgar, slang word for an unpleasant female

Trathnona maith - (traw-no-na-mah) - "Good After-noon/Evening"- a common greeting

Tuatha de Danann - (two-ha de dan-an) "The Shining Ones"- a magical race of ancient, gifted Fae with royal bloodlines. They currently compose *I Idir's* ruling council under the Monarchy of The Morrigan, Queen Maeve

BABY 1

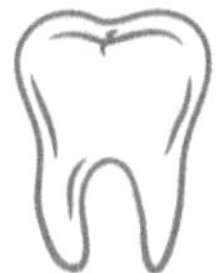

REPEAT PERFORMANCE

IT'S true what they say about newlyweds: they are two burning souls in the heat of love, reveling in the joy of a lifetime of passion and on a path to discovering a deep, heartfelt connection. It's the stuff fairytales are made of. Mostly. We'd been home from our honeymoon fiasco only two days when my amazing, sweetness-to-the-core, cinnamon-roll husband asked me to marry him. Again. I know this sounds incredibly romantic. Truthfully, it wasn't. As I had hoped, my darling *Mo Shiorghra* is over the moon about the prospect of being a Daddy, but it didn't take long for his Tax Man-side to take control. We had barely unpacked our suitcases when the "Numbers Guy" began to list various priorities which needed to occur before the "wee bairn" made his or her appearance. At the top of the list was the tenet that we marry legally according to the laws of Massachusetts and in the eyes of the rest of the Mundane World.

Realistically, he's right about the need for us to have a civil ceremony here in Salem. It had always been part of our plan. We'd already begun telling people that we were engaged before we left for our Otherworld handfasting and had intended to eventually elope after we'd been together for a more reasonable amount of time. However, according to my fated mate's sensibilities, knowledge of Baby Fitzpatrick's impending arrival required we speed up that plan since he's now focused on insurance issues, tax requirements, medical power of attorney, housing logistics, college savings, etc, etc, etc...

He's not wrong, of course. It's the sensible, adult thing to do. However, I'll be the first to admit that after our disastrous, short-lived honeymoon, I was very much anticipating some quality sexy time as a new couple before we became a responsible family of three. I might also have been a bit more enthusiastic about his second proposal had he not chosen to do it while I sat on the edge of our bed eating saltines to ward off the morning sickness that just had begun in earnest here in my 7th week. Nonetheless, I did say yes, assuming we'd do it in a month or two down the line. Not a chance. My Tax Man declared that the best birthday gift I could give him would be to consent_to Mundane-marry him on his 36th birthday, August 4th…less than two weeks away.

That's how I ended up standing here now, queasy and uncomfortable in 2-inch heels, inside a private room of the Hawthorne Hotel in downtown Salem, Massachusetts. In all honesty, Declan did the planning for the entire event: He arranged for the Black Knight himself, Sheriff Ted Beckett, to marry us in a simple civil ceremony, surrounded by our local friends and family. We exchanged plain gold bands, though since the wearing of wedding rings by Fae men is not a traditional Otherworldly custom, I don't expect to see it on the Tax Man's left hand much after today. Mel has graciously agreed to step aside as my Maid of Honor so that my sister, Claire, could enjoy the role this time around. My big sis's joy at being part of the occasion has made my physical discomfort a little easier to endure.

Although the Sheriff did an eloquent job with the ceremony, I am shocked that I don't feel the same heart-pounding, spiritual emotions I did at our handfasting. Perhaps my soul has a stronger connection to my Fae roots than I'd ever realized. During his vows, Declan spoke directly to my mind, declaring his undying love and commitment, not only to me, but to our unborn baby as well; that part got me right in the heart, so I couldn't help but to sniffle, which I suppose everyone in attendance expected.

Originally, we'd agreed to wait to tell people about the baby, hoping to get past the first trimester before making the big announcement. In addition, the Tax Man was so mortified regarding the pineapple incident that he made me solemnly promise not to spill the beans about his "blind stupidity" (his words, not mine). Unfortunately for him, nearly everyone on the planet has a cell phone they're not afraid to use. Videos of Declan's epic fruit throwing moment, along with his public announcement of our big news to an entire planeload of people, went viral, rendering the possibility of keeping these events just between the two of us a "no-go".

Thus, while the waitstaff is serving pre-dinner champagne and *hors d'oeuvres,* I see My Beloved entertaining a group of rugby mates with a demonstration of how he pitched that damn pineapple. Although they're speaking in the Otherworld language, there apparently is no proper word for swingers, so he is forced to use the English vernacular. He feels me watching him and gives me a wink along with mentally sending me several suggestive plans for later this evening.

Despite my reluctance to have yet another party to celebrate our joining, this one that my Tax Man has planned all on his own is proving to be quite a lovely affair. I sip a glass of sparkling cider in lieu of champagne and let myself relax a little and enjoy the moment. Considering everything that has happened during the past eight weeks, I probably should have known better than to let my guard down even for a mere moment. As I turn to speak to Claire about when Declan and I should cut the wedding cake, I catch sight of my highly dysfunctional in-laws, the infamous Lord and Lady *Nuada,* entering the room.

BABY 2

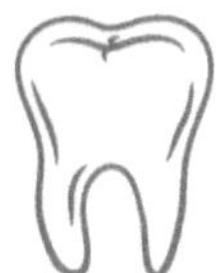

GUESS WHOSE COMING TO DINNER?

I FERVENTLY HOPE the shock regarding the unexpected arrival of my in-laws is not written across my face like a giant circus banner. Claire leans over and whispers, "Who the hell are those people? They look pretty 'hoity-toity,' even for this crowd."

"That's Declan's parents...Lord and Lady *Nuada*," I explain, my voice strained and choked.

"Holy shit...those two are your new in-laws? They look like they both have a stick up their ass. I can tell by the look on your face that you weren't expecting them."

"Nope. I wasn't." I watch as my twice over new husband approaches me. It's obvious that, unlike me, he is not shocked by his parent's appearance at our present celebration. I smile sweetly, but the mental message I send him is anything but pleasant. *"Damn it, Declan! If you knew Lord and Lady Nuada were going to show up here today, why the hell didn't you give me a heads up?"*

Declan kisses my cheek and takes my hand. *"I am sorry, Love. I was made aware of their plans only a few hours ago. I did not wish ta' add ta yar already growin' stress level. 'Tis a vera bad thing for a developing bairn."*

"Listen, Tax Man...I'm not some china doll you need to keep in bubble wrap. I am an adult woman capable of handling my own emotions. You and I need to sit down and talk about how we are going to handle the next nine months!" I am working very hard to keep the smile plastered on my face while wondering if perhaps I'm over-reacting. Declan has every right to have his parents here if that's what he wishes. It's his wedding day as much as it is mine.

"We will talk later, Lass. Soon. Ya' have my word on it."

"Sooner than later, Tax Man," I demand.

I feel a mix of annoyance and angst in his thoughts. *"I have already given ya' my word, Rosalinda. Now, please...I'm askin' ya' ta' tighten yar' shield and trust me."*

His use of Rosalinda hurts my feelings. Declan only calls me by my full given name when he's annoyed with me. If that's how he's going to treat me on our second wedding day, then so be it. Maybe I'll keep my shield up for the whole damn day. Maybe the whole damn week. I take his proffered hand, and we walk together to the entryway to greet his parents.

Lord and Lady *Nuada* make a stunning couple. The *Tuatha De Danann* are an attractive race, and in their expensive designer clothing, Declan's parents exude an air of old money and good breeding. Still, having seen them in the Otherworld where their comfort level is more natural, I can tell they are stiff and uncomfortable in their

Mundane clothing and trappings. Lady *Siobhan* always leans to the pale side of coloring, but today she seems far more translucent than usual, her red lipstick presenting as a dark slash across her face in contrast to her fair skin. His Lordship gives the appearance of a European-born CEO, with his long auburn hair generously sprinkled with gray and braided neatly down his back, a hold out to his Fae traditions. He is decked out in what I guess to be Ferragamo, its long lines better suited for the tall, lithe, Fae build.

Otherworld tradition dictates that the Lord and Lady be greeted with a waist bow from their heir and a curtsy from me. However, as we are in the Mundane World surrounded by a mixed group of Fae and human guests, Declan forgoes the customary bow and offers his *athair* (father) his hand instead. There is a flash of disdain on Lord Callum Fitzpatrick's face, but he returns the handshake nonetheless. Then, Declan kisses his *mathair's* (mother's) cheek. "I am blessed by your presence here today, *Mathair.*"

I wait for Lady *Nuada's* usual scathing remark and am more than a little surprised when it is not forthcoming. She stares at her son as if she is looking right through him and ignores me all together. "Greetings on your birthday, Lord *Mac Nuada.* May the Universe continue to bless you."

Her polite comments throw me entirely off my game, and for a second I almost lose hold of my mental shield. I feel Declan squeeze my hand, and I take a deep breath and refocus. My Tax Man obviously senses that things are very tense. Wishing to change the weird vibes passing between the four of us, he takes control and speaks just loud enough so the people currently nearby can hear. "It is good that you could be here today, Father and Mother. Come...let us get you some refreshments and introduce you to our friends and family."

Following proper Otherworld protocol, he first takes them over to speak with the Black Knight and his wife, the *Banphrionsa* of *I Idir,* Lady Dear Heart. Everyone notes their current situation and refers to each other by their Mundane titles, though I can tell that Lord *Nuada* is impressed by the fact that such distinguished, high-ranking Otherworldly guests are in attendance. My husband then takes his parents over to meet my sister, Claire, and her husband, Scott.

That's when things get really strange. Lord Callum takes one look at my sister and freezes. He mumbles something under his breath in the Old Language, and I recognize the word *Aine,* my mother's Fae name. It takes me a full thirty seconds to realize what's going on here. Though Claire didn't inherit a single Fae magical gene, she physically resembles my deceased mother almost identically. Her willowy figure, high forehead, and hazel green eyes are testaments to the Tooth Fairy Fae she should have been but by the decision of the Universe simply is not; that dubious honor went to me. It was the second child who inherited our mom's magical DNA but whom unfortunately resembles her short, round, human father. My red hair and pale complexion are the only throw backs to my tooth fairy roots. Upon seeing my sister for the first time I only can imagine Lord *Nuada's* deep disappointment that the Universe decreed the second of *Aine's* daughters for his son and not the one who is the spitting image of the only woman Callum Fitz-patrick claims to have ever loved.

BABY 3

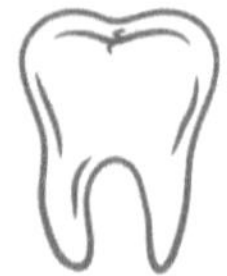

HAVING YOUR CAKE

MY FATHER-IN-LAW FAWNS over my sister *ad nauseam*. I can tell that Claire, as well as her husband, Scott, are uncomfortable with Lord *Nuada's* up close and personal attention. I wait for Declan's *mathair* to say something to him, or at least to poke him in the ribs, but she remains quiet and still, a strange ghost of her usual, caustic self. Even my own hubby appears oblivious to his father's rude behavior, so I'm relieved beyond belief when it's announced that lunch is being served in the adjoining room. I'm hoping now maybe his Lordship will divert his scrutiny elsewhere. In keeping with my general bad luck, this turns out not to be the case.

Had I been thinking clearly, I would have realized that since we'd opted out of a bridal table we undoubtedly would be seated with our immediate families. Each table is arranged with seating for eight; thus, our table is set for Declan and me, my sister and her husband, the Black

Knight and Lady Dear Heart, and, of course, my in-laws. Holding a tight mental shield, I manage to suffer through the soup and salad courses without revealing my growing annoyance over Lord *Nuada's* creepy preoccupation with my sister. I desperately want to say something to my husband, so I'm thrilled when the photographer pulls Declan and me away from our meal to take photos of us with the cake before it's cut and passed out to the guests.

In between poses, I whisper into the Tax Man's ear. "Can't you do something about your father?"

Declan looks confused. "I'm not sure what ya' mean, Lass. All things considered I believe it has gone vera well so far. My *mathair* has been unusually polite, and his Lordship is being more social in a Mundane gathering than I would have expected."

"That's exactly my point, Declan! He's behaving more than just 'social' towards my sister. He's flirting outrageously with her! I can't believe that you don't see it."

He looks at me with a mixture of sympathy and a tad of annoyance. "I know yar' tired, Love. It's been a long day. A long week, in fact. But I think yar' overreacting. My *athair* is just bein' polite to yar' family. He's no longer as comfortable in the Mundane world as he once was, so perhaps his knowledge of human culture is a bit rusty. Besides, yar' sister is half his age. Why would ya' think he'd be flirtin' with a lass so young? In front of my *mathair*, no less?"

I smile sweetly for the camera as we pose, beribboned cake knife in hand, while I growl into his ear: "Because Claire is the spittin' image of my mother, Tax Man! You remember my mother...*Aine*...don't you? Your father's one true love? The one that tragically ended up not being his *Mo Shiorghra?*" It all comes down to that dirty little family secret Lord Callum Fitzpatrick revealed to me before the handfasting ceremony. Although I faithfully told the Tax Man the entire story as soon as I learned of it, it wasn't anything either of us were in a hurry to discuss in the ensuing weeks. Now, the whole ugly tale has come roaring back to haunt us.

My groom turns his head and looks back at the table, finally noticing exactly what I've been seeing; though Lord *Nuada* is relating some humorous anecdote to the entire table, his eyes are resting solely on my sister. Declan turns back to me and says, "Please, Love, can this not wait until..." He never finishes his statement. All the guests have begun tapping on their water glasses, an old-fashioned Mundane custom that requires the bride and groom to immediately stop whatever they're doing and lovingly kiss each other. My Tax Man paints a forced smile on his handsome face and leans over to kiss me.

BABY 4

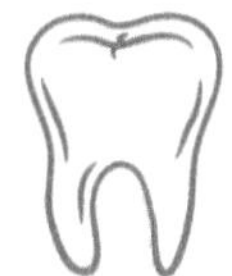

... AND EATING IT TOO.

DURING THE RIDE HOME, I am more than grateful that Declan planned our civil ceremony and small reception for a Saturday afternoon instead of opting for a long, evening affair. I have plans to return to my dental practice the following Monday after the weeks-long hiatus and look forward to being able just to relax and chill at home for the rest of the weekend. Having an afternoon event also allowed us to avoid the music, dancing, and socializing that normally occurs during an evening reception. After watching my poor sister hide in the lady's room for the better part of an hour just to avoid Lord *Nuada's* impertinent behavior, I was no longer in the mood for further wedding festivities.

In addition, my Tax Man and I are not on the best of terms right now. The logical side of my brain, the one with the post graduate degrees and medical background, understands that my hormones undoubtedly are going absolutely crazy as I start my eighth week of pregnancy, but the new bride side of my brain resents that my spanking-brand-new husband is not taking my side and is ignoring my concerns over his father's inappropriate, touchy-feely actions toward my older sister. Plus, I haven't forgotten that he called me Rosalinda. On our frickin' wedding day, no less!

We manage to escape the reception unencumbered, leaving Claire, Scott, Mel, and Duncan to deal with the gifts, the centerpieces, and the rest of the trappings. We needed only to cart home the top layer of our wedding cake to serve, as Mundane tradition mandates, on our first wedding anniversary. My logical brain tells me just to keep my mouth shut about my husband's family. Hormonal me goes ahead and kicks logical me in the ass and proceeds with a conversation I know will not end well. "Do you realize that your parents never even mentioned the baby, Declan? Not even a single word of 'congratulations.' I find that extremely annoying since your father couldn't seem to stop talking about how you needed to 'get busy' and knock me up with your heir."

My *Mo Shiorghra* lets out a long sigh which annoys me even more. "Rosie...Love...I've explained this to ya' already. It is considered vera bad luck in Otherworldly tradition to celebrate a new *bairn* before its gestation has reached the twelve-week mark. I am sure that once we are beyond that point my parents will plan some type of celebration. Until then, 'tis not our way ta' annoy the Universe with excessive 'braggin.' I've already been scolded by ma' *athair* regarding my celebratory behavior on the airplane. I do not wish to hear my *Mo Shiorghra* scold me as well."

I understand what he is saying. The Fae, especially the *Tuatha de Danann,* are extremely superstitious. This, coupled with the fact that I know my Tax Man is especially hinky about our baby due to the tragic stillbirth of his twin brother, works to put the logical side of my brain back into control. Instead of my planned tirade, which definitely would not have led to anything good, I mumble, "Whatever," and turn up the radio's volume.

When we arrive home, I don't wait for the Tax Man to try to carry me over the threshold or any such nonsense. Instead, I scurry inside, drop the box with the top layer of our wedding cake on the kitchen counter, and head upstairs to shower and change my clothes. Alone. I put on a pair of my rattiest pajamas, even though it's only 5:00 in the afternoon, and I turn on the TV. I am surprised but thankful that Declan leaves me alone for a while, and eventually I doze off.

I am awakened by him sitting on the edge of the bed, holding two slices of cake on small plates. It takes my half-asleep brain a few seconds to realize that the pieces look suspiciously like the top layer of our wedding cake. "I thought ya' might like ta' share a piece of our weddin' cake with me, Love. We never got a chance to eat any of it at the party," he says sweetly.

I can't believe what I'm seeing. "Declan, did you cut into the top layer of the cake that I brought home in the white box? The one I put on the kitchen counter?"

"Aye. Where else would I get it from?"

I don't know whether to cry or rage. "That was

supposed to be saved and frozen for our first anniversary celebration! You've gone ahead and ruined the whole damn thing!"

The Tax Man looks at me like I'm making shit up. "'Tis the silliest thing I've ever heard, Lass. Who would want ta' eat a cake that is a year old? It will surely not taste as good as it does now."

"It's a Mundane tradition, Declan," I huff. "But I suppose all Mundane traditions are stupid compared to Otherworldly ones, right? Say it, Tax Man, because I know that's what you're thinking."

My Beloved puts a hand to his forehead. "For the life of me, Lass…I don' understand why ya' are so damn cross with me today. 'Ken ya' not just eat the cake here in this moment and enjoy it?" He pushes the plate toward me.

I take the plate from his hand. "So…what you're saying is…you just want me to 'enjoy' this cake?"

"Aye. If that's at all possible, Rosalinda."

And that was the last straw. Rosalinda, again. "Okay, Tax Man. I'll 'enjoy' this piece of wedding cake that was supposed to be saved for our first anniversary." Then, I scoop up a dollop of buttercream frosting and flick it directly at him. It hits him squarely on the left cheek. I know; it's childish behavior… but it feels good. Real good!

At first, Declan looks shocked, my action catching him off guard. Then, he raises a single eyebrow in that 'way' only he can do. "Did ya' just throw a wad of cake at yar' husband…your Beloved…your Lord?"

He should have known better than to use that Lord crap with me…not when we are sitting here alone in the Mundane world. "You betcha…your high and mighty…

Lordship." Then I whip another glob at him, this one catching him directly in the chest.

I don't expect his neutral expression. "I see, then, how this will be, my Lady," Declan replies. Before I can comment further, he takes an entire handful of cake from his own plate and throws it directly at me, hitting me in the chest as well. The cake and icing slide down into the top of my pajamas.

"I can't believe you just did that," I say. "You...Mr.-Ever-So-Polite-Because-I-Have-A-Stick-Up   -My-Ass... Fitzpatrick."

He shrugs with the barest of smiles on his face. "Ya' should never underestimate ma resolve, Lady *Mac Nuada*. I donna like ta' lose."

Things go south from there, with both of us flinging cake at one another and wrestling about trying to stuff the dessert in places dessert never was meant to go. We laugh so hard that we cry, and when we finally stop, the two of us, along with our bed linens, is a sticky mess. I look across at my Beloved who is covered in buttercream frosting and ask, "And now who do you think is gonna clean this mess up?"

My Tax Man grins, oozing that sexy, boyish charm I fell in love with from day one. "I have a vera good plan, Lass." He leans over and unbuttons my pajama top, then begins to lick up the cake he stuffed down my boobs. Looking towards me he winks and adds, "I told ya' we needed ta' enjoy this cake today, Love." And that's how my day ended much better than it had started.

BABY 5

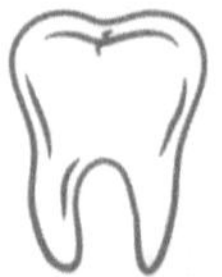

WILL PIZZA NIGHT MAKE IT RIGHT?

THERE'S something to be said for a husband who's a total neat freak and one who is magically gifted to boot. By the time we finish showering, Declan has already cleaned up the cake mess and remade our bed with fresh linens, using magic, of course (I know…don't hate me). We are both surprisingly, or not surprisingly, hungry; the small filet we ate at our wedding luncheon a distant memory. Because it is still my Tax Man's birthday, I encourage him to choose what to order, since my cupboards and fridge are too bare for me to create anything celebratory here at home.

I mentally cross my fingers that Mr. Health Nut doesn't choose the Good Earth Cafe, an organic, new-age spot he enjoys and I detest. To my palate, everything I've ever ordered from there has tasted like tree bark. Thankfully, my *Mo Shiorghra* feels like going big tonight, opting for pizza from Bambolina's, a wood-fired, Neapolitan-style restaurant a few miles away. Me and Baby Fitz-patrick do a happy dance hoping we both don't share any late-night heartburn.

Declan and I spend the rest of our Second Wedding Night cuddling on the sofa and munching pizza between bouts of teenage-style, make-out sessions. Our mountain hideaway handfast night undoubtedly was one for the books, but this night at home on the sofa with my Tax Man is pretty darn special too. I expect that if that damn commercial hadn't aired when it did, and if I hadn't been just that tad bit overly hormonal, we may have ended the night much more agreeably. Instead, a simple 30-second sales pitch for a local assisted-living home facilitated a shitload of niggling, unanswered questions and differences of opinions that landed squarely into our living room.

The short ad showed images of happy senior citizens playing lawn bowling outdoors and enjoying meals in a cheerful, communal dining room. Something in that commercial must have triggered Declan's sense of guilt. He looked at me with a solemn expression and said, "I am vera sorry, Love, for the way ma' *athair* acted today. I am ashamed of his disrespect toward both ma' *mathair* and yar' sister. I 'ken not understand what nonsense has gotten into his head."

I do my best to be sympathetic, though Lord *Nuada* really had pushed my buttons earlier in the day. It also reminds me of our families past shared history, a topic I try not to revisit too often, since its implications keep me up at night. "I know, Sweetie," I reply. "It's not your fault. Your parents are...well...overwhelming. I'm sure we'll figure out how to keep them from…" What I really want to say is "from wrecking our lives," but instead proffer a more diplomatic, "structuring our future."

Declan grabs another slice of pizza and chews silently for a few seconds. He swallows and then adds, "Lord *Nuada* is like a dog with a juicy bone, Lass. Once he's gotten somethin' in his head, 'tis hard to pull it from him. I am worried that now that he has seen yar' sister and knows she's here in the Mundane world, he will find multiple reasons to visit."

I actually hadn't thought beyond today. All I had been able to do was to wish for that damn reception to be over and for Lord and Lady *Nuada* to go back to *I Idir*. But my husband is absolutely right. The Fitzpatrick men are stubborn. Very stubborn. I have first-hand knowledge of that. There's no reason to think Declan's *athair* will give up his obsession with my sister Claire…or his feelings toward my deceased Mother, particularly since he's been carrying them around for so many years. "Can't you speak with him, Declan? You need to remind him that my mother is long dead and that my sister is an entirely different person. Plus, she's fully human, AND married to another man with whom she has two children!"

The Tax Man is drumming his fingers on the arm of the sofa in a musically rhythmic pattern. This is a habit I've noticed he does subconsciously when he's stressed. It's obvious he doesn't want to have this conversation with me. He weighs his words carefully before answering. "What you are asking of me is far' mar' difficult than ya' 'ken imagine, Lass. Callum Fitzpatrick is ma' Liege Lord, and I am his heir. 'Tis a complicated relationship, Love.

Yes, he is ma' athair, ma sire, and when I was a wee boy, we shared many special moments together. But when I came of age, things changed. I took on the mantle of Lord *Mac Nuada* and all of the responsibilities that come with it. 'Tis how the Universe has set ma course."

Suddenly, an ugly, horrible, scary thought crosses my mind. I put a hand on my still flat belly and blurt out exactly what I'm thinking. "Shit! What if this baby is a boy?"

My husband looks at me startled. "Do ya' already know whether the *bairn* is a boy or a girl, Love?"

I make a face. "Of course not! It's still too early. But I'm sure Dr. Brannigan will be able to tell us in a few weeks."

He smiles broadly, then leans over and kisses me. "That will be an exciting day for us, Rosie Lass."

I don't mention that Mel and Claire already told me they want to host a top-notch Gender Reveal party. Bigger issues are afoot. "You're missing the point, Declan. I...would be thrilled if this baby is a boy...but I don't want our son to have to go through that...that awful magical ceremony you were forced to endure that ruined your life for over twenty years!"

The smile on Declan's face that appeared only a moment ago now is gone, replaced with something between a frown and a grimace. "I was not 'forced' to do anything, Rosie. 'T'was somethin' I willingly accepted as part of ma' birthright. 'It eventually led me ta' ya', and I am happier than I can ever remember bein.' I could only hope for such a fortuitous outcome for ma' own first-born son."

The thought of my child suffering through years of

loneliness like the Tax Man makes me queasy. I've always dreamed of having a real family...not the pseudo-hierarchy nonsense of the Fae Ruling Class. "Declan...what about the mistake the Universe made with our parents? Three people ended up with sad and disillusioned lives just so we could be together. Does that seem right to you? Is that really what you want for your own child?"

Now my Tax Man just looks sad, and I feel guilty for making him feel this way, not only on his birthday, but on our Second Wedding Day as well. I secretly want him to tell me that he agrees with me one hundred percent and that everything will be okay. However, I am not at all surprised when he shrugs his shoulders and says, "I canna' change who I am, Lass, nor what responsibilities the Universe has destined for me. That the future will be as it is meant to be is all I 'ken promise ya."

BABY 6

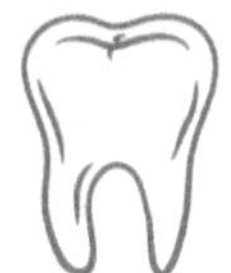

A NEW DAY

NEITHER THE TAX Man nor I sleep very well that night. I feel him tossing and turning for several hours. My brain refuses to shut down, reviewing the various "what ifs" and "might happens" until the early morning hours. I hear Declan get up while it's still dark. When I check my phone, the time is 5:20 AM, one hour earlier than the time for his usual run. I feel terrible about all of the fussing that occurred, and I am pretty sure that a good portion of the blame rests on me. Yes...my husband's father acted a nuisance. And yes...I have countless concerns over how Declan's role in the Otherworld's Ruling Class will affect our family's future. Nonetheless, I am usually more level-headed and open-minded than my behavior yesterday indicates, and I promise myself that I will think before I act and speak, especially while on this hormonal roller coaster ride.

However, this doesn't mean I've changed my mind

about what I will or will not allow to happen to any child born to Declan and me. I still feel passionately that the ridiculous coming of age ceremony dictated by *I Idir's* Ruling Council is barbaric and cruel and counter to the usual Fae philosophy of individual freedom. However, this is a bridge that needn't be crossed anytime in the near future and only matters if we have male children. Fourteen years is a long time, and a lot can happen between now and then. The Morrigan slowly has been trying to pull her people into a more modern-age way of thinking, and it is my hope that Otherworld law eventually will do away with some of the nonsense it's held on to for far too long.

I decide to do my best to act charming and sweet today no matter how icky I might feel. Rising earlier than normal, I shower and braid my hair in the complicated Fae style that I know my husband finds especially fetching. (Though I secretly believe he likes taking it all down even more than he enjoys seeing it on me.) I pull out my rose print blouse with the sweetheart neckline that I wore during one of my earliest meetings with the Tax Man, knowing full well he'd later confessed that this particular article of clothing made him want to ravish me on the spot.

When my husband finally walks through the kitchen door, after a longer than normal morning run, I am waiting for him. He looks startled to see me since I am not an early riser unless required to be, and he's perhaps a tad leery of the mood in which he might find me. "Good morning, My Love," he says. "'Tis a surprise to see ya' up so early and lookin' like the goddess Herself. To what do I owe the pleasure?"

"No special reason other than to wish my beloved *Mo Shiorghra* a beautiful Sunday morning," I say sweetly.

The Tax Man eyes me somewhat suspiciously. I suppose I can't blame him. I was pretty much a she-wolf a mere twelve hours earlier. "Look, I know I was overly harsh yesterday, and I feel badly about my…negative attitude. I realize you went to a lot of trouble to make our Mundane wedding a lovely event. Plus, it was your birthday, and I didn't act very lovingly toward you. I'm sorry if I played a part in spoiling the day."

"There's no way ya' could spoil anything far' me, Lass. Not ever." He steps forward to embrace me but then realizes he stinks to high heaven. One cannot run for two hours without working up a good sweat. "Ya'll have ta' take a rain check, Love. I'm afraid I am not vera huggable right now."

"Oh…I'm all in for rainchecks Tax Man. There's not a chance in *Dubnos* (hell) I'd let you forget about any of your…rainchecks."

This comment causes him to laugh out loud, and the sound of it makes my heart swell. "I will be mar' than happy ta' make good on it, Lass," Declan says. "Now, how 'bout I go and take a quick shower and then I would vera much like ta' take ma 'new bride out far' Sunday breakfast, if ya' think yar' stomach is up far' it?"

"That sounds lovely, Sweetie. I'm actually not feeling half bad this morning. I was also hoping you and I could stop at the market to pick up some fresh produce and meat. Our cupboards are completely bare."

My husband stops on the stairs and turns around to ask, "Are ya' talkin' about goin' ta' the place I took ya' that other Sunday?"

"Yes. Steve's Quality Market. I don't buy my meat anywhere else," I say. A tingle runs through me remembering the last time we went there. It was a *muy caliente* (very hot) memory. I wonder if my hubby remembers it the same way I do.

"Da ya' think Jimmy the butcher will be there today?" the Tax Man asks.

"I would guess so. He usually works on Sundays."

"What about the butcher's son?" he queries.

This is a loaded question. I can just tell. "I don't know, Sweetie. I've never met him. Why do you ask?" I know damn well why he's asking me this, but I'd like to see where the Tax Man is heading with his line of questioning.

He smiles at me. "No reason. Just curious." Then he turns back and heads upstairs to take his shower, whistling some Otherworld tune under his breath.

BABY 7

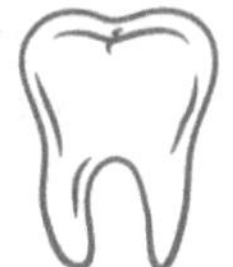

SHOPPER'S RHUMBA- THE SEQUEL

THE TAX MAN comes bounding down the stairs like a man on a mission. What that mission entails is lost on me, but whatever it is, he's dressed to the nines for it. Wearing a pair of linen dress pants and a crisply pressed dress shirt (obviously tailor-made because it fits his longer, Fae torso and arms perfectly) he strolls toward me while putting a watch on his wrist that I think cost more than my car. He is a mouth-watering sight, and suddenly I forget all about breakfast and shopping. I'd much rather stay home and rumple that dress shirt. I also wonder what the hell Rosie Parker ever did in the Universe's "good works category" that earned her a life-time supply of the Tax Man. It's mind-blowing.

"Are ya' ready to go, Lass?" he asks.

I look down at the cotton skirt and sandals I'm wear-ing. "I thought I was, but after one look at you I'm wondering if I should go back upstairs and put on a dress…or something a little nicer."

He leans over and kisses me. "Don't go changin' a thing, Love. Ya' look entirely too fetchin' already. Anything mar' and we'll never leave the house. Plus, ya' know perfectly well that yar' wearin' ma' favorite blouse. I look forward ta' enjoyin' the grand view all mornin'."

"You look exceptionally…yummy yourself, Sweetie. Did our plans change? I thought we were just going out for breakfast and to the market."

"Aye. That is still the plan. I thought I shud' look like a proper husband ta' ya' since we may run in ta' yar'… acquaintances," Declan explains.

I note that he's wearing the wedding band from our ceremony yesterday. Yes indeed. The Tax Man is pulling out all the stops this morning. I'm beginning to understand what's going on here, but as I've resolved to be sweet and charming all day long, I don't say a word about his attempt to show off.

We select a cute little cafe near the house for breakfast. People stare at us, throwing side-way glances when they think we're not looking. Okay, not people, women. Women are looking. And they assuredly are not looking at me, unless it is to ask themselves "How was SHE able to land HIM?" I suppose I can't blame them. I had the same exact thought myself twenty minutes earlier. My Tax Man is a hottie. This is something I'll just have to get used to. *Eat your hearts out, bitches. He's all mine.*

Declan stays true to his health-conscious routine and orders steel-cut oats with soy milk and fruit with a side of whole-grain avocado toast. He apologizes for his multiple choices by saying he's extra hungry today. I suppose this would be a feast to someone who ordinarily only drinks grass smoothies on most mornings. His foodie wife, on the other hand, orders blueberry pancakes. A whole stack of them, with a side order of crisp bacon. I can just hear all of the tisking going on inside my head from the female observers around us.

We keep our conversation light; we don't talk about babies, or in-laws, or Otherworldly responsibilities. I chat excitedly about returning to my practice, and Declan tells me how his rugby team has fared without him these past few weeks and that they need to replace their Openside Flanker because their current one is moving to Hong Kong for business. In essence, our breakfast time is the calm before the storm.

Declan drives to Steve's Quality Market without the aid of his GPS, obviously recalling its location. The parking lot is empty since it is still fairly early on a Sunday morning. I don't see Stella the cashier at her usual post by the door, and I am a little disappointed as I know she'd be thrilled to hear the news regarding our nuptials. The Tax Man pulls out a cart for me, and we hit the produce section. He picks up two good sized cantaloupes and grins at me, and I know he is recalling our first trip here together. I, on the other hand, just want to get the shopping done as quickly as possible and return home so that I can wrinkle up my husband's expensive, tailored shirt.

I reach into my purse for my list but then realize I've

left it in the car. "Shit. I left my grocery list on the car's console. Can you hand me the keys so I can retrieve it?" I ask.

"I'll get it far' ya', Love. Ya' said it was on the console?"

"Yes, Sweetie. It's in the cup holder. Thanks." Declan heads to the parking lot, and I push the cart toward the meat counter hoping that my butcher friend, Freddy, is working today, as he's another one with whom I definitely want to share my good news. It appears he's not, as a young man with longish, dark hair is placing a stack of pork chops into the case, showing off an arm full of ink. He looks up and smiles at me. He's no slouch in the looks category, if in a dark, bad boy kind of way. "What can I get for you, Beautiful?" he asks.

"Is Freddy here today by any chance?"

"'Fraid not. Pops is taking a few weeks off, but I'd be more than happy to help you, Bella Mia," the man answers. "The name's James Carlisi, but my friends call me Jimmy."

Realization dawns on me. This is Freddy's son. The one who was getting out of prison. The one Freddy the Matchmaker wanted to fix me up with. "You're Freddy's son, aren't you? Your father spoke often about you. I'm his friend, Rosie."

Jimmy puts his elbows on the counter and gives me the head to toe once over. "Well, he sure didn't mention you, Beautiful. I would've definitely been more excited about this job if I'd known my Pops had customers that look like you." He gives me a boyish grin and winks at me just as my husband returns with my grocery list. I don't need to turn around to know *Mac Nuada* is pissed. I can feel the hostile energy rolling off of him.

Declan hands me the slip of paper without breaking eye contact with Jimmy. "Here is yar' list, Love. Is yar' friend workin' today?"

I put my arm through the Tax Man's. "Freddy's on vacation, Declan. This is his son...Jimmy." I don't mean for my voice to come out squeaky, but I can tell my *Mo Shiorghra* is feeling more than a little...possessive, and this encounter has the type of vibe that suggests things could go south very quickly.

"Aye, the butcher's son. I see yar' done servin' yar' time then?" my husband asks.

It's a very rude thing to say, and I cringe while also squeezing his arm. Hard. Jimmy makes a face at what obviously was meant as an insult. "You got me at a disadvantage, Mick. You seem to know more 'bout me than I know 'bout you."

Before Declan can say anything more, I jump in. "Jimmy, this is my husband, Declan Fitzpatrick. We just got married yesterday. I was hoping your father might be here today. I wanted to give him the good news in person."

The butcher eyes the Tax Man. I can guess what he's thinking. My husband is not a small man, and there's no doubt he's in great shape. Jimmy isn't stupid. He smiles blandly and shakes his head. "Well...isn't that wonderful news, though I'm rather surprised that you'd want to spend your honeymoon out and about doin' the grocery shopping, 'Dick-land'...married to a babe like Rosie here."

Jimmy mispronounces my husband's name, making it sound like a vulgarity.

I feel Lord *Mac Nuada* tense up next to me as he tries to step forward, but I push myself in front of him. "I'd like two of those pork chops, Jimmy. Oh…and 2 small filets as well."

Freddy's son gives my husband a look before turning around to prepare my order. The Tax Man has his mouth pressed into a thin line. I hold my breath the entire time until we finish our shopping, while Declan plays the role of Silent Sam.

When we get to the car I say, "There was no need to be defensive, Sweetie. Or so rude. The man was just trying to be…friendly."

He gives me one of his annoyed, cranky Declan looks but doesn't respond. There's no use in making matters worse, so I keep my mouth shut during the ride home. We carry the groceries into the kitchen, but before I can put anything away my husband scoops me up and carries me directly upstairs and to our bed. Putting me down, he stands at the side and says, "I plan on thoroughly ravagin' ya', Mrs. Fitzpatrick. If yar' still angry with me and ya' don' wish ta' be ravaged, then ya' must speak up now."

"I'm not angry with you, Declan," I say.

"'Tis not an answer, Lass. Either it's a yes ta' ravagin' or a no."

I might be a tad annoyed, but I'm sure as hell not crazy. Who in their right mind would ever say "no" to being ravaged by their hottie of a husband? "I'm saying positively 'yes' to being ravaged, Mr. Fitzpatrick."

"Excellent choice, Mrs. Fitzpatrick." He grins and begins to unbutton his shirt.

"Wait," I say. "Can you leave the shirt on?" He looks at me quizzically. "I've been dying to rumple that nicely pressed shirt all morning," I murmur, as I grab his hand and pull him onto the bed. "You can let the ravagin' begin now, Tax Man."

BABY 8

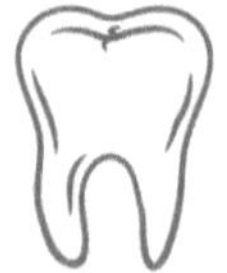

KNIGHTY NIGHT

I AM THRILLED to be back at my dental practice. I've truly missed my young patients, along with sharing my days with Mel, as well as the camaraderie of my devoted staff. Everyone has been super supportive of Declan and me and the new addition to our family. However, I'm not going to lie; I did not anticipate just how exhausted I'd be by the end of each day. In the past, no matter how long or busy of a day I had, I faithfully went home and prepared myself dinner. I never was one to fall into the bad habit of picking up questionable fast food on my way home. Nonetheless, between the bouts of morning sickness that aren't limiting themselves just to mornings and the albatross of early pregnancy fatigue, I find myself falling onto the sofa as soon as I open the door. I have no idea how I will ever manage my nightly Tooth Fairy duties when I am expected to return to them in another week or two.

My husband suggests that perhaps he could use his

Ruling Class influence to get me excused from my birthright commitment to *I Idir*. I flatly refuse the offer, which I think secretly relieves my Tax Man who solemnly believes in upholding the Otherworldly philosophy of service to the Kingdom and not shirking one's responsibilities, even when they are difficult to bear. How can I look down upon the elitism of the Ruling Council and then practice it myself when the going gets tough? I may be the *Mo Shiorghra* to House *Nuada's* heir, but I'll be damned if I'll turn into one of those pampered pet wives who uses her position to sit on her ass and not help her own people.

This philosophy sounds great in theory, but as I sit on my sofa picking at the remnants of my Chicken Egg Foo Young with eyes at half mast, a call to service is the last thing I desire. Then, the doorbell rings.

I'm not looking forward to this particular visitor, because I soon learn it is not someone who typically is the harbinger of good news. Fae protocol requires Otherworldly guests who are not family to ask for specific permission to enter one's home. Declan offers to answer the door. From his expression and quick response, I can tell he already knows who's there and that he would rather I stay put.

The Black Knight's voice is highly recognizable, as its timbre is much lower than my husband's. Actually, it's lower than most Fae men. I have mixed feelings regarding *I Idir's* intimidating judicial leader who also happens to be my husband's superior. There's no denying that the 27th Merlin is the Queen's right hand man and is absolutely devoted to the people of I Idir. Despite growing up unaware of his heritage, the Black Knight is surprisingly loyal and staunchly committed to the Otherworld cause over that of the Mundane world, even while staying balanced and responsible in his role as Sheriff of Essex County. Despite his devastating good looks and easy charm, I sense a backbone of steel and an air of ruthlessness in the man that can be frightening. As both the Black Knight of *I Idir* and the Sheriff of Essex County, Ted Beckett always gets his way…no matter the cost.

Declan gives the man permission to enter our home, and the two of them greet each other with general chit-chat that includes the topic of how I am feeling. While my husband purposely lowers his voice, I still can hear him say the words "vera cranky" to which the Sheriff answers, "I get it, Fitz. Those first few months are a headache. It's like the woman you love moved out, and some monstrous fiend took her place."

It's annoying to be discussed within hearing distance, and I say just that. Loudly. "You know that I can hear both of you perfectly fine, right? I suggest, gentlemen, that you come into the parlor so I can join the conversation."

The Black Knight follows my husband into the room. Declan looks a bit sheepish about being caught gossiping about me and quickly asks if I want him to warm up my herbal tea. I start to stand up to greet my guest according to proper protocol, but the Knight waves me down.

"No need to get up, Lady *Mac Nuada*. I'm familiar with the fatigue that accompanies the first trimester. My own Lady slept away most of those early days when she was expecting our Mairead."

I gladly accept his offer to stay seated. I really am

THAT tired. "Please sit down. Make yourself comfortable. Can we offer you some refreshment, Lord Merlin?" I ask.

He takes a seat in the arm chair across from the sofa. "Please don't fuss, dear Lady. I actually came to speak to you…and I hope you'll just call me 'Ted.' "

Not in a million years would I ever feel comfortable calling the Black Knight of *I Idir*, son of the reigning Merlin, by his first name. I skip it all together and ask, "Me? I can't imagine what I'd be able to help you with."

He smiles, and somehow, I know I'm going to be swallowed up into something of which I do not want to be part. "I thought we might talk about the agreement we made before your handfasting, Lady *Mac Nuada*. You do remember that, don't you?"

BABY 9

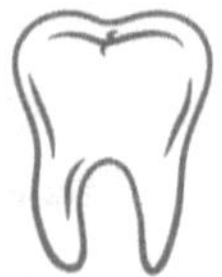

MAKE ME AN OFFER

I KNOW exactly what the Black Knight is getting at. He's referring to the night of my Bachelorette Party. The night I was arrested at a dive bar hosting a male strip revue that also was offering, unbeknownst to me, more than just dancing. At the time, I'd frantically brokered a deal with the Black Knight hoping that I'd be able to keep knowledge of my bad choices from my Tax Man. I brokered the arrangement before I knew Declan had followed me to the bar and already knew about everything that had gone on. The Black Knight was completely aware of all of this, thus rendering his acceptance of my offer something he'd done in bad faith.

As of yet, I don't know what this man wants from me, but I'm already put-off by his bad taste and arrogance in mentioning that bogus deal he fully knew I made under duress and ignorant of all the facts. However, my Mama didn't raise an idiot. No matter how big of a jerk he might be, Ted Beckett is still the Black Knight of *I Idir* and a guest in my home. I know my Tax Man wholly respects him and considers him a close, personal friend. Even though I am, to quote my husband, "vera cranky" in my new roles as expectant mother and Lady *Mac Nuada*, I measure my words carefully. Smiling sweetly, I say, "Of course I remember our agreement, your Lordship. What an amusing evening that must have been for you and my husband. I'm glad I was able to provide you with such merriment at my personal expense."

I expect to receive a mental poke from my husband or at least a dirty look. Instead, he and the Black Knight look at each other and burst out laughing, which, of course, annoys me even more. "Maybe I should put on a clown suit since you both find me so amusing," I exclaim as I stand up to leave. "Suddenly I'm feeling unwell; if you'll both excuse me."

Both men quickly rise as well, and, upon seeing my face, my husband isn't laughing anymore. "Please, Dr. Fitzpatrick...I seriously didn't mean to insult or upset you," the Black Knight says. "Fitz here said his Lady was not to be underestimated and that you wouldn't react well to me reminding you of 'our little deal,' but I couldn't resist having a bit of fun. I actually thought it would help break the 'protocol ice' between us. *I Idir* truly is in need of your service, Lady *Mac Nuada*. Please, at least let me explain why I've come."

"This is important, Lass," the Tax Man adds. "All I ask is that ya' hear the man out. Then ya' 'ken decide how ya' wish ta' proceed. I respect that ya' are yar' own person. 'Tis one of the things I love most about ya'. Please know that I will fully support whatever decision ya' make."

I'm still pissed about being laughed at, but I remind myself that these two men have more history together than Declan and I do, and I need to remember that I'm actually the new person in his life. Plus, I'm just a tad curious about what *I Idir* possibly could want from a tooth fairy, one with limited magical skill despite her new Ladyship title. I sit back down, and the Tax Man takes my hand in his. "Apology accepted, Sir Knight. Now, what is it you think I can provide the Kingdom?"

"First, it would make me feel much better if, when we're alone like this and not in a formal, protocol setting, you would agree to call me 'Ted' or 'Beck.' That's what the members of my intelligence teams call me, and I'm hoping to persuade you to be part of that group."

When I register what he's just said, I think this guy must be completely out of his mind! I know nothing about intelligence work, and I absolutely don't see myself as a spy sort. "I'm honored you think so highly of my abilities...Ted." His name sticks on my tongue. The man controls *Caladbolg*...the enforcer sword of the Otherworld. Calling him "Ted" just seems...well...wrong. "But I'm a dentist. And a simple tooth fairy. My husband can attest to the fact that my magical skills are extremely limited. I'm not sure in what capacity I could offer your team any help in the field of intelligence."

"I need someone smart, logical, fearless, and, most importantly, loyal to the Otherworld cause," the Knight says. "I consider myself a good judge of character, and your recent interactions with Erik Ashton and the Chechens stand as testimony that you are endowed with all of these characteristics. The fact that the Chechens were able to infiltrate the Tooth Fairy Corps as easily as they did is proof that we need intelligence liaisons in every branch of Fae business here in the Mundane World. We need to catch these types of security breaches before they get to the point they did with the Chechens and the tooth fairies."

I agree with the Black Knight's thought process. Knowing the terrorists were able to get to Erik so easily proves the need for tighter security; however, I'm not sure how I can do that as a lowly Cadet. "What you're saying makes perfect sense, and I agree wholeheartedly about the need for tighter security in these difficult times, but I don't have much access to the goings-on within my Corps division," I remind him.

"As a Cadet...no," he says, "but as a Captain you would."

Now the man is talking pure nonsense. "I'm sorry... 'Ted,' but one does not jump from Cadet to Captain overnight. No one in their right mind would believe I was capable of making such a giant leap, not with my limited magical expertise or lackluster performance reviews. Everyone will assume my 'fast track' is due solely to my recent handfast to House *Nuada's* heir, and it will cause all of my fellow tooth fairies to resent and distrust me. That's neither a good nor logical technique to get inside information."

Declan and the Black Knight look at each other. "I told

ya' she is vera, vera smart, Beck," my husband brags. "My lovely Lady always sees things other people miss."

"Beck" gives me his devastating, dimpled smile that never puts my mind at ease. "You are absolutely correct, dear Lady. That's why Her Majesty and I have come up with a perfect plan to make your promotion to Captain a completely logical and reasonable conclusion."

BABY 10

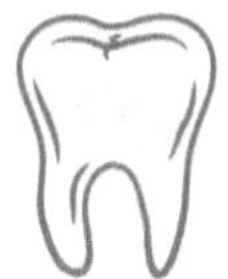

ROSIE THE HERO

MUNDANE OR OTHERWORLD. It doesn't really matter. Politics are politics no matter what dimension one calls home, and in my mind, the whole concept is nothing more than a three-ring shit show. Despite its Ren Faire culture, its adherence to centuries-old traditions, and the reality that its entire population is magically gifted, hanging onto one's governing power is just as tricky in the Otherworld as it is in the Mundane. The fact that The Morrigan has managed to sit on the throne of *I Idir* for over six hundred years is a testament to just how adept she is at playing the game. Our Queen Maeve is definitely a badass, and though I highly respect her genuine commitment to our people, she scares the freaking bejesus out of me.

Knowing that she's behind a plan to place me as a spy in the Tooth Fairy Corps doesn't leave me with the option to bow out gracefully. Having Her Majesty take notice of me among the vast population of *I Idir* is remarkable. Having her remember me for the wrong reasons would be a nightmare. Adding the Black Knight into this royal mix, who is no slouch in the used-to-getting-his-own-way department, makes this an offer I can't refuse.

Similar to what goes on in the Mundane world, the people of *I Idir* don't always learn the absolute truth about what their Queen is doing or the things in which she is involved. The Chechen incident and infiltration of the Tooth Fairy Corps by Mundane terrorists bent on Other-world access was information conveniently withheld from my fellow *Idirians*. Only a handful of insiders knew exactly what had gone down in Salem, MA. Thus, my previously unknown role in the fiasco has become the perfect cover for my unrealistic promotion from Cadet to Captain. The plan is to award me the Kingdom's Medal of Valor for my service in apprehending the traitorous Erik Ashton, a story which will be adapted and spun to include only the details The Morrigan and her Head of Security want revealed. In gratitude, Her Majesty will promote me to the rank of Captain, with no mention of the intelligence work I am supposed to carry out.

Although the Black Knight presents this opportunity to me as a choice, anyone with half a brain knows perfectly well that turning it down is not an option. Therefore, I agree to this new challenge as I'm sure all of the involved parties knew I would, and I accept an invitation to the awards ceremony in *I Idir* to take place at the beginning of September.

Although my husband restrains his exuberance regarding this turn of events, I know secretly he is doing the dance of joy. My being part of the intelligence community means that my Tax Man will no longer have to keep any part of his spy jobs a secret from me. Also, the Medal of Valor presented to me as Lady *Mac Nuada* would be a boon to his House's reputation and was sure to please his Lordship father. Most importantly, though, my promotion to Captain means a cushy, desk job for my pregnant self in lieu of household tooth retrievals, something that makes the New Daddy happily relieved, and if I'm being perfectly honest, a blessing for my exhausted self. Proper protocol requires a quick "seal to The Throne's deal," and thus with my signature on the formal document, along with a wax impression of Her Majesty's profile and a boat-load of bullshit compliments, I find myself the newest member of *I Idir's* intelligence network.

BABY 11

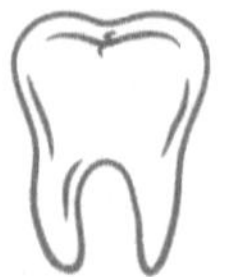

PICTURE THIS

THE TAX MAN squeezes my hand as we currently sit in Dr. Robyn Brannigan's Mundane world office. The Fae physician officially confirmed my pregnancy shortly after Declan and I returned from our honeymoon disaster and had offered to pop in on me at home from time to time to monitor my care. As generous as that offer was, I wanted to experience all of the regular, Mundane trappings of my nine-month adventure, including monthly visits to the OB's office where I could sit and chat with other expectant mommies.

I can tell my *Mo Shiorghra* is nervous by the way the fingers of his right hand run imaginary scales on his thigh. I expect at today's appointment the Doc probably will do an early ultrasound to determine whether I'm having more than one baby. Twins run in my family. My sister, Claire, has a set of infant twin boys. The odds of having twins grow higher as a woman ages, and at 33 years old, I'm right there in that sweet spot. It's a possibility I've considered, but for reasons I can't explain, I think there's only one baby in there. Though he hasn't said a word on the subject, given his personal history, I'm pretty sure Declan secretly is hoping we're expecting a single child. Despite my efforts to talk openly about the trauma of his birth and the tragic death of his twin brother, it's a subject he absolutely will not discuss. I don't want to have his twin angst hanging over us for an entire nine months, but the choice is not up to me. The Universe already has made its decision.

Sitting anxiously like this in Dr. Brannigan's waiting room, I philosophize on how frustrating it is to be kept waiting beyond one's scheduled appointment time. I make a mental note to discuss with Mel on Monday a system that will shorten the wait time for my own young patients. The Tax Man already has played an entire imaginary piano concerto…twice…on his thigh, and I can see that his typical patience is wearing thin. He leans over and whispers, "Does Robyn know how long we have been waitin' ta' see him? 'Tis not like him ta' be so…unconcerned regardin' other people's time."

"I thought we both decided we didn't want any special treatment? Apparently, this is how it is with obstetricians. Dr. Brannigan obviously is in high demand," I explain.

"I am beginnin' ta' rethink that decision, Lass. I 'ken not see waitin' this long every month," he grumbles.

"Sweetie, you don't have to come to every appointment. I just figured you would want to be here for this initial one with the sonogram. But I'm perfectly fine coming by myself in the future."

Declan looks at me with the type of horrified expression one would expect to see if I had asked him to ride a llama to Hades and back. Blindfolded. "It is ma' fatherly duty to be with ya' evera' step of the way, Love. And if it means spendin' ma' afternoons watchin' this home and garden television nonsense instead of seein' ta'' ma' clients, then 'tis what I must do."

I momentarily think he's joking, but I know full well what a Declan stubborn face looks like, and it's exactly the same as the one currently painted on his handsome features. I consider what it will be like to have my husband as my constant, scrutinizing shadow for the next seven months and involuntarily shudder, to which he quickly responds, "Are ya' cold, Lass? Da ya' need me ta' get ya' a sweater or jacket?"

I cannot begin to express my relief when the nurse steps into the waiting room, obviating the need for me to explain the truth behind my 'shudder.' "Mrs. Fitzpatrick?" she calls.

Nurse Amy shows us to an exam room where we hurry up and wait some more until she finally returns. By this time, my Tax Man is about ready to crawl out of his skin at the lack of activity, and I'm close to wetting myself as I try to hold in the 32 ounces of water the staff had me drink an hour and a half ago. Nurse Amy is full of cheerful smiles and positive vibes. "Doctor has ordered an ultrasound for you, Mrs. Fitzpatrick. I'm going to have you lie right up here on this table and get you all ready. Dr. Brannigan should be in shortly. He'll be doing the procedure himself."

I get up to follow her directions and immediately

Declan jumps to help me. The nurse smiles and asks him, "First baby?"

"Aye," he says, both beaming and blushing.

"New daddies are the best," she says, helping me lower the waistband of my pants and pull up my shirt to expose my whiter than rice, flabby tummy. Nurse Amy gets me set up and turns to leave but not before sticking a gummed label to Declan's perfectly pressed, white dress shirt that reads "VID -Very Important Daddy."

I see him cringe. The Tax Man is extremely fussy about his clothes, and I have no doubt his shirt is some ridiculously expensive, custom-made piece which now will have glue residue stuck to it. Ever charming, he smiles politely and thanks Nurse Amy, though I hear him swearing in Gaelic in my head.

Finally, Robyn Brannigan steps into the room with my chart in his hand. At this point, I have to pee so badly that I hope the two men don't plan on a long Otherworldy catch-up session. The doctor notes the sticker on my husband's shirt and laughs. "I see Amy has gotten to you, Fitz. She does love those Daddy stickers." Then, being the professional he is, he turns all his attention to me. "How are we feeling, Dr. Parker? Any spotting or cramping?"

"Nope," I answer. "Everything's been going fine."

"Good to hear. Now, let's get a look at how things are coming along, shall we? This is going to feel cold," he adds, as he squeezes gel onto my abdomen. "Today, we're primarily looking to see if by chance this is a multiple pregnancy. It's too early to determine sex yet, though I'm sure his Lordship will want us to be on top of that."

I know the doctor is referring to my father-in-law and

his anticipation of another heir for House *Nuada.* I don't meet my husband's eye. I am in no hurry to discover our baby's gender. Truthfully, we haven't discussed that topic since the night of our Mundane wedding. The cold gel combined with the pressure the Doc is placing on me down below forces me to bite my lip and hold my breath so I don't accidentally piddle my pants. He runs the transducer over my skin, and I can see the image on the screen next to me. I can't help breathing a sigh of relief. It's a single baby. No twins. I look over at Declan and hold up one finger. The look of pure, genuine relief on his face almost breaks my heart.

BABY 12

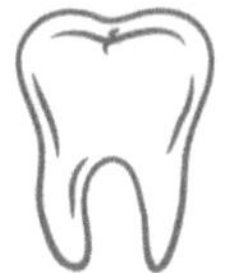

MI CASA ES SU CASA

DECLAN and I put my recent sonogram print-out in a small silver frame on the nightstand next to our bed. My husband affectionately has named our baby Peanut, going as far as to hold a real nut in the shell next to the image to strengthen his comparison. The way he pronounces it, "payknot," always makes giggle, though for all his teasing about not being able to see a "real *bairn*" in the image, I have caught him intently studying the photo with an expression of pure wonderment when he thinks I'm not looking. I do not believe I am over-exaggerating when I say that my "Very Important Daddy" is a vera, vera happy lad.

Knowing that I'm only carrying a single baby has been a big relief for the both of us. Less complications, fewer chances of something going wrong at delivery, and the absence of traumatic memories is a plus in every conceivable way. And even though calling our baby Peanut sounds goofy, it's a nice, non-gender moniker that helps us avoid discussing the ramifications of our baby's sex.

When I first realized I might be pregnant, one of the biggest worries I had was not whether I was carrying a boy or girl. Rather, it was the remote possibility that my baby would be born completely Mundane like my older sister, Claire. I couldn't begin to imagine having a child that would be completely left out of the world and culture in which their parents, especially their father, are so deeply rooted. It would mean that our son or daughter would never be able to experience the Otherworld in person. Thankfully, Doctor Brannigan put my mind at ease after analyzing my initial blood work. The hCG hormone level was much too high for me to be carrying a completely Mundane fetus. It wasn't yet possible for the Doc to say whether our Peanut would fall more to his father's *Sidhe* side or to my *Fiacail* genetic structure, but I figure we can cross that complicated bridge when we get to it. I seriously am not looking forward to the reaction of my in-laws if it happens that their heir with the *Tuatha de Danann* pedigree produces a common tooth fairy child.

But today I haven't been thinking about any of that. Today is Wednesday, and I've made special plans for this, my coveted day off. Declan has a client appointment in the morning in Swampscott and then is going to Boston for a shareholders' meeting in the afternoon. This leaves me with an entire day to rearrange the bedroom furniture to see whether we might be able to create a small nursery area somewhere within this space. The Tax Man had, for all intents and purposes, moved into my home shortly before our handfasting, and every time I turn around, I find more of his things have made their way from his expensive three-story townhouse into my cozy one bedroom-with-loft bungalow.

Of course, that is absolutely A-Okay with me. I'd fallen in love with my house the moment I first laid eyes on it, and I'm thrilled my new husband considers it his home as well. Unfortunately, its lay-out doesn't allow much extra room for a seperate nursery unless I'm willing to give up my dollhouse and crafting space and Declan can forgo any type of home office, neither of which is a reasonable solution. Forgoing any type of personal space won't work for us at all. In the meantime, I've been thinking that with a little bit of creative maneuvering, I might be able to expand my walk-in closet to create a very tiny, but totally sweet nursery to solve our space problem.

I carefully place Peanut's photo on the bed so the frame's glass won't break as I move the nightstand across the room. I have music blasting in the background as I work, so I don't hear my husband drive up, unlock the front door, or head up the stairs. I finally hear a male voice shout out, startling me and making me knock the bedroom lamp off the nightstand.

"Alexa, stop! Feckin' hell, Rosie! What in damn Dubnos da' ya' think yar' doin'?"

"Jeez, Declan! You scared me! You can't go jumpin' out at pregnant ladies like that! It's not good for us," I shout back.

"Ya' know what else is not good far' pregnant ladies, Rosie? Pregnant ladies ought not be movin' heavy furniture around because it surely is takin' risks doin' so. Plus, it also happens ta' scare the livin' shit out of thar' ever-lovin' husbands when they come home and see it takin' place without them!" the Tax Man growls.

"It's really not that heavy, Sweetie. Honest." I stop what I'm doing and hug him. "You being home is a 'vera' nice surprise, though." I add a kiss to my welcome.

He returns it warmly, but adds, "Don' ya' go tryin' to butter me up, Mrs. Fitzpatrick. Ya' know vera well that I am annoyed with ya' far' not waitin' until I was home ta' help ya'. I 'ken not understand why ya' are willin' ta' take such risks when 'tis not necessary."

"I'm sorry, Hon. I just wanted to see if my idea for turning the closet into a nursery possibly could work."

My *Mo Shiorghra* looks at me as if I've suddenly grown two heads. "Ya' wan' ta' put our little 'Payknot' in the closet as if the wee *bairn* were a pair of shoes or one of ma' dress shirts?"

"Duh! It wasn't like I was planning to leave the clothes in there, Declan. Seriously, sometimes you have absolutely no…vision."

"'Tis where ya' are vera wrong, Love. I've given it a lot of 'vision.' It is completely obvious ta' me that now that we have a little 'Payknot' on the way, we will need ta' look far' a bigger home."

Sell my beloved bungalow and move somewhere else? The Tax Man is talking like he's a couple of digits short in his asset column!

BABY 13

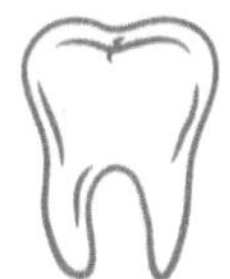

THAT'S THE WAY

IN MY OPINION, the Tax Man gives up his idea of buying a larger home far too easily. I know him better than to think he'll just forget about a plan he deems superior to mine. It makes me a bit suspicious and keeps me on my toes. To maintain marital peace, I offer him a vague promise to keep an open mind if the perfect Fitzpatrick Family Abode just happens to present itself. Meanwhile, I secretly plot to find multiple flaws in every house he shows me. Yes. I realize this makes me sound like a conniving bitch. The truth is, I love my husband to the very depths of my soul. I am absolutely convinced he is my one true *Mo Shiorghra* and that the Universe brought us together for a purpose. However, Lord *Mac Nuada* is also a *Sidhe* force to be reckoned with, a traditional Fae male always used to having his own way, and a member of the *I Idir* ruling class with a family history going back over nine hundred years. If I don't wish to become his ever-loving, wifely doormat, I surely will need to keep one step ahead of him.

On this beautiful September morning, there are other things foremost on my mind. My bogus awards ceremony in *I Idir* is only a few weeks away, and the majority of gowns I purchased back in June are now much too snug in my bust and my waistline. I contemplate looking for a Fae seamstress who could let out the seams of my favorite few, but Declan insists I should purchase new ones for this auspicious occasion. My Very-Important-Daddy is no longer okay with Mel and me taking the train into Boston by ourselves, so he invites Duncan along with a plan for the four of us to drive into the city together and make a fun day of it.

I love the idea, if and only if, I can find something acceptable to wear for this Saturday city outing. I look at the pile of clothes on the bed that I've already tried on and discarded, deciding that none of them are anything I care to be seen wearing in public. It isn't as though I had a fashionable figure before this pregnancy, and now, still in my first trimester, I have no baby bump to mark my impending motherhood. What I do have is an already-gone waistline lying under boobs that would give Dolly Parton a run for her money. I pull the last summer dress I own out of the closet, the linen green shift I ended up wearing commando the first time I met Declan's parents. It's a tad snug in the bust, but unlike my other choices, at least this dress zips up all the way. However, looking in the mirror, I want to cry. I resemble an upside-down, neon traffic cone, with all of my width on top and my skinny legs sticking out underneath.

The Tax Man walks into our bedroom, dressed and looking, as usual, as if he's just stepped off the cover of GQ. He finds me sitting on the edge of the bed, picking through the pile of rejected clothing. "Yar' not ready, Love?" he asks.

I want to spit back something along the lines of "does it look like I'm ready, Captain Obvious?" But I don't. It's not Declan's fault that the Universe has saddled him with a *Mo Shiorghra* that bears a strange resemblance to a city garbage truck. "I can't go," I say. "I have nothing to wear. Everything is too tight, and this dress looks hideous on me."

Like every father-to-be before him, Declan tries his best. "Ya' da'not look hideous, Love. I would tell ya' if ya' did. Yar' positively radiant, and I adore the way ya' have braided yar' hair."

"Stop, Tax Man. We both know I look like a damn traffic cone. I don't know what possessed me to buy this putrid color in the first place."

"Stand up for a moment, will ya', Lass," he asks.

"Why?"

"Humor me," he says.

I give a dramatic sigh and stand up. Declan puts a hand under his chin and walks around me. "The dress has good lines and it surely gives ya' a vera nice shape. It's the color that's off."

"Duh," I answer, sounding like a certified bitch even to my own ears.

My husband ignores my sarcasm and runs a hand downward in front of me. Before my eyes, the lime green changes to a pale celery color with a tropical leaf pattern a shade darker. The leaves draw the eye away from the fact that I have a less than stellar waistline, and the color is more complimentary to my skin tone than the lime. Seconds later, I'm wearing a short bolero type sweater that matches perfectly. Declan explains, "It is cooler in the city, especially in the evening, Lass. I donna' want ya' to be chilly in those short sleeves."

Now I want to cry again, but for different reasons. My husband is spot on with his make-over. I love how I look in this outfit, and knowing that Lord *Mac Nuada* never uses his magic frivolously, I realize it's a sign of how much he wants me to be happy. "Oh Declan! It's perfect! Thank you!"

He smiles broadly. "I am vera glad yar' pleased, Love. I will wait far' ya' downstairs. Duncan and Mel should be here shortly, and then we can be off on our little adventure."

BABY 14

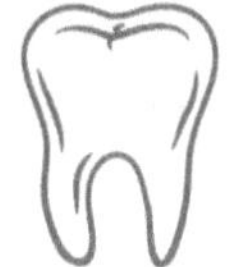

...THE BALL BOUNCES

IN HINDSIGHT, I should have covered my Tax Man's mouth when he began uttering the word adventure. Spending most of our time in the Mundane world as we do can sometimes lead us to forget key tenets of Otherworld philosophy, even important ones like the belief that all words hold power. The Fae typically speak extremely carefully, believing that spoken words can influence the choices made by the Universe. Like a lot of our inter-dimensional cohorts, it's been easy for us to fall into the habits and speech patterns of the humans with whom we share the Mundane existence. According to the Enlight-ened Ones, one should always strive to use definitively positive words in conversation, and since the Oxford Dictionary defines adventure as a typically hazardous activity, I should have expected that our outing would not proceed as planned.

The trip starts out perfectly fine, as spending the day

with Mel and Duncan always holds the promise of a good time. Since Declan and his *gancanagh* cousin have healed their contentious relationship, they've become more like brothers, and when they are together, my beloved Tax Man loses some of his ingrained seriousness and prim sense of propriety. Declan is always lighter of heart when Duncan is around, and I thoroughly enjoy seeing the boy shine in my man. Thus, we often spend our downtime with my BFF and her new significant other in a pleasant atmosphere of camaraderie.

Because it is a Saturday, the weather is glorious, and we are in no particular hurry, my Tax Man takes MA-1A, the coastal, scenic route from Salem to Boston. Duncan and Mel keep us laughing with their funny stories, and I can see that the two of them share a very similar, wicked sense of humor. My good friend seems deliriously happy these days, and I'm pretty sure the Fae man sitting next to her is the reason. I try not to think of all the ways this could go wrong. Although Declan's cousin is nothing short of crazy hot and perfectly charming, with a smile that lights up every room and a face that turns heads, he is, by birth, a *gancanagh*, a Fae incubus who, by nature, is a natural seducer of women. I have a deep-seated fear that he will end up hurting my dearest friend, even though Mel continually professes that she is well aware of who and what Duncan is and that they are only friends with benefits. Still, I see the way she looks at him and hope my BFF is not on the road to heartbreak highway.

We arrive in Boston and the Festive Boutique just before lunch time. The city's streets are full of people enjoying the day, and I'm surprised by how busy the

Mundane side of the store is. The woman at the counter doesn't notice us, and when we reach the front of the line the clerk is startled by my husband's appearance. "We didn't expect you today, your Lordship. Master Leon generally doesn't work Saturdays, but I can contact him if you need something," she says quietly as not to share her comments with the Mundane customers milling about.

Master Leon is my husband's tailor, the one that makes sure the Tax Man's designer clothes fit his tall, lithe frame perfectly. "No worries, Tavia," Declan politely answers. "'Tis ma' beautiful wife in need of apparel today. I hope that Madame Woodly is available this afternoon?"

"Of course, Lord *Mac Nuada*. I've already let her know you're here." She pauses and then adds, "It seems everyone is very much looking forward to Lady Rosalinda's medal presentation as well as the celebratory Ball afterward. We have several important clients shopping with us today. If you'll please make your way to the usual third dressing room on the right with the red curtain, Madame Woodly will be there to meet you."

"Thank you, Tavia," Declan says as he takes my hand and the four of us head to the back of the store. Once we are outside of the clerk's hearing, I turn to my husband, shooting him a look and ask, "What the hell was that woman talking about? What celebratory Ball?"

BABY 15

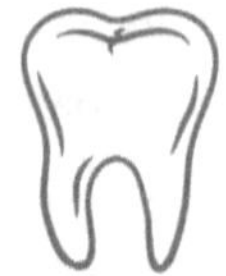

BOYS WILL BE BOYS

My Tax Man smiles blandly at me. "I was hopin' ya'd be surprised when the formal announcement was delivered by raven-gram, Love. I didna' wan' ta' miss seeing the look of excitement on yar' face at havin' such an honor bestowed on ya' by Her Royal Majesty."

I stop and look at him incredulously. "Really, Declan? That's what you thought?" My annoyance and sarcasm is hard to miss, and Mel and Duncan discreetly continue walking, giving my husband and I some needed privacy.

Unwilling to take chances that someone might hear us, Declan speaks directly to my mind. *"Please...can we discuss this at home when we are alone, Love. I swear to ya' that I only was made aware of this planned celebration a few hours ago. I know yar' uncomfortable with this whole 'award' scenario and with bein' the center of attention, but 'tis for the good of I Idir. It is not like we can refuse a gifted token from Her Highness. This Honor Ball was specifically her idea. Ya' shud' take pride in the knowledge that The Morrigan has taken personal notice of ya'. She chooses har' inner circle vera carefully."*

Frankly, the last thing I ever wanted or expected was to be part of the Queen of *I Idir*'s inner circle. In fact, I easily could have gone through life without ever having The Morrigan know who I was. Our Queen is a very demanding, imposing woman. To be under her watchful eye means having to swallow a lot of shit. That really isn't Rosie Parker's style. However, the truth of the matter is that I'm not just Rosie Parker, D.D.S., anymore. I'm Lady *Mac Nuada*, mate to House *Nuada*'s named heir. Everything I do and say now reflects not only on my husband, but on his House as well. In a culture built solidly on honor, tradition and service, saying no thanks to duty, especially as a member of the Ruling Council, is not an option; but that doesn't mean I have to be happy about it. I answer my *Mo Shiorghra* in the same intimate fashion I've finally gotten accustomed to. *"I agree, my Lord. This is neither the time nor the place to be discussing such things. I am content to wait until we are in private to discuss this turn of events further. Until then, I shall do my best to wear the happy face you ask of me."*

Hubby makes a sour face, though I'm not entirely sure whether it's because I've called him "my Lord", a title he doesn't relish between the two of us, or that I have said we would continue the discussion further when we get home, or even, perhaps, because I have promised to be cheerful for the rest of the day. I don't wait for him to find out. I turn on my heels and enter the dressing room with the red curtain, popping out into the boutique's Fae salon.

Tavia the clerk wasn't kidding. The place is hoppin'

with more shoppers than I have ever seen here before. People stop and stare when Declan and I enter. Some wave, some approach to congratulate us on everything from our handfasting to the upcoming ceremony, and some pointedly ignore us. Every dressing room is full, and there is high-end, Otherworld clothing on racks throughout the sales floor. The fact that so many people are fussing in preparation for this Honor Ball exacerbates my unease about it. On a side note, I'll admit I am one hundred percent relieved that I let Declan help me choose my outfit this morning; I would have been unbelievably mortified had I worn that hideous lime green dress and had so many people see me in it.

Madam Woodly joins us immediately. "Lord and Lady *Mac Nuada*, welcome to Festive Boutique! I'm honored to help you with your apparel selection for the upcoming Ball." She waves a hand around the room. "As you can see, everyone in *I Idir* is very excited. Are you in need of apparel as well, your Lordship? I can contact Master Leon if you'd like."

"That won't be necessary, Madame Woodly. I am perfectly set for the celebration. 'Tis just the ladies in need of help today," my husband explains.

I turn to speak to Mel but catch the small group that ignored us when we came in now snickering amongst themselves. I'm not the only one that sees this. Duncan is staring back at them with a look of intense dislike, and my BFF is considerably less jubilant than she was before we came through the red curtain. My husband's cousin turns to Declan and says, "'Tis foul luck to find House *Mac Badh* in attendance, my Lord. That man is a pompous ass as sure as the sun rises. Ya' are aware he still holds to the same weary grudge from yar' handfasting?"

"Aye. He is not unlike a fox who has been thwarted in his attempt to steal Master Farmer's hens," Lord *Mac Nuada* responds.

"What grudge, Declan?" I ask, once again caught off guard about Otherworldly goings on, though I recognize the man as the one who intended to kidnap me in the ridiculous steal the bride game during our handfasting reception.

"He dinna' like that I out-foxed him in the traditional mate stealin' game, Love. The man hates ta' lose almost as much as I do," he explains.

I don't much like it when Lord *Mac Badh* leaves his group of cronies and comes toward us. I like it even less when he reaches the Tax Man and says, "No surprise to see House *Nuada* once again puttin' on airs not rightly deserved."

BABY 16

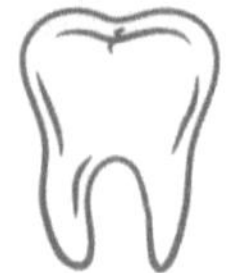

UP FOR THE CHALLENGE

I DON'T NEED a telepathic connection with my husband to realize that the young man's comment will quickly turn a few ill-chosen words into a huge battle which basically boils down to who's metaphorical Lordship's dick is bigger. From birth, Fae men are extremely competitive and full of personal family pride. The *Tuatha De Danann* take these natural instincts, found in human males as well, to a whole new paranormal level, and since both men are heirs to two of the most influential Houses in *I Idir's* Ruling Council, their disagreement has the potential to lead to an outright vendetta. In addition, Lord *Mac Badh* is distantly related to the Queen, a point to which he never ceases to remind people and yet another reason to steer clear of starting shit with him.

"A fine day to yourself, *Mac Badh*," Declan replied. "'Tis a wonderment to see ya' here in the Mundane world. I will dare to guess that yar' gracious sire has given permission for ya' ta' venture outside the safe boundaries of *I Idir*? A celebrated surprise indeed."

Lord *Mac Nuada's* reply to the other man's rude remark is a cutting personal attack that is out of character for my husband and one I understand only because Declan previously had enjoyed sharing with me gossip regarding his Lordship *Badh's* intense prejudice against any and all things regarding the Mundane World. Many residents of the Otherworld have a love/hate relationship with the human plane of existence. For the most part, the Fae hold the Mundanes and their culture in complete disdain. But the discovery several centuries ago of a rapidly declining birthrate between fully Fae couples forced a reliance on humans that the Fae cannot get around. To help convince her people that having mixed blood children was the only way to save their species, The Morrigan herself conceived a child with a human male, starting an impressive line that continues into today's modern times. This proved to be even more beneficial than first thought when it eventually was discovered that mixed-blood offspring suffer less physical cellular damage crossing back and forth between the dimensions than full-blooded Fae. It soon became a badge of civic pride to further the population of the Otherworld with human and mixed-blood partners and offspring. Like my own husband, *Mac Badh's mathair* is half *Tuatha De Danann Sidhe* and half Mundane of Irish heritage. The Universe has, of course, fully sanctioned these types of unions, and it has been considered a huge stroke of blessed good luck when one's *Mo Shiorghra* is chosen from a mixed gene pool which, hopefully, will lead to the conceiving of children.

However, in the case of Lord and Lady *Badh* it is whispered that the Mrs. had far too many handsome male friends in the Mundane realm, causing his Lordship to keep his entire family, his Lady included, firmly ensconced in the Otherworld, thus assuring that any children the union produced were truly his. While Declan and his counterparts were encouraged to live, study, and acclimate to Mundane culture, Mac Badh and all his siblings, as well as his supposed roving-eye mathair, were firmly placed under his athair's thumb, so that a trip to the human plane for anyone in that House was a rare event.

The fact that the Tax Man used this particular insult to wound *Mac Badh's* pride demonstrates just how much offense Lord *Mac Nuada* has taken over the man's implication that the honors being bestowed upon me by The Crown are bogus. From my point of view, my hubby's reaction is a bit hypocritical since we both know that the real reason for my award and promotion relates solely to propaganda for *I Idir's* hidden intelligence network. If Declan's rude behavior is on behalf of that secret agenda, my Tax Man is just being a very good actor/spy. On the other hand, I'm well aware that the Tax Man's personality and House pride doesn't allow for any disparaging remarks suggesting that Lord *Mac Nuada* is anything less than perfect when it comes to honor.

Mac Badh's face reveals no emotion, but his aura turns

a deep red and black, signifying that Declan's comments have made him extremely embarrassed and angry. Yet, it isn't House *Badh's* heir that pushes the silly argument to a whole new level; rather, it's the young Lord's companion. He steps forward and drops his dirk, oddly not at the feet of my Lordly husband, but rather at the feet of his cousin, Duncan. "*Mar Chosaint ar onoir Theach Badh, iarraim Dushlan Aisiocaiochta* (In defense of the honor of House *Badh*, I call for a Retribution Challenge)."

I only understand the words honor and retribution, but I can tell by Mel's face that whatever was said doesn't bode well for her friend with benefits. My BFF's skin has gone a shade paler and her eyes widen. Duncan, on the other hand, smiles broadly and bends down to pick up the dirk. Taking the knife in hand, the *gancanangh* places the flat end of the blade to his forehead and says, "*Dushlan glactha* (Challenge accepted)," before tossing the blade down at the other man's feet.

Mac Badh's man retrieves his dirk and announces, "I will send a raven-gram with the details upon my return to *I Idir.*"

"I await such details with great anticipation," says Duncan

At that moment, Madame Woodly scuttles towards us, agitation clearly evident in her expression. She addresses both my husband and Lord *Mac Badh* using stern tones. "Your Lordships, I find it very distressing and embarrassing to remind you both that Festive Boutique is a designated neutral zone. You must take your disagreements someplace else."

"Gracious apologies, Madame Woodly." Declan offers. "You have my word that there will be no further hostility in your place of business." My husband looks toward *Mac Badh*, who nods in agreement to this statement. However, I know this is only the beginning of these so-called hostilities.

BABY 17

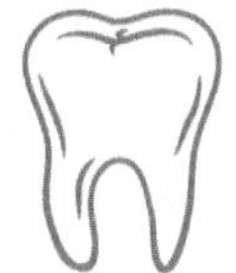

FAMOUS LAST WORDS

FOR THE NEXT two hours we four do a fine job of pretending we actually care about what Mel and I will wear to my silly hero's award presentation and subsequent Royal Ball in my honor. I had a difficult enough time following the damn Otherworld protocol and procedure for my handfasting and am not looking forward to repeating it on an even grander scale. I will be forever grateful to Madame Woodly and my fashion-conscious husband for helping me select attire that is both proper and attractive, as I am oblivious to the latest style trends among the Fae hoity-toity.

Out of respect for the proprietor, Declan and Duncan remain silent regarding the challenge between House *Badh* and House *Nuada*. I, on the other hand, have a million questions and concerns, and Mel still looks as if she's been sucking on a sour lemon. My husband sends me a mental message explaining that we will discuss it when we have some privacy during dinner, though I don't understand how he thinks we'll have any confidentiality in a crowded restaurant.

After we've finished at Festive Boutique, we walk the three blocks to the restaurant instead of re-parking our car. The Tax Man has promised us a fun evening, though he's given no hints as to what we can expect. I'm pleasantly surprised to find he's chosen a Japanese restaurant with tatami seating. The kimono-clad hostess leads us to a private dining room with rice paper walls and cushions on the floor, and I look forward to an enjoyable evening, even while the challenge nonsense hangs over us like a dust cloud.

We settle ourselves around the low table and allow Declan to order for everyone in flawless Japanese. Hearing her own language come so perfectly from lips belonging to a face so obviously not Asian, must tickle our waitress's fancy because she giggles behind the menus and bows low in apology for doing so. When she leaves, the Tax Man and his cousin speak in rapid-fire Otherworld Gaelic, high-fiving each other and laughing at jokes neither Mel nor I can understand. "English please, gentlemen! We ladies would love to join your conversation," I scold.

"I am sorry, Lass," my husband apologizes. "I'm near to burstin' with humor over *Mac Badh's* puffed-up attitude." His comment causes Duncan to stick out his chest and puff up his cheeks in mocking imitation of the other Lord, causing Declan to laugh even harder.

My BFF makes a disgruntled face. "That's so juvenile, Duncan."

"Do not be so hard on him, lovely lady. I am as much to blame for laughin' at his antics and thus eggin' him on," said Declan.

"I'll leave the job of commenting on your behavior to your wife, my Lord," Mel answers.

My husband turns to me and asks, "Did you not find *Mac Badh's* pompous posturin' amusin' as well, Love?"

"Frankly," I say, "I think the whole thing is ridiculous. You and *Mac Badh* have words, but Duncan and the other Lord's man have to fight your battles for you. It makes you both look arrogant and cavalier. I would like to think you'd prefer to handle your own disagreements."

Duncan jumps in before Declan can respond. "I'm sorry to disagree with ya', Rosie, but Fitz here has no other choice. As ma' cousin is ma' sworn Liege Lord, 'tis ma' honor and duty to take on such challenges far' him."

"He's right, Lass," Declan explains. "I am prohibited by *I Idir* law ta' engage in any physical battle with another House's Lord or heir. The Houses of the Ruling Council must stand united in appearance and their leadership must stay above petty disagreements. However, since honor is everything in the Otherworld, it is expected... and even encouraged...far' members of our inner House circles to take on these challenges in our stead."

"Do not worry an ounce over me, dearest Lady," Duncan adds. "I am able to best *Mac Badh's* man, Fergus, in most any type of competition. I do not wish to brag, but I am vera skilled in most every type of Otherworld weapon. All except the ancient long sword, but 'tis not likely Fat Fergus will select it as his first choice. The long sword requires a great deal of agility and speed and *Mac*

Badh's Fergie is not known to be quick with a blade. I do not have the least bit of concern over this challenge, and neither should ma' two favorite ladies lose any sleep over it either," the *gancanagh* says with a wink.

The waitress enters with my ginger ale, everyone else's sake, and our first course. We heartily tuck into our food, but despite Duncan's bravado, all I can think about is the old adage regarding famous last words.

BABY 18

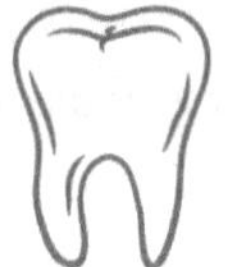

MUCKING UP THE MORNINGS

Morning sickness is a common ailment for many expectant mothers. I was hit with bouts of nausea early in my pregnancy, only a few weeks after conception. It was my first physical clue that the Tax Man and I might be on our way to becoming parents. When it stopped almost entirely following our honeymoon, I congratulated myself for having handled it so damn easily; I was the modern Madonna who didn't let a little tummy upset rule her life. Worse yet, stupid, senseless, cavalier me had the bravado to say this out loud, to my husband, using those exact same words. This was a dumb ass move for which I want to slap myself.

As any follower of the Old Ways learns, making such statements like that out loud is an open invitation for the Universe to prove the speaker wrong. Thus, as I start my fourth month, it is entirely my fault that I spend half of my day with my head stuck in the toilet and the other half feeling just plain lousy. Luckily, my young patients and their parents are sympathetic to my appointment schedule falling behind, and Mel has been great at keeping things in the office from falling totally apart. It's my husband who, besides yours truly, is having the most trouble with this phase of my pregnancy. He does his best to help by holding up my hair while I'm sick even though the smell makes him gag, making me countless cups of ginger tea and rubbing my feet. (Truthfully, the foot rubs don't relieve the nausea, but I'm not stupid enough to tell him that; the Tax Man gives the most excellent foot massages.)

Declan has questioned Dr. Brannigan so often about my excessive morning sickness, I'm surprised the good doctor hasn't told my husband to knock it off. Instead, he has assured us both that though uncomfortable, the feelings of nausea are perfectly normal, and, if anything, they may be a sign that our Peanut falls more to the *Tuatha De Danann* side of the genetic lottery because the HCG levels, and thus the constant gastro upsets, are much higher in pregnancies in which the fetuses are heavily *Sidhe*.

If it hadn't been for the upcoming awards presentation and ball that required my perky presence as its guest of honor, I'm sure we would have been able to weather our way through this stage of pregnancy without any drastic measures. However, the days preceding us having to leave for the Otherworld became some of the worst I'd experienced, which caused Declan to pace the house, swearing up and down that he would meet with the Queen personally and explain that I was too ill for such going-ons.

We both knew that excuse wouldn't fly. This entire

dog and pony show was vitally important to The Morrigan and her Black Knight in the furtherance of their war against Mundane terrorism. The natural symptoms of a normal pregnancy would not stand as an excuse to cancel events that all of *I Idir* has been looking forward to for weeks. I just needed some help in getting through the next few days, so we once again looked to Dr. Brannigan in order to find something to lessen the horrible queasiness.

As a medical professional myself, I can attest to Doc Robyn's remarkable patience and understanding in response to our repeated questions and concerns. The good doctor made a special house call on his day off, spending a great deal of time calming my nervous Very-Important-Daddy, reiterating that what I was experiencing was very normal and indicative that our baby was actively growing. He also confirmed our thoughts that the idea of my not attending the events this weekend in *I Idir* because of my pregnancy wouldn't go over well, and since Dr. B knows The Morrigan better than most, we have no reason to doubt him.

"I understand what ya' are sayin', Robyn, but ma' first concern is far' ma Rosie and our *bairn*," my husband counters. "The Lass suffers so greatly that I ken no' bear to ask her ta' be paraded around the Court far' three days. Is there not somethin' ya' can give her ta' lessen the tossin' and turnin' in har' gut?"

"The ginger tea hasn't helped at all?" the Doc asked.

I start to answer, but the Tax Man cuts me off. "Ma beloved *Mo Shiorghra* has drunk so much tea, 'tis a wonder the Lass hasn't floated clear away. It helps far' an hour at most, but then ma' dear Rosie is back feelin' wretched. I ken no' believe someone of yar' standin' doesn't have anythin' better ta' offer."

Though I appreciate his devotion to me, my husband is beginning to border on rudeness. "Declan, Sweetie, I'm sure Dr. Brannigan has my best interests at heart. There's no need to be so gruff."

The Very-Important-Daddy looks slightly taken back. "Truly, Robyn, I donna wish ta' cast blame, but 'tis hard to watch ma' Rosie Lass be so miserable hour after hour, day after day, and not be able ta' do anythin' far' har'."

"No offense taken, Fitz. I understand you're just concerned about your family. Please know I have Lady Rosalinda and her baby's well-being at the heart of everything I do. There is something I can suggest for short term use...just to help her get through the upcoming commitments in *I Idir*."

"That would be helpful, Doctor. What are you suggesting?" I ask, hoping for a reasonable solution.

"It's my guess that your morning sickness is being exacerbated by your angst over the upcoming events. I can totally understand how that might cause you additional stress. I'm thinking that perhaps monitored doses of *Fiodoir Aisling* might be just the thing."

Both my husband and I stare at the young physician as if he's lost his mind. Declan shakes his head in either disbelief or disagreement. I'm not sure which it is, but I'm just as shocked as my husband at Dr. Brannigan's suggestion. "Wait...," I say, "you want me to ingest 'Wacky Weed?'"

BABY 19

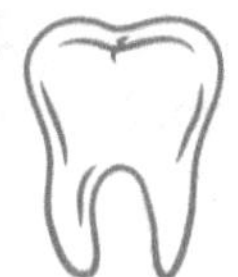

DOCTOR'S ORDERS

DOCTOR B LAUGHS OUT LOUD, something he does not often do in his professional personae. "I don't think I've ever heard it called that, but I suppose it does release the boundaries of one's… inhibitions."

My husband interjects. "Is not its use limited by law ta' Druid magical prophecy work, Robyn? As I recall, the members of the Ruling Council were compelled ta' outlaw it far' any other purposes after things got too far out of hand during the 17th century."

"Yes, you're correct, Fitz, but it still can be prescribed to the Fae for medicinal reasons, both physically and magically, under the care of a physician, though I know for a fact it's been readily available on the black market since it was outlawed. It's not the drug itself that causes the harm, but the situation in which deviant Otherworld citizens use the drug on unsuspecting Mundanes. It causes a multitude of problems for the leadership of many

Otherworld countries," Brannigan explained. "However, I don't foresee any problems receiving permission from the Black Knight to use it under these conditions, as Lady Rosalinda's presence this weekend is so critical to The Crown's initiatives. As I recall, the Lady Dear Heart also suffered from acute morning sickness when she carried the youngest *Banphrionsa,* and Her Majesty offered her *Fiodoir Aisling* in tea form. I do not predict Herself will disagree with my prescribed treatment."

The Tax Man is still not convinced. "I ken no' believe that an herb as powerful as the 'Dream Weaver' would do no harm ta' a developin' bairn! I have seen it put fully grown men into states of wild abandon."

"For pure Mundane mothers and babies, I would absolutely agree," the doc said. "But Fae fetuses, even those with mixed bloodlines, seem immune to the plant's... relaxing properties; the Fae placenta has a unique filtering system that's not present in human physiology. This has been commonly known for over eight hundred years. Pregnant female druids freely used it for their divinations back when conception among the Otherworld population was more robust. Trust me, Lord *Mac Nuada,* I would never risk the safety of your Lady or your child. The plant is entirely safe." The doctor turns to address me. "Have you any experience with the Mundane THC or CBD, Lady Rosalinda?"

In truth, I wish that Brannigan hadn't put me on the spot like this. My husband is as straight as an arrow; he's not even much of a drinker while treating his own body like a temple. I'm not sure how he'll react to my revelation that I am, in fact, quite familiar with it. I hesitate and my

Tax Man gives me a questioning look. I hear him in my head. *"Ya' need ta' be honest with Robyn, Rosie. He's yar' physician. I have no intention of judging your life style before I was a part of it, just as ya've been acceptin' of mine."*

As far as I'm concerned, my occasional experimentation with legalized marijuana is an entirely different issue than his screwing half the female population of Salem, but he's right about the need to be honest with the doctor caring for me and my baby. I give a little cough. "I've smoked a few joints, eaten a few edibles. When it became legal, of course. Not before that."

"And what was your reaction to the drug?" the doctor asks.

I shrug my shoulders. "I suppose like anyone else's, I guess. The edibles took some time to kick in but put me in a complete stupor. The symptoms took longer to wear off as well." I don't even look over at my husband. Despite his claim that he wouldn't judge, I can feel his disapproval float across the room. He makes faces whenever I eat a damn fast-food burger. I know he isn't okay with my sampling of pot, even if it was before he was in the picture.

"That's good to know," Brannigan replies. "We obviously don't want you smoking anything, so I will give you the plant in edible form. The fact that you react strongly is important. Let's go with the lowest dose possible. Just enough to take the stress away and get the morning sickness under control." The Doc stands up. "I'm going to get right on this so you can experiment with the dosage a bit before you leave for *I Idir*. I'll send a messenger with your medication later today."

BABY 20

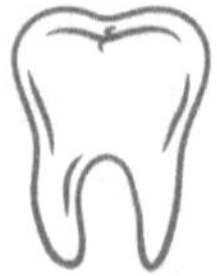

OF RECREATION AND RAVENS

THE TAX MAN and I are out of breath. The good kind of out of breath. We both lie on our backs staring at our bedroom ceiling, sweaty, exhausted, sated puddles of post-coital bliss. "That was fun," I critique.

"Aye," my spouse concurs. "Vera fun. Though 'tis a good thing that Robyn has not given ya' unlimited refills on the *Fiodoir Aisling*. I am sure ya' would end up killin' me before our Paynut' is barn. The wee babe would undoubtedly end up fatherless."

I give his bare thigh a playful slap. "You know better than to say shit like that out loud, Declan. The Universe might be listening."

"I am only teasin', love. There could never come a day I would not welcome yar' advances."

That's not the part of his statement I am concerned with. "No…I mean the last part of your comment."

Declan thinks for a moment before answering, the

light bulb finally going off in his head. "Yar' right, Love. I shad' not be so damn careless with ma' words. Do not hold ta' any worries, Lass. Paynut's father has no intention of bein' anywhere but here with his family." He flips onto his side ta' look at me. "Ya' seem to be more in tune with the old ways these past few months. I wonder if it is the impendin' arrival of our *bairn* that is makin' ya' more aligned with the Great Mother Goddess, *Danu?*"

"Maybe. I'm not sure whether it's that, or your House sigil inked on my back, or even whether it's just plain, old pregnancy hormones doing their job, but I do feel more spiritually connected now than I did before I met you," I confess.

"'Tis a good thing…us bein' fated mates. It can only serve ta' help each of us find our destined purpose," my Fae husband theorizes. "Livin' in the Mundane world dampens our Fae connection ta' the natural Universe; together we are more grounded to who we are."

This is a typical Declan thing to say: magically logical, sensible, and worthy of a man comfortable in his Fae skin. I, on the other hand, have spent nearly all of my life hiding my Otherworld heritage, denying my birthright, and avoiding relationships with *Sidhe* folk except, of course, for Mel. To be thrust headlong into Fae culture and political structure has been a difficult adjustment for me, and though I believe my husband loves me as much as he says he does, I don't think he really gets how much of a culture shock this has been for me. The prescribed *Fiodoir Aisling* has heightened these dormant Otherworldly feelings in me far more quickly than that which I am comfortable. However, my increased libido, sense of euphoric happiness, and lack of grueling nausea outweigh any hesitation I have regarding my new found spiritual nirvana.

"All joking aside, Lass, I am vera happy to see ya' feelin' so much better. Robyn was wise ta' suggest the Dream Weaver ta' combat yar' mornin' sickness. I surely owe him an apology. I may have been, perhaps, a mite impatient with the man. I think a bottle of good Scotch whiskey is in order as a 'thank you.'" The Tax Man tilts his head at me and asks, "Have ya' experienced any prophetic dreams yet, Love? *Fiodoir Aisling* is known ta' reveal secrets of the future ta' souls who have ingested it."

"Don't be silly, Sweetie. I'm a tooth fairy, remember? We don't possess that level of magical skill. I still have trouble transporting myself to specific locations in *I Idir*. I don't suspect I'll be having 'premonitions' any time soon, even with daily doses of 'Dream Weaver,'" I say with the absolute certainty of someone who knows diddly squat about metaphysical soothsaying. "I'm happy enough not to be spending the majority of my day with my head in the toilet."

We're startled by a sharp rapping on our bedroom window; in my experience, this can only mean one thing. Declan rolls to the side of the bed, "I'll get it," he says. "I'm guessin' it will be the details of Duncan's challenge with *Mac Badh's* man."

He pads to the window, comfortable in his nudity, and opens it. Sure enough, there on the sill sits a nasty, Otherworld raven with a rolled-up scroll in his beak. The bird gives me a beady-eyed stare, and I pull the covers up tighter around my naked self. The ravens of *I Idir's* inter-dimensional message service are creepy, rumor-mongering assholes, and on almost every occasion I've witnessed, they've never arrived with news I've been happy to get. From the look on my husband's face, today's message is more of the same.

"Feckin' hell," he says as he peruses the length of the parchment. "Those dirty, low-down, bastards…"

BABY 21

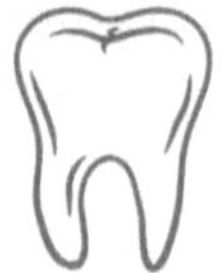

HOW IT IS BETWEEN FRIENDS

WHAT SHOULD HAVE BEEN a few days of chilling before the big celebration in *I Idir*, now has turned into a frantic rush for Duncan to train with the long sword. This particular weapon has not been used actively in the Otherworld for nearly two hundred years, and the only *Sidhe* that still train with it are members of the Ruling Council and the Royal Circle. Its selection for the challenge between *Mac Badh's* man and Declan's cousin is nothing more than a well-planned attempt to put my husband on the losing end of this competition, a position that the Tax Man absolutely detests and which everyone in *I Idir* knows.

This is the reason that instead of some private R and R time of the type I prefer, Mel and I have ring side seats in my veiled backyard as *Mac Nuada* gives his cousin a crash course in a weapon Duncan's never handled before. Granted, there are worse ways to spend a summer evening than stretched out in a lawn chair with a cold lemonade, watching two half-naked, top specimens of Fae masculinity swing big ass swords at each other. The late summer temps aren't the only reason we are fanning ourselves with paper fans. To quote my husband, it is "vera, vera appealin'."

There's little doubt that Duncan is extremely athletic and quick on his feet. Unfortunately, he has a slightly smaller build than Declan, who is two inches taller and fifteen pounds of pure muscle heavier. The Otherworld-style long sword has a double-sided blade that is 46 inches long and weighs just under five pounds. It is meant to be a double-handed weapon with a cruciform hilt that requires a great deal of arm strength and stamina to wield. Considering that Duncan is entirely new to its use, he isn't doing too badly, but one would be naive to think that *Mac Badh* hasn't been planning this challenge since my husband bested him in his attempt to kidnap me at our handfasting reception. No doubt *Mac Badh's* man has been training intensely these past six weeks while waiting patiently for his Lord to find an excuse to declare this bogus challenge.

"Duncan is doing pretty well, don't you think," I ask Mel.

"I suppose," she answers, her mind obviously else-where. "I'm not much into Otherworld weapons." My BFF has been unusually quiet, odd behavior for her in a situation like this. She's always adored watching Fae men compete in any type of sport and normally is far more enthusiastic than she's been this entire evening.

"Is everything okay?" I ask. "You seem to be someplace else tonight."

She hesitates a moment and then sighs before spilling the beans. "Duncan has asked me to move in with him."

I shouldn't be as surprised as I am over this piece of news. Mel and Duncan have been inseparable since Declan and I discovered we were each other's *Mo Shiorghra*, or fated mates. However, during this entire time, Mel has sworn that the two of them were just really good friends with benefits and that nothing serious was going on between them. Being the supportive pal I am, I've been happy for her, believing she realized their relationship could never be a permanent one.

Duncan Fitzpatrick *Nuada* is a *gancanagh*, a love talker or seducer of women, traditionally considered an incubus among Otherworld *Sidhe*. He was born this way, a genetic heritage gifted from his maternal grandfather, who, like all of his type, never committed to his grandmother and had little to do with the raising of the daughter he sired, who became Duncan's mother. Isabelle, Duncan's mom, handfasted a Fitzpatrick of House *Nuada* and their union produced Duncan. I don't know his family personally, but I've been told by Declan that though his cousin's parents were thrilled to be expecting a coveted child, they were a tad disappointed to find that their first-born son, and, as it turned out, their only child, was a genetic throwback to his *gancanagh* ancestor, a situation that doesn't bode well for building strong family lines.

I personally adore Duncan. He's the prettiest man I have ever laid eyes on, as well as charming and funny with an unbelievable zest for life. He's also incredibly loyal to my husband and the four of us spend a great deal of time together. But I know my Mel desperately desires a traditionally monogamous handfast, and, should the Universe allow, children and a family of her own. As much as I care for Duncan, it is not reasonable to think with his *gancanagh* heritage he can give my best friend those things she's dreamed of since she was a little girl.

As much as I hate the role, I have no choice but to play devil's advocate. "You're not seriously considering it, are you Mel? We've talked about this. You swore to me you weren't going to get serious about him. You know I care for Duncan, but he is what he is. The Universe decided that thirty-two years ago. He can't change who he is even if he wants to. Trust me. This won't end well for you."

Mel makes a face I've seen too many times before when I tell her something she doesn't want to hear. I try to soften my approach. "At least give yourself some time to think about it. Don't run into this decision willy-nilly."

No sooner than the words leave my mouth then I can tell this was the absolute wrong thing to say to her. Mel's face scrunches up like she wants to cry, but instead of weeping, she almost snarls at me, "That's some totally hypocritical shit, coming from you Rosalinda Parker! You went and handfasted the first Fae man you ever slept with! How much thinking did you do on the matter? You went and got yourself knocked-up less than two weeks after meeting him. Goody for you that he ended up being *Sidhe* royalty! It must make it so much easier to pass judgment on the rest of us lowly beings."

I've been on the receiving end of my friend's anger before, but today her words cut especially deep. "Ouch," I say, this being the only response I can muster, but she must read the hurt on my face.

She puts her lemonade down on the table and stands up. "Look, I'm just gonna split, okay? I've got the worst headache. Tell Duncan I'll call him later." Then she turns and walks out of the yard without looking back.

BABY 22

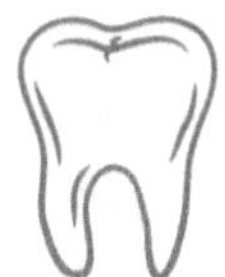

FRIGHTS AND HEIGHTS

FOR SOME REASON, naivete perhaps, I'd expected my husband to support the advice I gave Mel about her plans to move in with Duncan. I'd assumed it was a strict tenant of matrimonial loyalty to take one's spouse's side in arguments where others are involved. I should have known better. When he's not playing at being Mr. Super Spy, the Tax Man is a staunch pillar of blunt honesty, to the point that he can be what some people might call abrasive. I just call it being an ass.

From the first day I met him, I could tell that Declan Phineas Fitzpatrick didn't mince words, so much so, that after our first meeting regarding my IRS problems I determined him to be an overbearing, pompous jerk, albeit a deliciously handsome one. It took a week together in forced proximity to understand fully that Lord *Mac Nuada* says what he means and means what he says, a trait totally foreign to Mundane culture, but considered honorable among Otherworld traditions. Knowing this, I should have been better prepared when he told me in no uncertain terms that I had no business telling Mel...or Duncan for that matter...how to live their lives.

"'Tis none of your business who Mel spends her days and nights with, Lass. I don' recall that she ever told yourself that ya' were bat shat' crazy ta' commit to a man ya' knew far a mere six days," he says in that Lordship voice that gets under my skin. "In fact, as I recall, Mel has always been a true friend to ya' when ya' needed one most. My thought is that ya' need ta' apologize and keep yar' thoughts ta' yourself even if ya' mean well by them."

This, unfortunately, is how we begin our trip to *I Idir* for the sham celebration and stupid royal ball; by me giving my husband the fully silent treatment and his Lordship suggesting that perhaps I was a mite over-wrought, and recommending that I take a booster dose of the Dream Weaver, advice which only works to make me even crankier.

Visits to *Dun Siorai,* Declan's ancestral home, have never been a walk in the park for me, but with all eyes on House *Nuada* because of both my award ceremony, the honorary ball, and the highly-charged challenge with House *Badh,* the atmosphere around the estate now is especially tense, to say the least. Upon our arrival we are met by his father's man, Corvot, who informs us that Lord *Nuada* is in meetings at *Crann Bethadh* and that Lady *Nuada* is currently indisposed.

I can tell my husband is annoyed by our less than stellar homecoming, but I consider it a lucky break. I would like to settle in before dealing with Declan's highly dysfunctional family. Our quarters look the same as I remember them from our handfasting stay, with the addition of yet another over-sized armoire which I guess holds our clothes for the various official functions. I don't bother to check, as I pretty much could guarantee that, like everything in the mansion, all is exactly as it should be. Mistakes and oversights simply are not allowed at *Dun Siorai*.

It was late afternoon in *I Idir* when we arrived, and a complete traditional tea is laid out on the small dining table. This was a welcome sight as we'd left before 7 AM Mundane time without the benefit of breakfast. Over tea, I nonchalantly ask Declan if he knows where Mel is staying.

After hesitating a moment, seemingly to choose his words carefully, a sure sign I won't like his response, he relays, "Mel is stayin' with Duncan in his quarters on the west side of the estate." He takes a long sip of his tea and adds, "And I'm gonna ask ya', Love, ta' simply leave them be. My cousin has a big challenge in front of him on the morrow, and the last thing he needs right now is added drama ta' distract him."

As he must have expected, I find this suggestion that I cause drama super annoying. "Seriously, Tax Man, I resent that you think the simple and honest advice I gave my best friend is so-called 'drama.' I've been her confidant for twenty years. I just want what's best for her. If you were to be honest with yourself, you'd admit as well that Duncan is not the best choice for Mel."

He raises that single eyebrow, something that must be genetic because I sure as hell can't do it. "As I recall,

Love…my parents thought the same thing about ya', and I'm sure ya' haven't forgotten how we both reacted ta' their unsolicited…advice."

"That's entirely different," I argue. "We are each other's *Mo Shiorghra*. Your parents were arguing against something set in place by the Universe."

I should know better than to argue with the Tax Man. He always needs to have the last word. "And who's to say that the Universe does not have plans for Duncan and Mel as well? Not every decision comes with inked proof so easily read." My husband is referring to the *Nuada* sigil magically inked on my right shoulder blade, the sign marking me as his fated mate. "Should our friends be denied a chance at happiness because they weren't fortunate enough ta' have the magic of the natural world bring them together?" he asks me bluntly.

There's nothing I can say to that without sounding like a magical elitist, something I vowed never to do despite marrying a man who can trace his *Tuatha de Danann* heritage back a thousand years. I remain silent, and the Tax Man adds, "If for no other reason than because I asked ya', Love, please don't make things more difficult this weekend by fussing with Duncan and Mel. Let them figure out their relationship on their own."

"As you wish, my Lord," I answer, knowing it annoys him when I use his title.

He sighs and changes the subject. "I need to check on the horses. Would ya' like ta' come along ta' the stables with me?"

"No," I say. "I'm tired. I think I'm going to rest a while before dinner."

"A vera wise plan, Love," he placates. "I'm sure the trip here wasn't easy on ya' or our Paynut'. A few hours of rest will do ya' both some good. I won' be long, Lass. Perhaps we can 'rest' together when I return."

I don't answer, so he puts his cup on the saucer, rises from the table and kisses the top of my head before heading out the door toward the stables. I finish my tea and stretch out on the bed, doing my best to close my eyes and rest, but I find sleep impossible because I have too much on my mind. I decide that I need fresh air and exercise, so I grab my shawl and wander outside. Remembering Declan had said Mel and Duncan were staying on the west side, I purposely head east, not in the mood to run into either of them right now. I set a course toward the cliffs that overlook the sea, one of the most desolate but beautiful spots on all of the *Nuada* property.

It's a bit of a climb, and I work up a good sweat by the time I reach the top. I feel the imminent arrival of autumn in the air, the wind coming off the water bearing a slight drop in temperature. I expect a stunning view, and that's what I get, the wide expanse of blue-green, churning water below the dark-shadowed, craggy rocks of *Carraig an Bhroin* (Rock of Grief). What I don't expect is the realization that I am not alone. At the very end of a rock that juts precariously over the water, stands a woman, her clothes whipping to and fro in the wind. My heart beats faster at the notion of how absolutely unsafe and terrifying her position is with the strength of the wind and the instability of the rocks underfoot. I want to call out, but I'm afraid of startling her and causing her to lose her balance. Strangely enough, I don't have to say a single word. The woman must sense my presence and slowly turns her gaunt face towards me. My poor heart goes from beating fast to standing completely still; the woman on the cliff, a step away from sure death, is Declan's mother, the Lady *Nuada*.

BABY 23

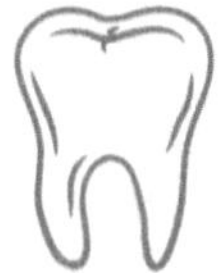

SIOBHAN

Lady *Nuada* snarls at me. "Go away, tooth fairy. I don't want you here."

I should be offended that despite my handfasting her only son and carrying her first grandchild, my mother-in-law still is unbelievably rude to me. But frankly, what stands out to me is how terribly thin she's become. *Siobhan* Fitzpatrick has always been tall and lithe like most of the *Sidhe* population. Last month, at Declan and my Mundane wedding celebration, I'd thought she'd looked thinner than usual. Today, however, standing on this cliff, she appears almost skeletal.

I have an extremely bad feeling about this scenario; something tells me I must ignore her admonition to go away. "How 'bout you come closer and tell me why you want me to 'go away,' Lady *Nuada*?" I suggest.

"Leave now, silly girl, if you know what's good for you." Declan's *mathair* shouts over the howling wind and churning waves as she moves closer to the edge of the rock she's standing on.

A plan materializes out of nowhere. "What did you say?" I scream back, taking quiet, baby- steps forward. "I can't hear you over the wind."

By the time she turns around to face me I'm close enough to grab a handful of the wool cape fluttering behind her. The instant I touch it I'm filled with an over-whelming sense of despair and unhappiness. She and I lock eyes. Hers are the same moss green color as my husband's, but they are framed in deep, sunken circles and filled with such pain that it sucks the breath from me. She tries to pull her cape from my hands, but I hang on to it with all the strength I can muster.

"Why must you make this harder for me than it has to be, tooth fairy? You should be pleased to rid yourself of me," she whispers, her voice hoarse and low.

And there it is: a situation I understood in my heart but didn't want to believe. Lady *Siobhan* came here, to this desolate spot, to end her life. A fall from this height against the rocks below surely will break her neck, the only way to permanently kill a Fae of *Siobhan* Fitzpatrick's bloodline. The realization that I have stumbled upon my husband's mother as she's attempting suicide has me fully rattled, but I'll be damned if I let her throw her life away like this.

"You mustn't do this, Lady *Nuada*. It goes against everything you believe in! Your family needs you…your husband…your children. Think of the grief you will cause them." I know I'm babbling, but I have no proper training in what to say in a situation like this so I'm just winging it.

I pat my belly. "Think about this new grandbaby! Don't you want to be part of its life?"

"Family? What do you know of my family, stupid girl?" she growls. "A loveless marriage with an indifferent husband... daughters who bring me nothing but heartache, the youngest...my baby... banished because of her madness of mind. This is no family, tooth fairy. It is an abomination. You have tied yourself to a House full of secrets and pain, a damaged clan of misfits. If I am no longer here, perhaps his Lordship can find a different mate, one who reminds him more of your dead mother."

Maybe it's the dose of Dream Weaver I took earlier today; maybe it's my maternal hormones kicking in; but for whatever reason, I understand that the words she is spitting at me come from a dark place inside of her, and I refuse to let them change my course of action. "Haven't you sacrificed enough already, Lady *Nuada*? Don't let his Lordship's selfishness take anything more from you. You have a chance to start new with this grandbaby. I won't let you give up on that! You are the only grandmother our baby will know."

"This baby surely will hate me just like his father," she whispers. "That is something I will not put myself through again. You cannot ask that of me."

This has to be one of the most difficult conversations I've ever had. It's no secret the relationship between Declan and his mother is a strained one. Both of them have wounded each other so deeply and so often that I'm not sure things between them ever can improve, but I have to try, for my husband's sake as well as for our little Peanut. "Declan doesn't hate you, Lady *Nuada*."

"You really are a stupid girl, aren't you tooth fairy?" she snaps. "Of course he hates me. From the day he was born, the same day his twin died, Declan would stiffen and wail every time I picked him up. I am sure that, like his father, Declan blamed me for the death of his twin. My son knew I was somehow cursed. Our bonding went so poorly, his father took him from my arms and hired a nurse to care for him. From that moment forward, things soured between us. He loved his *athair*, but he's never had any use for the woman who birthed him."

I've never been fond of Lord Callum Fitzpatrick *Nuada*, but at this moment, I think I dislike him more than ever. What he did to his mate was beyond cruel, taking her baby from her because of what may have been the postpartum depression of a grieving new mother combined with a very colicky baby who picked up on his mother's anxiety. I'm glad his Lordship is not here, because I'd be tempted to give him a good slap.

"Lady *Nuada*...you are aware that I'm in the medical field, correct?" I ask.

"I know you fuss around with Mundane teeth. That is not a medical doctor," she counters.

Okay. I get it. *Siobhan* Fitzpatrick is definitely hard to like, but she's not the first one to disrespect my profession as secondary. I'm ready for her. "For your information, Lady *Nuada*, I took the same basic medical training as doctors who go into other specialties. That being said, what you are relating to me about your experiences with Declan have sound medical reasons. You were not a bad mother. Most probably, Declan suffered from colic." I leave out the part about postpartum depression. No use getting her self-blame all riled up again.

She looks at me questioningly. "Truly?" she asks.

"Absolutely. I can show you the facts clear as day in some of my old medical textbooks. Dr. Brannigan will second everything I tell you if you wish to speak to him about it." I put an arm around her shoulder, and, despite her instant stiffening at such a familiar touch, I lead her away from the cliff's edge. "I can explain everything to you. You weren't to blame for Declan's infant behavior, and you are absolutely and unequivocally not to blame for the death of his twin. But can I suggest we head back to the house first? I really gotta pee."

BABY 24

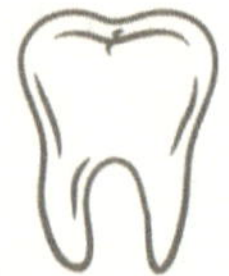

LITTLE SHOES TO FILL

AT LADY *NUADA'S* INSISTENCE, I keep silent about what occurred on the cliff yesterday. Truthfully, I don't feel good about doing so. Prudence dictates that someone in addition to me should know that Declan's mother is suicidal, but since our relationship is already a difficult one, I don't discuss the event. Whenever I give my word like I did with her, I always do my best to keep it. However, I plan to closely monitor her behavior over the next few days, and if I see she seems to be struggling again, I may have to seek some advice from Dr. Brannigan. As a physician, and a Fae one at that, I pretty much can guarantee Robyn will not breach the privacy of his patients.

Luckily, Declan is too preoccupied with the competition between his cousin, Duncan, and *Mac Badh's* man, as well as my award ceremony later in the day, to pay attention to anything else. It's also the reason I'm sitting alone in our quarters so early in the morning on my supposed big day while my husband is getting one last training session in with Duncan. I'm trying not be overly annoyed about his obsession over this silly challenge with another House's young heir. I've known from the first day I met him that D.P. Fitzpatrick's competitive edge is three times more intense than any man I've ever known, Fae or otherwise. His must win mentality sometimes can be difficult to live with. Frankly, it's been the basis for the few serious arguments we've had in our short relationship. But I know I have some faults of my own that drive Declan crazy, and all marriages require a constant battle of give and take, so I just roll my eyes when he's not looking and accept the man as he is.

I just finish showering and dressing when there is a sharp knock at my door. I assume it's my breakfast, but instead I'm greeted with the sour face of Master Hobart, Lady *Nuada's* personal page. He gives me the perfunctory bow afforded by my title and hands me a small box tied with twine, both yellowed with age.

"My Lady wishes for you to have this," he says in his usual disdainful tone. Then, without waiting for me to respond, he turns on his heel and leaves.

It takes a few minutes to wrap my head around the idea that Declan's *mathair,* a woman I've secretly called Dragon Mama since day one, has sent me a gift. I take the box to the table tond am just about to settle down and open it when I am again interrupted by yet another knock at the door. This time, it actually is my breakfast, so I wait until the tray is unloaded onto the table and the kitchen staff leaves before pouring myself some tea and then getting back to the mystery box.

The knot is complicated, and it takes me a few minutes to un-work it. When I finally open the box, the contents leave me stunned. Inside are a pair of very tiny, exquisite baby booties, made from the softest lamb skin I've ever felt. The infant shoes are intricately embroidered with what looks like flowers, but on closer inspection, actually are Fae magical sigils stitched into the shape of Other-world blooms. To describe the booties as a piece of art doesn't do them justice. Inside the box is also a note written in an ornate, feminine penmanship...

> *Lady Mac Nuada,*
> *These were Declan's and his athair's before him.*
> *I thought you might want to have them.*
> *Lady N*

I pick the booties up and hug them to my chest. To my mind, Lady *Nuada's* sending these to me could have two impossibly different scenarios: either Declan's *mathair* has decided to embrace her role as our Peanut's grandmother, or the troubled woman is giving away treasured things before taking her life. The problem is, I can't be sure which of these two scenarios are true.

BABY 25

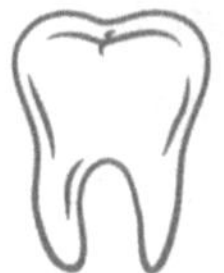

THE LONG AND SHORT OF IT

MUCH LIKE LIFE in the Mundane world, major sporting events are a big draw for the Fae population. Though the actual competitions are different in nature, the people of the Otherworld seem to enjoy the thrill of victory and the agony of defeat nearly as much as their human counterparts. The fact that this particular event pits two of the Ruling Council's most prestigious Houses against each other makes interest widespread and just about everyone in *I Idir* has come out to view the spectacle.

The viewing stands, set up especially for this match, are a sea of flapping maroon and gold pennants for House *Nuada* and white and purple ones for House *Badh*. I find myself seated in House *Nuada's* personal box without the benefit of my husband's company, as Declan has left me alone while he attends to some final words with Duncan. As usual, my sister in laws and their respective spouses ignore me. Lord and Lady *Nuada* arrive shortly after Declan leaves, and though I am nervous about seeing Lady *Siobhan* after our meeting on the cliff and the arrival of her gift to me, it seems I have nothing to worry about as she glides past me without a single word, disregarding me to the point of not even making eye contact.

His Lordship stops in front of me momentarily as I struggle to my feet for a proper curtsy. "Do not trouble yourself to rise, Lady Rosalinda. How fare thee? Are things progressing well with this pregnancy?"

"Aye, your Lordship. The baby and I are doing fine. Dr. Brannigan doesn't expect any complications."

"Good to hear, though I would have expected you to look a bit rounder by now. Are you eating properly?" he asks in his usual condescending tone.

"Yes, my Lord," I answer, wanting to say something equally rude but wisely holding my tongue.

"Good. Proper nutrition is key to a healthy *Nuada* offspring. I await the news of the baby's gender with much anticipation. My mages all say House *Nuada* will have a new heir soon."

It's the last thing I want to hear. Up until this moment, I have been manifesting my desire for a healthy baby without the additional petition for a specific gender. But the thought of my child having to adhere to the archaic Otherworld traditions that were set upon my husband makes me queasy. If our Peanut is a girl, we can avoid all that nonsense. "As the Universe desires, my Lord," I say, "so it shall be." I smile up at him sweetly.

He nods and moves toward his seat, signaling that I have been officially dismissed. I am grateful when I see

Declan making his way toward the House box, and when he sits down next to me, I ask, "Is Duncan ready?"

Lord *Mac Nuada* makes a face. "As ready as he will be, Lass. I would have liked another week or two of trainin', but Her Majesty was insistent about this competition being held today. The Morrigan loves pageantry and undoubtedly an event like this will excite the citizens in advance of the ceremony and the ball."

"I'm sure Duncan will do his best, Sweetie." I hesitate a moment, and ask the question that I really want the answer to. "Did you see Mel?"

He leans back in his seat. "Aye. Miss Mel is as anxious about the outcome of the match as the rest of us, though she does her best to be supportive. It is obvious that what his lady thinks is vera important ta' ma' cousin."

I feel as if the last part of that statement is aimed directly at me and my doubts regarding the relationship between my BFF and his cousin, but I let it slide. Instead, I ask, "Did you invite Mel to come sit with us?"

"I did, Lass. But she has decided ta' sit among the general crowd…as not ta' be a distraction ta' our Duncan."

I know Declan is trying to spare my feelings. Mel isn't sitting with us because she is still upset with me. I feel an ache in the back of my throat over the discord between my oldest friend and I, but there's no way I'm going to start boo-hooing in front of my in-laws. I sniff and look away, working to grab hold of my hormonal emotions, a symptom of my pregnancy that I find even more difficult to deal with than the ongoing morning sickness.

Thankfully, there is a flourish of trumpets and all eyes are now on the two men in the center of the arena. As tradition dictates, both men are shirtless and kilted in their family plaid. I'm not gonna lie...even as a pregnant, married woman whose beloved husband is sitting right next to her holding her hand, the sight of them takes my breath away. There's no getting around the fact that *Sidhe* men are vera, vera attractive, and dressed this way, can really get a girl's libido running, which I'm sure is one reason there are so many ladies in the audience today.

Apparently, I am not shielding quite as well as I should, because my husband gives me a smirk and I hear him say, *"I will keep your admiration of the kilt in mind, my Love."*

I blush but respond by simply giving his hand a squeeze. We watch as two attendants carry out the designated weapons of choice. I am not all that familiar with Otherworldly weaponry, and though I realize by the nature of its name that a long sword is undoubtedly large, it seems disproportionately huge to my eyes. But what alarms me most is the obvious sharpness of the double-edged blade glinting in the afternoon sun, and the unsheathed, deadly point at the sword's end. Not wanting anyone to hear me, I speak to Declan telepathically. *"Wait...those look like genuine long swords. Someone could end up truly getting hurt! If this is simple pageantry like you said earlier, why aren't they using dull bladed training swords?"*

Lord *Mac Nuada* looks at me oddly before responding out loud. "Trainin' swords? What challenge would that provide, Lass?"

BABY 26

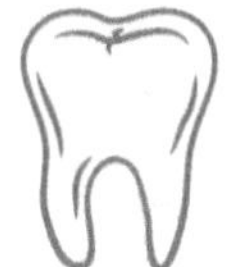

PROVIDING A CHALLENGE

I'T'S NOT easy to end the life of a Fae. Their physiology, though similar to humans, is far more complex. It's tied directly to their genetic bloodline, and their regenerative powers often are determined by their magical skill level and their personal mindset. Contrary to myth, the Fae do age, but at a much, much, slower rate than their human counterparts; and despite not falling prey to most Mundane illnesses, they can suffer from a handful of cancer-like blood diseases such as the one that took my mother, though research on these have made some recent advancements.

As fabulous as this sounds, the Fae's remarkable genetic structure does not give them a free pass to live a life devoid of pain or injury. When their magical abilities are weakened or destroyed for any number of reasons, their natural healing abilities are greatly limited, and there is always the possibility that these injuries could lead to permanent damage. Some Fae have been known to give up their will to live instead of choosing to go on with a life-altering disability, either magical or physical.

Although he doesn't have the overwhelming *Tuatha De Danann* bloodline of my husband, Duncan is more than 75% genetically Fae. It is unlikely he will die from today's longsword battle, unlike what almost happened when he took that brass bullet to his groin protecting me. The weapons being used today are created from Fae safe elements, and there is little chance Lord *Mac Badh's* man would attempt to take Duncan's head. To do so would be an automatic death sentence for him delivered by the Black Knight's *Caladbolg* and would cause his House great shame. Nonetheless, today's little challenge, as my husband so nonchalantly calls it, could cause Duncan some extremely painful injuries, a potentially long recovery, and even possible disfigurement since the Fae facial skin is highly susceptible to scarring.

There's no doubt that both men participating in today's nonsense are well aware of the risks, but with competition firmly ingrained in the Fae male psyche, one would be hard pressed to find a single man in the viewing stands who wouldn't do the same for the pride of his own House. As I previously mentioned, there are more women here today than one would have expected to see prior to a big social event later in the evening, but I assume it's because the two swordsmen involved are very easy on the eyes and currently unmated.

The opponents are introduced and the challenge begins. I admit to not knowing a thing about longsword battle, but even I am able to see that things are moving rather slowly. Duncan seems to be strangely…well…hesitant. Nothing *Mac Badh's* man does to try and engage him in direct battle seems to work. I begin to hear the murmurings of a bored crowd, and I mentally ask my husband, *"Doesn't Duncan seem a bit...uhmm...timid, Sweetie? He and Mac Badh's man look more like they're dancing than battling."*

I see a slight turn of a smile on his lips. *"Patience is a winner's game, Lass."*

Frankly, it's a presumptuous non-answer, and I find his silence annoying. I turn back to the competition, as bored as the rest of the spectators appear to be. People have taken to conversing with those around them, and many have left their seats in search of refreshments. This tedious dance between the two men goes on for another seven or eight minutes, and I consider going to find myself something to eat. *Mac Badh's* man appears annoyed and it's clear he's lost some of his determined focus. I stand up to leave, but Declan takes my hand and pulls me back into my seat. Before I can protest his unusual manhandling, everything in the arena changes.

Duncan suddenly spins around, placing himself in the back of *Mac Badh's* man, Fergus. This catches Fergus off guard, and when he turns around to face Duncan, the pivot on his left foot is wobbly. Duncan takes advantage and lowers his sword to the left, making his opponent move on the foot that wasn't firmly set and causing him to roll his ankle. Fergus regains his balance quickly, but I notice that he now moves on that particular foot a little more gingerly. Normally, a small injury like a rolled ankle would take seconds for a *Sidhe* male to heal, but most of his energy has been, and still is, directed toward Duncan, so the healing process undoubtedly will take longer than usual.

This Duncan now in the arena is a whole new opponent. He moves with lightning speed, and his thrusts are aimed carefully. He catches Fergus across the right shoulder, and a bloom of red spreads across the *Sidhe's* arm. Fergus is sweating hard now and undoubtedly wishing he hadn't expended so much energy playing keep away with Duncan in the early part of the match. I look over at my husband, whose expression hasn't changed the entire time and realize this has been Duncan's plan from the start: wear down his opponent until he loses his fighting adrenaline while expending a lot of energy without success. This explains my Tax Man's cryptic answer about patience being the winner.

Fergus tries delivering a few strong thrusts at Duncan but cannot make contact. Then, in a move that happens so fast it's only a blur, Duncan hits his opponent across the right knee, and the man goes down in pain. He doesn't get up; blood is now pouring from both his shoulder and his knee, and his bad ankle is turned at a funny angle. He pulls a white rag tucked into the waistband of his kilt and lays it at his feet signaling his surrender. Duncan lowers his sword and bends to help the man up, and the two opponents take their bows before a cheering crowd.

Next to me, Lord *Mac Nuada* rises and joins in the thundering applause, and in my mind I hear him say with just a touch of lordly swagger, *"And that, dear Lass, is how it's done."*

BABY 27

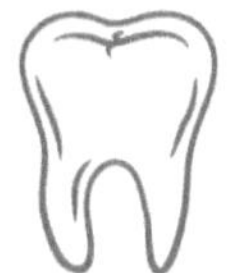

TAMING THE BEAST

A HAPPY TAX Man is an amorous Tax Man. Mine is very happy this afternoon. After the formal awards ceremony, while the last pastry is barely consumed and the final toast is jubilantly raised in my honor, his Jr. Lordship has us rushing back to the *Nuada* ancestral home as if he were on fire. That's because he most definitely is. On fire, I mean. I'd never turn down a roll in the hay with an amorous Tax Man, especially when it's real hay in a deserted stable, but if my husband notices I am a tad distracted he politely doesn't point it out; he just works even harder at his task. He's awesome like that.

It's not the bogus awards ceremony that's on my mind. That went very well, all things considered. The Black Knight greatly embellished the story regarding my courageous sacrifices to bring down a Chechen terrorist group attempting to breach the Otherworld. Yes, it's true that I was almost shot by my traitorous Tooth Fairy Supervisor.

It's also true that I was captured and held hostage by a Chechen terrorist group with an Otherworld conquest on their agenda. However, it wasn't like I volunteered for any of that; it all just sort of happened. In full honesty, at the time these incidents were occurring, all I really could focus on was if and when my handsome tax accountant might try to get into my pants and whether it would be more than a one-time thing.

It seems pretty silly, as well as slightly dishonest, for me to be fussed over, when in truth, I had nothing to do with anything. Still, my cooperation with the royal game plan has made everyone happy, including Her Majesty, The Morrigan, whom one always wants to please if at all possible. According to Himself, the Queen made a definite point of saying to a crowd of insiders that someone should "tell the little tooth fairy that her loyalty has been noted by The Crown." Obviously, it's much better to be on Her Majesty's good side than her bad.

No, I don't have any lingering angst over the awards ceremony. Rather, I'm completely besides myself over the terrible wedge that continues to linger between Mel and me. I tried speaking to her after Duncan's victory, but when she saw me heading her way, she hurried off in another direction, obviously working hard to avoid me. She attended the ceremony, clapping politely with the crowd, but Duncan attended the reception alone, providing a lame excuse that his lady was feeling under the weather and was hoping to lie down before tonight's celebration.

It's that very celebration, this evening's hoity-toity ball, that's also giving me a bad case of anxiety. Events like royal balls are not my cup of tea, and generally I count on my BFF to help me get through the stress of such overwhelming events. Mel could make a car wreck festive just by being herself, and I know that if she shuns me like I believe she will, it will take every ounce of fortitude I have not to fall apart into a hormonal mess. Discussing this with Declan is not an option. He's already been his usual blunt self over the opinion that I should leave my best friend alone and let her process everything at her own speed. He believes that when Mel makes her decision about the state of her relationship with Duncan, she'll undoubtedly move on to patching things up with me.

I suppose the Tax Man is right. What Mel needs now is space, and it does seem rather selfish to make this all about me. I need to pull myself together before the housemaids arrive to dress my hair and help me with my ball gown. My husband already has finished dressing and is off meeting with his father when my stomach suddenly churns and I find myself running to the commode to be sick, something that hasn't happened much since Dr. Brannigan prescribed the *Fiodoir Aisling.*

Up until this moment, the Dream Weaver drug has worked miracles in keeping my morning sickness and anxiety at bay. However, today has been at the top of the chart stress-wise, and I wonder whether perhaps I might need a booster dose. My throwing up like I just did seems to support this hypothesis. As someone in the medical field herself, I know that patients need to strictly follow their doctor's orders regarding medication, but the thought of being sick in front of all of *I Idir* makes me shudder. I've done the research and am quite satisfied that while exceeding the prescribed dosage might make me a little loopy, it won't do any physical harm to me or our baby.

The threat of possible embarrassment is a bigger worry for me. I take the vial of edible *Fiodoir Aisling* from our trunk and pop another chewable in my mouth. From experience, I know it will take an hour or two for the drug to kick in, and by then the festivities will be in full swing, so this extra little shot of happiness will be just the thing to get me through this stress-inducing, ridiculous event. Satisfied with my decision, I brush the vomit taste from my mouth just as there's a knock at our chamber door announcing that it's time to dress for the ball.

BABY 28

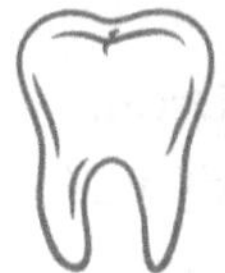

A DREAM GETS WEAVED

TURNS out that my husband is not the only one who can be vera, vera happy. It takes nearly two hours, but the *Fiodor Aisling* finally kicks in and I find myself the belle of the ball...literally. I actually greet the Tax Man's Dragon Mama with a kiss on the cheek, dance a waltz with my imposing father-in-law, and even compliment all of Declan's sisters on their choice of gowns. His Jr. Lordship looks at me oddly on more than one occasion but doesn't question my new-found social confidence. If anything, he seems relieved not to have to remain glued to my side all evening, since his role as House *Nuada's* heir requires him to make the rounds of all the members of the Ruling Council and their entourages.

Mel and Duncan are here of course, but only my husband's cousin greets me. This time, he doesn't make any excuses for his lady's avoidance of me. He simply ignores the topic altogether. I am relieved that the falling

out between my BFF and me hasn't damaged the relationship between Declan and his liege man or Duncan and
myself. Both men wisely have decided to keep their noses
out of their significant other's business, and Mel's beau
doesn't appear to hold it against me that I wasn't a fan of
their moving in together. My heart still is breaking over
the fact that my oldest and dearest friend and I are at
odds, but the extra Dream Weaver dose keeps my
hormonal emotions safely under wraps, and I am able to
get through the evening without dissolving into an
embarrassing puddle of tears.

I make several attempts to talk alone with Lady
Siobhan in order to gauge the woman's current mental
state, but she keeps herself safely surrounded by her
daughters and an older woman whose name I can't
remember. Truthfully, she looks much better than the last
time I saw her, every bit the reigning Lady of House
Nuada. This evening she has broken with tradition and is
not garbed in the House's colors of maroon and gold.
Rather, she's dressed in a stunning green, satin gown that
makes her eyes shine like clear, faceted, emeralds. When
Declan stands next to her to greet her in the expected
manner, their resemblance to one another is astounding,
and I can't believe that I ever thought he resembled his
Lord father in any way. Despite the manner in which the
two of them relate to one another, the Tax Man is one
hundred percent his Mama's boy. I put a hand on my own
belly and wonder who our Peanut will resemble. Truthfully, I don't care who the baby looks like…as long as she's
a she and not a he, an admission I can't possibly ever
make out loud.

Throughout the evening, I spend several hours on my feet, dancing with at least one male from every Ruling House, careful not to slight any of the key players. I even dance a fast-paced Fae reel with Duncan, making it through the entire eight minutes of the twisty, turning moves before seeking rest in a comfortable, overstuffed chair on the side of the dance floor. I literally fall into the cushions, completely out of breath, and send Duncan off to fetch me a cold tankard of apple juice. By the time he finally comes back through the heavy crowds, I'm having a hard time keeping my eyes open. The *Fiodor Aisling* is known to help the body relax into an almost euphoric state, while also fighting stress and keeping the waves of nausea at bay. Since I've taken an extra dose today, I now find myself completely relaxed and very sleepy. I take a few sips of the cold drink, then close my eyes for what I expect to be a short cat nap of a minute or two.

Instead, I fall into a complete, heavy REM sleep that soon gives way to dreaming. *In my dream state, I find myself standing in a prison of some sort. I know it's a prison because I am looking through metal bars, staring at a man in horrible physical condition, chained both hand and foot to a stone wall behind him. His head is slung down onto his chest, and his arms are covered with cuts, burns and bruises that match similar wounds on both legs. His head is shaved, he's covered in filth, and the little bit of clothing covering him shows a body suffering from starvation. He is a heartbreaking sight, and I feel tears of pity well up in my eyes. I try calling out to him, but no sound seems to emerge. I will myself to make the words a reality, and eventually I push the syllables out into the air... "Hello...can you hear me?" There's no response. The man doesn't even pick his head up to look at me. I try to put more force behind my attempt to speak. "You there...please answer me. I want to help you."*

Slowly, the man picks up his head, straining from obvious pain and agony. For a second or two, the lighting is too poor and I can't make out the man's features. Then, a door opens behind me and a ray of light falls directly on the poor soul's face. It's a face I know extremely well...that of my beloved husband. Immediately, I open my mouth and begin to scream...

BABY 29

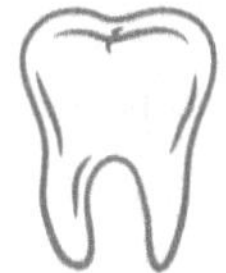

WHEN THE FUTURE MAKES YOU SICK

SO MUCH FOR not embarrassing myself. My insane screaming makes quite an impression on the multitudes of *I Idir's* movers and shakers present at the ball, and not in a good way. Half out of it and still howling, I am eventually shaken fully awake by my husband, whose face is now ghostly white as he keeps repeating over and over again, "Rosie, Lass, it's okay…wake up, Love…it's me, Declan."

It takes me a minute or two to come fully awake and out of the stupor left, I assume, by the extra dose of the *Fiodor Ainsling*. Seeing my Tax Man whole and in one piece, every beautiful, ginger hair still in place on his head, nary a bruise anywhere, makes me throw my arms around his neck. "Oh Declan, thank the Universe you're okay. It was horrible!" Tears are running down my cheeks as I pat him all over, making sure he is truly uninjured.

"Of course, I'm fine, Love. 'Tis only a bad dream, is all,"

he gently says as he wipes my teary, make-up smeared face with a linen napkin. "You must have dozed off and had a nightmare."

A crowd gathers around us, and Doctor Brannigan pushes his way through the mob to get to me. Without saying a word, he checks my pulse at my wrist, then places his hand on my forehead and then on my belly. Without a doubt, I'm sure he notes my very dilated pupils and the red tinge to the whites of my eyes, but he doesn't comment. Instead, he announces, "Everything is fine. The Lady and the *bairn* both are well, though perhaps it would be best for Lady *Mac Nuada* to return home to rest. This has been a rather long and stressful day for an expectant mother. I believe a good night's sleep is in order."

"Aye. I agree," his Jr. Lordship chimes in; "we shall take your sound advice, Robyn, and immediately head home." His voice is calm, but the words come out strangled. Before I can stand on my own, the Tax Man sweeps me up and carries me off to a waiting carriage that's appeared out of nowhere in front of *Crann Bethadh.*

Once we are alone, I attempt to apologize. "I'm sorry for ruining the evening, Declan. It was just such a horrid dream...and it felt so real." Recalling it again makes my heart beat faster, and I snuggle in closer to him, reassuring myself that it was only a stupid dream.

"I feel yar heart still racin', Rosie. Da ya' wanna' ta talk about it, Lass?" he asks. "It might help ya' move past it."

Truthfully, I don't even want to think about it, and the thought of verbalizing the events makes me queasy, but I hate to keep things from him, especially something this frightening, so I take a deep breath and begin. "I was in this dark place…a prison of sorts, and there was a man chained to the wall and moaning. He was so badly beaten and in such pain that I couldn't bear it. I began to cry even though I couldn't see his face." I hesitate, taking small, shallow breaths, getting to the words I don't want to say.

Declan prompts me to continue. "Is that all, Love? I can understand ya' feelin' sympathy for the poor man and all. Yar' a warm and compassionate woman, and I love that about ya'. But yar' awake now, and there's nothin' ta' be afraid of. I'm right here beside ya'. I'll always be here for ya'. Yar' safe with me…now and always."

That's when it hits me like an open-handed slap to the face; the sudden realization that I most likely was under the influence of *Fiodoir Ainsling…* the Dream Weaver herb that Druids have used for a thousand years to induce prophecies. The notion that what I saw while sleeping might actually occur in the future chills me to my core. Just the possibility that Declan might suffer like the man chained to the wall makes me physically ill, and I call out. "Stop the carriage, please! I'm going to be sick!"

The vehicle barely comes to a halt when I throw open the door, lean out, and promptly vomit all the contents of my dinner. Declan hangs on to me to keep me from falling headfirst into the mess I've just made. "Hell, Rosie…yar' really sick," Captain Obvious declares as I continue to retch. "I need to call for Robyn to meet us at the house. Somethin' troublin' definitely is goin' on with ya'!"

"Wait," I insist. "There's something I have to tell you, Sweetie." I wipe my face on a cool cloth that someone handed me back at *Crann Bethadh* and sit upright in the carriage seat. I take both of my husband's hands in mine. "Earlier this evening I was feeling very nervous and my morning sickness was especially bad…so I took an extra dose of the 'Dream Weaver' prior to the festivities."

Even in the dark I can see the beginnings of the dreaded cranky Declan face. "Ah, Rosie…that probably was not a vera wise thing ta' do. No wonder yar' feelin' so poorly. Robyn's right…what ya' need is a good night's sleep and time far' the drug to wear off." He instructs the driver to continue on to the *Nuada* ancestral home and turns his head so as not to get a whiff of my vomit breath.

"Declan… there's a big part of this you're missing. I don't think what I had was a regular nightmare. I think it was a prophecy brought on by the *Fiodoir Ainsling*." He turns back to me and gives me his "sure, honey…whatever you say, Lass" look, but it doesn't deter me from telling him the rest of my dream. "Sweetie, the horrible reality is that the beaten man that was in my dream…the one inside the prison…was you."

BABY 30

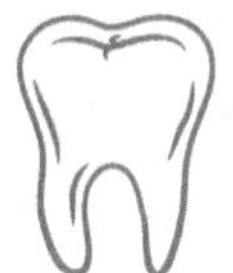

A RETURN TO NORMAL

As expected, none of the Otherworldly types take me seriously. Not my devoted Fae husband, not my highly qualified Fae obstetrician, and definitely not the three House *Nuada* druids who all declare that because of my more than 50% Mundane lineage, along with my sub-par tooth fairy magical skills, it's highly improbable that the *Fiodoir Ainsling* I consumed could ever lead to a genuine prophecy in someone like me. Even *I Idir's* current Merlin, Ambrose Myrdynn, who comes to see me as a favor to my husband, believes that the terrible nightmare is more likely the result of my very active subconscious processing all my worries over bringing a Fae child into the world, and thus not a dooming forecast of the future.

Frankly, I'm more than happy to take their educated word for it. Believing that the Universe has given me a sneak peek at such a terrible, futuristic event would just eat me alive, so writing it off as a bad nightmare is the way I prefer to go. Still, if anything good comes out of this mess, it's the fact that it's helped to get Mel and me talking again, if only at the most basic levels. My screaming performance at the ball must have really alarmed her, because she actually came to check on me at the *Nuada* ancestral home before we left *I Idir.* I can't say we are back to being the easy-going, best buds we were before my verbal faux pas, but at least we're talking. It's a start, and makes everything at my office less tense.

With the whole ceremony nonsense behind us, life returns to normal, or as normal as it gets when you have one foot in the Mundane world and the other in the Fae Otherworld. My dental practice continues to grow at a remarkable rate, and at Declan's advice, I'm looking into taking on a partner, which will surely make things easier when the baby comes. I'm also a week into my new position at the Tooth Fairy Corps, and I'm surprised how much I actually enjoy the supervisory role my new royally-granted promotion gives me. I've developed a good relationship with the tooth fairies under my supervision, and in my opinion, my updated duty roster is a lot more equitable than the one I found myself working under. Even though it's no secret that I owe this job to political connections, my co-workers appear to acknowledge my experience in smoothly managing a large group of employees as I do in the Mundane world, and for the most part, they all seem to find me to be open-minded and fair.

I say for the most part because there is one young tooth fairy team member who I get the distinct feeling just flat out doesn't like me. Lt. First Class Marcella

"Marcy" Alexandra Kilcrabtree gives me the business every chance she gets; questioning my decisions, disregarding any advice or suggestions I make, and rolling her eyes at me when she thinks I'm not looking. I'm doing my best to try and build some type of working relationship with this woman, because despite her ornery personality, "Marcy", as she prefers to be called, is extremely bright and a stickler for details. She keeps hand-written notes on every tooth she extracts, turns in her retrievals as soon as she nabs them, and has an uncanny photographic memory. She's an absolutely top-notch tooth fairy and there's little doubt she will move up through the Corps quickly.

None of this should come as a surprise. Marcy is a recent graduate of Harvard Law School and is currently employed with the IRS. Her records say that she's also a certified CPA. I keep meaning to ask Declan if their paths have ever crossed and if he knows her. Maybe he could give me some insight on how to best get around her prickly side. Until then, I have little choice but to keep a cheerful smile plastered on my face and do my best to get along with Ms. Marcy-Know-It-All. The last thing I want is for the Black Knight and the others to think I can't handle this new position or the side spy job. I still haven't lived down my screaming Banshee act from a few weeks ago and the less people hear my name, the better it will be for my growing little family.

BABY 31

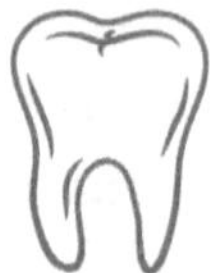

PUTTING OFF THE INEVITABLE

I TRULY HAD MEANT to ask Declan about tooth fairy Lt. Marcy Kilcrabtree. Honest. But then the whole brouhaha about the gender reveal came up, and, frankly, that's where I focused all my attention. Dr. Brannigan notified me via Mundane text message that at this point in my pregnancy, he could determine with 100% accuracy whether our baby would be male or female, and whether our Peanut would lean toward his father's *Sidhe* blood line or toward my tooth fairy heritage. Thus, he wanted us to make an appointment to go to his office for the exam and learn its results.

Reading his text made me go weak in my knees. This common gestational stage has caused me the most anxiety I've had since I knew for certain I was pregnant. Yup. Crazy as it sounds, my angst wasn't over the fact that I was starting a family with a man I'd known for less than five months, nor was it the stark realization that my new husband's family was a dysfunctional, crazy-ass mess. It wasn't even the usual working-woman's trepidation over how motherhood would affect my growing career. No. My worry was centered on the two things Robyn Brannigan now wanted to affirm; the sex of the baby I was carrying, and where the child fell on the Fae magical skill hierarchy.

I never thought I'd be the type of expectant mother who would prefer a child of one sex over the other; gender was never even a consideration for me regarding my motherhood dreams. I would have been equally happy having either sons or daughters or a mixture of both. That was until I learned of the hellacious ordeal Declan was made to suffer as the first-born male child of an Other-world Ruling House.

Technically, that title, and all of the expectations that went with it, should have gone to his first-born, twin brother, Dylan. But since Dylan was born with Declan's umbilical cord wrapped tightly around his neck, and did not survive the lack of oxygen, my husband was granted the title of Lord *Mac Nuada*, his father's heir. Along with this title came the expectation that at age 14, Declan would undergo a magical ritual that would render him completely unable to make any emotional connections with another living soul until he met the Universe's choice of his perfect mate. Though the same requirement is made of every Ruling House heir, I find it to be extremely cruel and an abomination forced on them by events that happened a thousand years before any of them were born.

The ordeal is bad enough when one must wait the

usual five or six years in what I term as emotional deprivation torture, since most House heirs find out who the universe has chosen as their mate by the time they are in their late teens or early twenties. However, in my Tax Man's case, he was forced to wait until the unheard age of 35. Thus, he waited twenty-one excruciatingly long, lonely years, until his Fated Mate, me, made an appearance in his life. I can't imagine the emotional suffering Declan was forced to endure; and although I am grateful to the Universe for binding the two of us together, this is not an ordeal I want for any child of mine. Furthermore, seeing how unhappy Declan's parents have been despite being chosen as Fated Mates, and how terminally sad the Universe's decision made my own mother, I'm also not a big fan of letting the Universe do the same for our little Peanut.

My husband, however, is deeply rooted in his Fae culture and tradition, and if this child is male, I have no doubt that his Jr. Lordship will insist that his own son adhere to the ancient ritual, and that my pleas, even in a society where women have equal rights under the law, will fall on deaf ears within the entire Ruling Council. I doubt even The Morrigan, a woman and mother herself, would take my side in this argument. For all of these reasons, I believe that life for all of us would be a hundred times simpler if Peanut turns out to be a little female tooth fairy.

Now facing the imminent revelation of reality, I'm desperately looking for a way to postpone, however briefly, what were, up to now, only possibilities before they become realities...to live in ignorant bliss for just a little while longer. I text Dr. Brannigan and say that life is far too hectic right now. Between an influx of new patients in my dental practice and a myriad of scheduling conflicts in my new role as Supervisor Captain in the Tooth Fairy Corps, I don't have a minute to myself. I can tell by the tone of his reply that he thinks my response is cagey, going so far as to remind me how important this information must be to my husband, but I'm no pushover, and he finally drops his insistence. This buys me only a little extra time to put off the inevitable and to work out a plan in case my hopeful hunch is wrong and "Pea-nette" actually turns out to be a "Pea-nut" Then, much to my relief, my dear sister, Claire, calls with an offer I simply can't refuse, and lucky me gets to stave off the reveal I'm dreading for at least another two weeks.

BABY 32

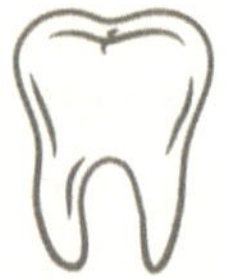

PARTY HEARTY

"'Tis the silliest thing I ever heard, Lass," my husband states, as he adds a handful of oyster crackers to his steaming chowder. "I'd rather we passed on Claire's vera kind offer."

Turners Seafood on Church Street in Salem is the Tax Man's absolute favorite place for classic New England Clam Chowder. I had hoped that enjoying an impromptu, weekday dinner out, complete with his favorite soup, on this chilly, October evening would help me achieve a positive reaction to my request. Apparently, it does not. "I don't want to hurt my sister's feelings, Sweetie," I counter. "This is something she has her heart set on doing for us, especially because she couldn't be part of our hand-fasting."

"We had a complete, second Mundane weddin' here, Rosie, and Claire was yar' maiden of honor. She was one hundred percent part of all the that plannin'." He stops to take a mouthful of soup before continuing. "Besides, wasn't that whole 'Bachelorette Party' fiasco also yar' sister's idea?" the Tax Man asks with a perfectly innocent face.

I give him the best stink-eye I can manage. It's hard to keep an annoyed expression when I'm looking at a face that melts my panties. "Seriously, Declan…you're going to bring THAT up? Again? You were really the one that caused all the trouble… posing as a male stripper! My sister had nothing to do with us landing in jail."

"I suppose yar' right about ma' involvement in that night, Love. But if I ken be perfectly honest, in ma' opinion the whole idea of lamentin' the demise of yar' single state by drinkin' too much and ogglin' half naked men appears a tad improper."

His assessment makes me giggle. "I can assure you, Sweetie, that there will be no drinking and no naked men at a gender reveal party. It's an entirely wholesome affair. Our family and friends will join us as we discover whether our Peanut is a boy or a girl."

The Tax Man makes an incredulous face. "I ken not imagine other people wantin' ta' give up their precious weekend free-time to watch us announce whether our wee *bairn* is a boy or a garl'. Seems a tad dull if ya' ask me, and no one's business other than the *mathair* and *athair*. I'm vera glad that to date, no one has ever asked me ta' attend such a tedious gathering," he says as he shakes his head.

"You don't understand, Declan. That's not how a gender reveal party works. Dr. Brannigan doesn't tell us… he tells Claire…and whoever else is helping her plan the party. Then, they decide on some adorably cute way of delivering the news to us in front of everyone."

Now my husband just looks plain horrified. "Are ya' sayin', Love, that someone other than you and I will know our intimate business before we do?"

I can't really refute his point. It is, in fact, exactly how a gender reveal party works. "Well...yes. But it's really a lovely celebration, Sweetie. Lots of decorations and good food...a joyful event with family and friends." I pull my cell phone out of my purse and bring up a popular YouTube video that I researched in advance. Handing him the phone, I say, "Here...watch this. It's a good example of what a gender reveal party looks like."

I should have realized that the Tax Man, being the logical, sensible, numbers guy he is, wouldn't settle for watching just that one, specific video I selected. I put my hand out to take back my phone, but he puts his finger up, signaling that he's not quite finished. I suddenly realize that on the left side of the screen there is a whole column of videos labeled Gender Reveal Disasters. I watch his eyes go wide as he selects a few and views them, several of which undoubtedly show one parent or another outwardly disappointed at the revelation of their baby's sex. He hands me back my phone and says, "I think this is a vera bad idea, Rosie, Love. I am askin' ya' ta' please reconsider. I don't want any bad memories attached ta' the birth of our wee Peanut."

As he says these words, I feel a sharp, stabbing pain on the top of my head, but it passes quickly and I shrug it off. "I don't understand why you have to be such a party-pooper, Declan. Who says our gender reveal party can't be awesome." I try not to look like I'm pouting, but I hadn't planned on Declan seeing those other terrible videos, and it's thrown up a whole new road block to my victory. I go to an impromptu Plan B. "Honestly, Hon, let's face it… we're no spring chickens. At our age, we're already considered 'late to the offspring party.' Who knows if we'll be blessed with any more children. If this is going to be our only pregnancy, then I want it to include all the celebrations and joy that come with the experience." Years later, I will probably think back to this statement and shake my head at the outrageous risk I took testing the Universe out loud as I had just done, but at this very moment I can only see the value of a good argument.

My husband is quiet for a full minute, weighing, I'm sure, the possibility of parenting a single child. The Fae birthrate has been low for centuries, and though the addition of Mundane blood to the mix has helped, *Sidhe* couples are given no guarantees. Declan's own parents produced six living children, one boy and five girls, but there is no assurance the same gift will be bestowed on the two of us. He hands me back my phone, and takes my hand in his. "If this means that much ta' ya', Love, then we will have this celebration as ya' wish. But promise me this…whatever gift of life the Universe sees fit to send to us, we will be grateful for it…even if it doesn't match our hearts' desires."

BABY 33

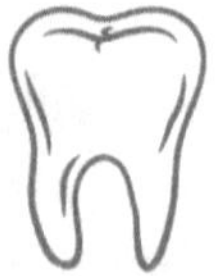

THE BIG REVEAL

I AM MORE than a little surprised when Claire tells me that she's holding our gender reveal celebration at the local community center and not her beautiful home in Swampscott. Granted, it's mid-fall in Massachusetts, and the weather isn't conducive to her and Scott using their fabulously landscaped yard or large deck to host the huge crowd she anticipates. Still, I'm a tad disappointed. My older sister as a hostess is a stickler for details, and somehow, I can't see a public rec center offering much in the way of ambience, and so I complain to my husband about it for days. In all fairness, I've been a complete nervous wreck for two weeks over finally finding out the truth about our Peanut. Pretty much everything sets my emotions off. It's a wonder Declan hasn't shipped me off to Siberia, as my moods have been changing drastically hour by hour.

As I should have realized, I've been unnecessarily

worrying about the appearance of the chosen venue. True to form, Claire has turned the open space into a fairyland of pink and blue, replete with twinkling lights, huge stuffed animals, and even a giant balloon arch. The tables all have floral centerpieces made with children's pastel building blocks and votive candles, and the buffet table even sports a large teddy bear ice sculpture. My sister has gone all out, and I can't help but to shed a few tears when I walk into such utter perfection.

The guest list is huge, a mix of Mundane and Otherworldly friends and family. Everybody who's anyone in our lives is here, including both of Declan's parents, who each scoffed at the idea and rudely commented that it was highly plebeian. No doubt my father-in law is here simply to gawk at my sister who strongly resembles the love of his life, our mother. As I've mentioned before, my husband's family is a bit...odd. Unfortunately, the two people I wanted most to be here, Duncan and Mel, are strangely absent. I ask the Tax Man about it, but he seems as surprised and disappointed about their lack of attendance as I am.

I was wrong that alcohol wouldn't be served. Cocktails of all kinds are offered along with non-alcoholic punch. The array of delicious appetizers is mind-boggling. Sadly, I can't enjoy any of them given my pending anxiety and rolling stomach. My fingers are crossed that the luncheon won't be served until after the big announcement is made so that I actually can eat something. At this point, I just want the waiting to be over.

For added fun, Claire and Scott even have set up a pink and blue booth to take bets on whether Baby Fitzpatrick will be a boy or girl. Every guest is allowed one vote, and the tickets are separated by gender in two big fish bowls. After the big reveal, one betting slip will be selected from the correct bowl, and the winner will take home a very expensive bottle of Irish whiskey, donated, I am told, by the Sheriff of Essex County, *I Idir's* own Black Knight. I smile when I see that the amount of tickets in the pink bowl far exceeds the amount in the blue one, and consider this a good omen.

After what seems like an eternity of socializing, Claire announces that all the guests should follow her. I look at Declan who just shrugs, and we tag along with the crowd, out of the party room, down a long hall and into...of all places...the community pool. I can't hide my bafflement. "Lordy, Claire, what the hell do you have planned? You're not gonna make Declan and me get into the water, are you?"

My older sister and her husband both laugh out loud. "No, silly! But we've planned something really special... just so you know how much we all love and care about the two of you and this much-anticipated new baby you're bringing into the world," she says. Music begins blaring from the PA system, and it sounds like trumpets from the Kentucky Derby. Suddenly, Mel and Duncan come marching out from the locker rooms, both attired in swimsuits, bathing caps and goggles, carrying floaty rafts and paddles; Duncan's whole ensemble is in the color blue, and Mel's, of course, is pink. A voice over the P.A. announces, "Let's get ready to rummmmmble...!"

Mel and Duncan put the rafts in the pool and climb into them. At the sound of a starting pistol, they both paddle furiously towards the opposite end, splashing and shoving each other, and making complete idiots of themselves for the benefit of the guests, who cheer, whistle and clap them on. Next to me, the Tax Man is grinning from ear to ear. He takes my hand in his and gives it a tight squeeze. "Ya' were right, Lass. This is a very special memory indeed."

My heart is in my throat. The race, in the beginning, is neck and neck, when Mel suddenly moves ahead, and in my mind, I secretly will her to paddle faster. She looks at me and smiles wide, and for the first time in weeks I know our friendship will survive my unwelcome advice about her and her lover. Then, with the pool's edge only a foot away, Mel abruptly tips the raft over and falls head first into the water, letting Duncan pass her up and ultimately moving his blue-self to the edge of the pool first. Declan turns and looks at me, and his joy at the news bubbles out of his head and over to mine. He hugs and kisses me to the cheers of the crowd. "It's a boy, Love. We have a son!" He suddenly pulls away and looks at his cousin. "Is he...?" not able to finish the question. Duncan grins and gives him the thumbs up sign. "Aye, my Lord. He's *Sidhe*. House *Nuada* will have a new heir!"

Lord *Mac Nuada* lets out a whoop as hundreds of blue balloons fall on the two of us from the ceiling. I don't know whether I want to laugh or cry. Instead, I watch the pink raft that once held my hopes for a happy family life, free from the trappings of cruel Fae tradition, float aimlessly in the center of the pool.

BABY 34

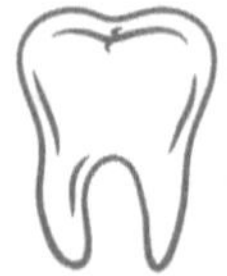

SUNDAY MORNING

Sunday mornings were made for this. I lay on my back, taking in the afterglow, still breathy and sweaty, watching the dust motes float in a rare beam of November sunlight. When I was a very young child, before I knew anything about my heritage, I liked to think those little particles I observed dancing in the sun around me were actually bits of fairy dust. Now the very idea gets my diversity dander up, the concept implying that we Fae people have clouds of dust following us around like that Pig Pen character in the Peanuts comic strip. As a dual citizen of both the Mundane and the Otherworld, I shudder at the notions humans have about the Fae.

Speaking of Fae, I caress the arm of the fine specimen of Otherworldly manhood lying next to me. "That was nice," I purr.

The Tax Man opens only one eye to look at me. "'Twas only 'nice?' Give me a few more minutes, Lass, and we shall see if I can earn a more definitive adjective from ma' beloved."

I should know better by now. Everything…and I mean everything…has a competitive nature to my husband. Even sex. "It's not a contest, Sweetie," I say. "'Nice' is good. Trust me, I'm a happy girl."

"Aye," he counters, "but if 'nice' is good, then 'mind-blowin' 'tis even better."

I don't know why I say it. It's bitchy, and petty, and bound to ruin the mood, but the words slip out anyway, and I regret them the minute they leave my mouth. "There's no need to try so hard, Declan. House *Nuada* has its heir. The deal's sealed." I instantly feel my *Mo Shiorghra* stiffen next to me. I've hurt his feelings and brought up a touchy subject that the two of us have carefully danced around since the gender reveal party two weeks ago foretold the birth of a son.

My husband rolls over and leans on an elbow. Both lush green eyes are now wide open, and I can see I've touched a nerve. "Is that what ya' really believe, Love? That our bein' together…the passion we share and the life we've created…is nothin' more ta' me than a means to further the legacy of House *Nuada?*"

I know my comment is both unfair and insulting to Declan, but I never like to be called out, nor apparently, have I learned when to leave well enough alone. "Of course not, Sweetie. I don't doubt that you truly love me. But you have to admit, our baby being male makes things easier for a lot of people."

He flops back down on his back and sighs dramatically. "Sometimes ya' drive me crazy, Rosalinda Parker

Fitzpatrick, and not in a good way." It's not a positive thing when the Tax Man uses my full name. The Fae wholly understand the power a name carries with it, so his using mine signals that he's very much upset with me. "I know that ya' are disappointed that our Peanut isn't a girl, and I am aware that ya' carry a lot of anxiety over what being a House heir will mean to our son," he lectures. "Though my heart breaks over the unhappiness ya' feel, I ken not pretend that I am not overwhelmingly relieved that I have been able to fulfill my responsibility to my House. If our baby had been a girl, I would have been just as thrilled to be her father, to love and protect her with my vera life. But if this *bairn* had been a girl instead of a boy, and we were never again gifted with any children, there would always be doubt in my head as to whether I was truly meant to be House *Nuada's* heir instead of ma' brother, Dylan. I would surely feel as if I'd stolen the title by a stroke of his bad fortune."

Now I just feel guilty that I've started the day off this way. Obviously, we needed to talk about our feelings regarding Peanut being a boy, but this certainly wasn't the best way to go about doing it. Plus, my timing really sucks.

"I'm sorry, Sweetie. I shouldn't have said what I did. You're right," I try to explain. "I was hoping for a girl so we wouldn't have to deal with all the...requirements that come with being a House heir, but I guess we'll just have to face this future issue together. I didn't mean to dismiss your feelings. It wasn't fair...or very loving, and for that I apologize."

He turns to look at me again over my growing belly.

"When ya' imply that ma' love and desire far' ya' has been based solely on yar' ability ta' produce an heir, it cuts me ta' ma' vera core, Lass. I love ya' ta' the depths of ma' soul, Rosie Fitzpatrick. You are ma' *Mo Shiorghra,* the bright light at the end of a vera dark tunnel and a vera special gift from the Universe that I surely don't deserve, but am forever grateful far'. I don't know how ta' make that anymore clear to ya', Love."

Now I'm sniffling and the lovely afterglow of earlier is a distant memory. With a morning that starts off this badly, one can only hope the rest of the day will be better, right? Nope.

BABY 35

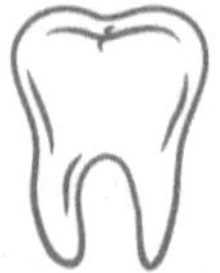

WHEN EVEN BRUNCH DOESN'T HELP

I DO what I usually do when I'm in the wrong and need to make things right; I offer a peace token. In my case, it usually involves cooking or baking. This morning's blunder requires both. Granted, my husband is less enamored of food than I am, but he understands that when I'm in my "I'm sorry mode," I'm also stirring in a good dose of "mea culpa" along with my cooking, and I believe he appreciates my efforts going back to the infamous basket of lemon-blueberry scones that started it all.

Keeping my husband's personal tastes in mind, I decide on a lobster and crab quiche with homemade crust, a blood orange compote, and some of his favorite Otherworld *eilic* (elk) sausages that I squirreled away and froze from our last trip in September. While I hustle around the kitchen, the Tax Man brings some business paperwork to look over, and we keep the conversation between us light and inconsequential. D.P. keeps me amused with banter about a wealthy client of his who is so thrifty, that he washes the throw-away, plastic silverware that comes with his carry-out orders so he can reuse them at home.

His office tale reminds me that I've yet to ask him about the new thorn in my side, the obnoxious woman giving me problems as a Tooth Fairy Corps Supervisor. While I pour the egg mixture into the prepared crust of the quiche, I make mention of it. "So...I've been meaning to ask if you might know this new tooth fairy assigned to my team. She's a real piece of work."

He doesn't look up from the page he's scanning. "I haven't kept up with Tooth Fairy business since we apprehended the Chechens, Love. No need to know, I suppose, but perhaps I might be acquainted with her. What's her name?" he asks, only half paying attention.

"I figured maybe your paths might have crossed within your Mundane business dealings. She's a tax lawyer with the IRS..." I add.

He looks up, suddenly interested. "With the IRS? Who?"

"Her name's Marcy Kilcrabtree...she's a tall, skinny redhead with a bad attitude." I can tell immediately that he knows whom I am talking about by his suddenly stiff body language and startled expression. "Ah..." I comment. "Then you do know her."

"Aye. I do. She ken' be...vera persistent. I'm sure she's quite successful working far' the IRS."

It's my turn to be interested. "So...how did you come to know her? I suppose you're right when you say you don't move in tooth fairy circles. We don't get many visits from Ruling Class lords down at the Corps." I sound much snarkier than I mean to be. I don't know what the hell has gotten into me today.

The Tax Man makes a face and I'm not sure whether it's because of my sarcastic comment implying that he looks down on tooth fairies, which I know isn't true, or if it's because he's had a relationship with Marcy and doesn't want to tell me. *OMG! Please don't let her be one of his previous conquests.* I do my best to shield my true feelings. There's no reason to escalate things without first hearing the whole story.

He shuffles his papers and pushes them aside signaling a serious discussion. My stomach suddenly feels icky, and the smell of frying elk sausages isn't helping. "About six years ago," the Tax Man begins, "I was asked by another member of our intelligence network if I would take on his wife's niece as an intern," he says. "The niece, who was studyin' to be a CPA, was havin' trouble findin' placement in har' field and such an internship was required for graduation. The man askin' far' the favor was a fine fellow, vera loyal and a real asset ta' the Black Knight's work, so I agreed ta' take the girl on, though I wasn't quite sure what was involved. It was only supposed ta' be far' a three-month period, and I assumed that it wouldn't be a terrible hardship far' me ta' do this acquaintance a favor. In hindsight, I suppose I should have required an interview with the girl beforehand, but I assumed she'd just be like any other college age woman, excited ta' be in a real-life work environment and eager ta' do well. What I didn't figure on, was her turnin' out to be so…uhmmm…forward."

I really don't like where this seems to be going. I turn

down the heat under the frying pan, and take a seat at the island. "Go on," I say.

"There was no doubt she was vera bright, with an almost photographic memory, and at first, I considered myself lucky ta' have such competent extra help. But after a few weeks, it began ta' become obvious that she was interested in...more than ma' guidance and business experience."

"How so?" I ask, not really wanting to know the sordid details but absolutely needing to hear them.

My husband grimaces and I start to fear the worst. "She began insistin' on workin' past the designated hours we'd set up at the beginning' of har' employment, stayin' long after Eleanor left the office far' the day. She was very clingy, and ta' ma' mind, there was far too much unneces-sary...touchin' on har' part; an arm pat here, an accidental brush there, with it escalatin' ta' offers of shoulder and back rubs. 'Twas makin' me vera uncomfortable. She was just a kid and her uncle was someone who trusted me not ta' take advantage of the situation. I knew I had to let her go before she put us both in a bad position."

"So you fired her?" I ask, hopeful this will be the end of the story.

"I found her a position with another accountant across town, a no-nonsense woman in har' sixties. Miss Kilcrab-tree was more than a little upset by the news, but when she took her things and stormed out of ma' office, I thought it would end there. Instead, a week later, I found her, waitin' in ma kitchen, lyin' on ma' granite island, naked as the day she was born. Feckin' hell, Rosie! I almost shot her thinkin' she was some kin' of an intruder.

It was all vera awkward and ugly. She implied ta' anyone who would listen that I 'led her on and then cast her away like a used rag doll,' which, of course, was a total falsehood. Nothing unseemly ever happened between us, nor do I feel as if I gave her any indication that anything would."

I am relieved beyond belief that there was no hanky-panky between my husband and Marcy Kilcrabtree, though I can easily imagine how a young woman might find herself overwhelmingly attracted to the incredibly handsome D.P. Fitzpatrick, decked out in his custom-fitted Brooks Brothers or Armani, just out of her reach. Lord *Mac Nuada* oozes sex appeal whether he realizes it or not, and even when he claims he isn't sending out signals, I've witnessed them myself. Apparently, at some point I've accidentally let go of my mental shields because these very thoughts are instantly read by the Tax Man.

He makes a face that fully registers his disgust. "Ya actually believe I did anythin' to lead this unhinged girl on, Lass? That I am somehow ta' blame far' the fantasies she dreamed up in har' crazy head?" I don't answer immediately...which to Declan's mind is just as much an answer. His brogue has gotten noticeably thicker throughout this entire conversation, something that happens only when he's worked up. Now, he lets loose with a whole string of Gaelic, letting me know just how unhappy he is with me. *"Tha mo bhean fhin den bheacd gu bheil mi nam racan beatha losal! Nach math sin fios a bhith agad* (My own wife thinks I am a low life rake! Isn't that nice to know)!"

He grabs the papers off the counter, adding, "She was

ten years ma' junior, Rosalinda…and a student under ma' supervision. I was just tryin' ta' be helpful and give har' a good foundation. Ta' have ya' thinkin' I'd be capable of ever takin' advantage of a situation like that…" He doesn't finish the sentence, just grabs his jacket from the hook by the back door.

"Wait…where are you going?" I ask. "Brunch is almost ready." Duh. Not the words I should have been saying.

"I guess I'm not vera hungry," my husband says. "I'm gonna head over ta' ma' office and catch up on some work," Declan says. "We'll talk later when I have a cooler head." Then, he quietly shuts the door behind him.

And there you have it, folks; explicit instructions on how to crap up a perfectly good Sunday morning.

BABY 36

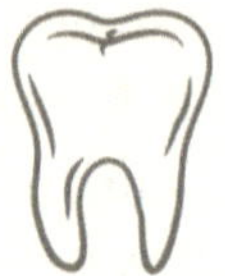

THE ALE AND PAIL

DECLAN IS GONE for several hours during which time I vacillate between being convinced that he's had enough of my hormonal bitchiness and has moved back into his own townhouse for the remainder of this pregnancy, or something terrible and awful has happened to him. Because of that horrible drug-induced nightmare I had at the Ball in *I Idir*, I lean toward focusing on the second option.

Despite all the grand magical types, (i.e Declan, Dr. Brannigan, my own Druid Master, the *Nuada* House mages, and even *I Idir's* current Merlin, Ambrose Myrdynn) assuring me that it was highly improbable for someone of my level of personal magical skill as a tooth fairy to generate serious "Dream Weaver" prophecies, I know how damn real that dream felt. There was more pain, suffering, terror and grief in that single dream than I'd ever experienced in any nightmare in my entire life, and the feeling of uneasiness it left me with still lingered three months later.

When Declan finally comes home later in the afternoon, loaded down with several bags and a huge bouquet of flowers, I'm so relieved that I burst into tears which in turn confuses the hell out of him. He puts all his parcels on the dining room table and takes me into his arms. *"Hush mo ros beag milis, ta gach rud go brea* (Hush my sweet little rose, everything is fine.)." In anticipation of our baby being bi-lingual, since early fall I've been studying Otherworld old Gaelic with a tutor, so I'm able to understand most of the words and realize he's trying to soothe me. "There be no need far tears, sweet Lassie. All couples have their disagreements. We are no different."

I don't dispute his take on the situation. I assume me going on and on about that damn nightmare again won't help matters. "I thought you left me and moved back into your townhouse," I sniffle. This close to him, I can smell the tell-tale odor of pipe and cigarette smoke, along with the stale, sour smell of Guinness. "Wait...did you spend the afternoon at a bar?" This thought shakes me, as Declan is a teatotaler when it comes to alcohol.

"Aye," he admits. "For a bit."

"I've been sitting here worrying about you all afternoon, my wonderful brunch completely ruined, and you were off drinking in a bar?" My voice takes on that awful shrew tone, and I want to swallow my tongue, but it seems to have a mind of its own.

"I was not there for the ale, Love. I went far' some sound advice," he explains.

"Advice? At a bar? From who?" I question.

"From Connor Dell," he says.

Connor Dell is a member of Declan's spy team. He's an easy-going, giant of a man, married to a wonderfully sweet *Sidhe* pixie. He also owns a traditional Irish style pub in the Derby Street area of Salem that's heavily frequented by Otherworldly types. "So...you were at the 'Ale and Pail' all afternoon...talking to Connor? About what? More damn spy 'shet'?" I question.

My husband makes a Declan 'cranky face,' obviously annoyed that I'm giving him the third degree, but then reigns in his exasperation, obviously trying really hard to remain pleasant. "No, Lass. Connor and his lovely Tessa have two wee bairns of their own. I was lookin' far' help with understandin' *iompar toirchis mna ceile* (a wife's pregnancy behavior)."

My husband's current heavy brogue and his switching back and forth between old Otherworldly Gaelic and modern English clues me to the fact that he's spent significant time with one of his own. However, I'm more than a little embarrassed that he's airing our dirty laundry among friends. "Really, Declan...I'm not crazy about you sharing the details of our marriage with other people."

"I didna' mean to embarrass ya', Love. But frankly, I am havin' trouble keepin' up with yar' mood swings. I've been a single man livin' on ma' own far' a long time. I want ta' be the best husband ta' ya' that I can, but I needed advice from someone I know who's ben' through the same thing and can tell me what ta' do."

The Tax Man looks so earnest about the situation that I tear up again. "I'm sorry I've been so moody, Sweetie. I can't seem to help it. One minute I'm fine, the next the whole world is wrong. Robyn says this is normal, especially when someone as Mundane as I is carrying a baby as genetically Fae as ours, but I know it's been difficult for us both. I perfectly understand that. Did Connor have any sound advice for you?"

"Aye," my husband, seemingly relieved that I'm not going into 'melt-down' mode again. "Dell explained ta' me that when a woman is carryin' yar wee bairn, she is always right, and the *fear ceile* (husband) is always wrong. He says it ken' not matter if I think I am not at fault. The wife is given' all that she has ta' bestow her mate with a gift beyon' measure…a family of his own…and that I shad' do whatever I can ta' make it easier far' ya' to get through the nine months…even when it seems yar' mate has gone completely *craiceailte* (crazy). I want to be that kind of *Mo Shiorghra* ta ya', Rosie."

It's a ridiculously sexist statement for the modern Mundane world, plus I'm not all that thrilled to be considered "completely crazy," but both my husband and Connor have far too much of the Otherworld in their souls to understand the nuances of modern Mundane philosophy. Plus, it's extremely sweet and reverent of them to consider the birth of a child as a precious gift. I hug him and say, "I love you, Declan Fitzpatrick. I will try very hard not to make the rest of these months an ordeal for you. I promise." I look over at all the bags and boxes he's carried in with him. "What's all this," I inquire.

He smiles. "More good advice from Connor Dell," he says. "'Tis what took up the majority of this afternoon's time. I have a fine plan far' the rest of the day, Love. A pleasant surprise. Let me show ya."

BABY 37

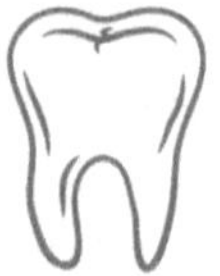

HIS LORDSHIP SAVES THE DAY

MY HUSBAND IS the king of romantic surprises. I don't mention this as an excuse to brag. It's just a flat-out fact that when his Lordship wants to sweep a woman off her feet, he knows exactly how to do it. I still get much too warm and tingly whenever I remember our very perfect handfast night. The Tax Man's plan for the rest of today might just come a close second to that special memory.

In typical dramatic Declan style, he leads me to a comfy chair in the living room and ties a silk blindfold over my eyes. My imagination runs wild with his use of an eye covering, wondering if he plans to get all Fifty Shades on me, though that's never been a preference for either of us, especially now that I have to pee every twenty minutes. I should have guessed that the Tax Man would read me better than that. When he takes the blindfold off, it's not to see any Red Room mock-up. There, in front of me, is a picnic scene spread out in all its glory on my living room rug in front of our blazing fireplace. I clap my hands together in glee. "You know me so well, Sweetie."

This, of course, is no ordinary picnic. Declan helps me down onto the floor pillows with the guarantee that he'll help me up again when we are finished. Now I understand where he's been all afternoon. "Ya' haven't mentioned any specific strange cravings, Love, so I just went with all yar' favorite Salem treats," he confesses, pleased as punch over my joyous reaction.

The Tax Man isn't kidding when he uses the word "all". There is lobster bisque from Eddie V's, fresh Spring Rolls with peanut sauce from Soall Viet Kitchen, linguini with a velvety smooth clam sauce from Bella Verona, Tikka Masala and lamb samosas from Passage to India, and for dessert, a rich, strawberry cheesecake from Caramel French Patisserie. Everything is beautifully plated on our good china and set out on the blanket, accompanied by a crisp, non-alcoholic, apple cider, chilling in our wedding gift ice bucket. "Oh sweetie…this is amazing," I gush, my mouth watering at the array of amazing smells.

"'Tis all directly from the restaurants themselves, Lass. I've only used enchantment to set it all up. I know how you dislike magically produced food," Declan proudly states.

I know perfectly well that these places are scattered all over Salem, miles apart, so ordering from each of them and then driving to pick them up took hours of time. It's so lovely, and wonderful, and romantic, that I want to cry, but I'm aware that boo-hooing is not the reaction that my Tax Man's is desiring in this special moment. Instead, I pat the floor next to me. "This is simply fabulous, Sweetie. Come sit next to me and we'll enjoy it together."

"Aye, Love. But ya' must promise me one thing," my husband asks.

"What's that, Hon?"

"When we have finished our feast, we will sit and talk, honestly and frankly," he states. "There are a great many topics that need airin' and I am tired of tip-toein' around them. We ken' not move properly forward unless we are honest with each other. I have watched my *athair* and *mathair* spend their years together in stubborn silence. I do not want that for us," he says.

He's right of course. We've spent most of our very short time together simply getting to know each other in the most basic of ways. We've had no time to really sit down and discuss our philosophies, as well as our goals and dreams for the long-term future. Little wonder that now that we are about to be parents, those missing pieces are staring us starkly in the face. I hate the idea that this lovely experience might end in disagreement, but Lord *Mac Nuada* is correct; we can't go on avoiding the touchy subjects that we undoubtedly may disagree upon. "It's a deal," I concede. "Feast first, then talk."

I put out my hand for him to shake on it, but he pulls me toward him and kisses me instead. "I want nothing more than ta' make ya' happy, Rosie Lass," he whispers. "Ya' know that, right? I'd be forever lost without ya', Love."

BABY 38

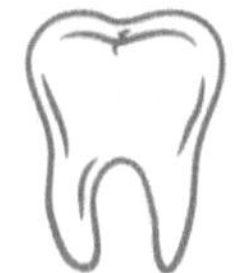

RESOLUTION

AND TALK WE DO; for more than three grueling hours on this blustery, November evening. I would like to have been able to say that the experience was satisfying and productive, but in truth, it was intense, difficult, and at times, downright painful. It's never been a secret that Declan and I are of two completely different mindsets about a whole lot of things. Despite my tooth fairy heritage, I've spent most of my life living a typical, Mundane experience, greatly influenced by my mother's negative view of the Fae culture and lifestyle. Though I now understand where her hurt and animosity was born and realize just how deeply Callum Fitzpatrick's betrayal hurt her, it's not an easy thing to change the prejudices that have shaped one's life well into adulthood. To this very day, my mom's feelings are still strongly imprinted on my way of thinking.

Declan, on the other hand, has been forced to live with one foot in each of the worlds when truthfully, he would have been most happy living his life completely in *I Idir* where his heart truly lies. His role as House *Nuada's* heir requires him to hold true to his ancient *Tuatha De Danann* heritage while modern reality makes it vital that he get a solid Mundane education and a full understanding of human culture. The vitriol of his parents' desperate unhappiness has left him with a warped idea of marriage and parenting that he's working very hard to overcome.

Thus, coming to agreement on several key topics was not easy, but we did manage to put to rest a few bones of contention. As to my disappointment over our baby's gender, both of us realized that it had nothing to do with my preferring one sex over another, and everything to do with our son's expected responsibilities as the next heir in House *Nuada's* line. I will never change my husband's commitment to his heritage. That's an absolute given. He is steadfast in his Otherworldly beliefs. Plus, as a believer myself in the Tenets of Magical Life, during our heartfelt discussion I finally came to the realization that the negative energy I was pursuing regarding the acceptance of my child for who he was created to be was selfish and harmful, and based entirely in one-sided, Mundane philosophy. There is no way to know what the Universe holds for our Peanut, and I do more damage than good by dwelling on the negative what ifs. Without blaming or mocking me for my feelings, my Tax Man helped me realize that I love this baby with a commitment I can't begin to describe and I've decided to be more open to the path the Universe has deemed for him.

In return, I help Declan understand how important my house is to me, and how much of myself I've put into making it a home. I agree that it doesn't offer the space a new, larger home might allow, but there's been so much change in my life so quickly, I feel that I need something familiar in which to anchor myself. My husband counters with the possibility of putting on an addition to the back of the house to give him more personal space, as well as remodeling the second floor to include a nursery. I'm not completely stupid when it comes to finances and business. I understand that we will never get the money back that we invest into remodeling this house as the Tax Man wishes. Not in this particular neighborhood of Salem. Being a logical numbers guy, I know this investment goes against everything Declan holds dear about money management, so when my *Mo Shiorghra* says to me, "My home is wherever ya' and our child are, Love. 'Tis all that is important ta' me," I about melt into one very large, pregnant puddle.

These are two major points that I am greatly relieved we have resolved. Unfortunately, those are the only two we can deal with at the end of a very long day. The abundance of rich foods has made me sleepy, although I am intrigued by Declan's promise to still change my description of our morning encounter from "nice" to "glorious". We never do get around to talking about possible names for our son, though my husband pretends to be serious about calling him *"Pis Talun,"* which you guessed it, means peanut. More importantly, we never do get around to discussing how to handle my disagreeable team member and Declan's former intern, Marcy Kilcrabtree. It will always remain unclear to me whether anything we might have said or suggested that day would have made a difference to the disaster that eventually occurred.

BABY 39

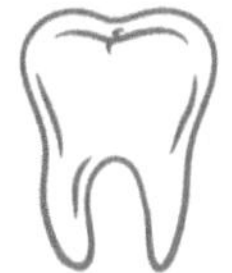

BIRTHDAY SURPRISES

GROWING UP, my family never celebrated the Winter Solstice. In deference to my dad's Judeo-Christian beliefs, December was entirely about Christmas and the Parkers always did it up in a big way. Our house was the most colorfully decorated on the block, our fresh-cut tree the largest among all of my schoolmates, and as a professional pastry chef, my mom's Christmas cookies were the prize gift of every family on our street. I was a teenager of sixteen before I had any experience with the Otherworld celebration that welcomes the return of the sun, and that was only because my mother finally gave in and let me attend a Solstice party at Mel's home.

Mel's parents are both half *Sidhe,* having met in *I Idir* at some festival or another when they were in their teens. Her mother is a well-known interior designer and her father is the CFO of an energy company in Boston.

Despite such prestigious and all-encompassing Mundane careers, both of her parents are highly committed to retaining their Fae identities, and Mel, their only daughter, grew up, like my husband, with one foot firmly planted in both worlds.

I'm not sure why my Fae prejudiced mother finally gave in and allowed me to celebrate with my BFF that year, but I came away from that experience with the shocking realization that many of the Christian and secular Christmas traditions in my own life had been swiped from the ancient pagan culture; the use of candles, holly and evergreens to decorate the home, the burning of the Yule log, wassail bowls and special holiday music have long been part of the Solstice celebration.

The following year, I boldly asked my parents if we could add the burning of the pagan Yule log to our own celebration. They agreed, always open-minded to allowing both Claire and I to follow our individual spiritual paths. Little by little, some of the traditions of the Otherworld made their way into the Parker home, and our celebrations became richer and more meaningful to me because of it.

Through the years that followed, I've become more comfortably aligned with the Winter Solstice celebration, though I haven't completely given up a few traditions from my early childhood. This year, our first major holiday together, the Tax Man and I have agreed to celebrate both Mundane and Otherworld traditions. Declan has promised me that for this year's Solstice holiday we'll stay home in the Mundane world and forgo any trips home to see his family which has me greatly relieved. Time spent with the Fitzpatricks under any circumstances, holiday or otherwise, is extremely stressful. Still, had I known ahead of time about the special holiday office party I was expected to attend, and had been given a choice between the two, I might have chosen Declan's family as the easier alternative.

The first mention of this impending fiasco came today, which also happens to be my birthday. The two of us had enjoyed a fabulous celebratory dinner at the Adriatic, a Mediterranean restaurant that's a favorite of mine. Back at home, my husband had romance on his mind, along with a stack of beautifully wrapped gifts, one of which contained a stunning hooded capelet made of the softest silver fur I believed to be fox, and lined with downy lamb's wool.

I could immediately tell by the unusual color and the careful hand stitching that it was an Otherworldly piece. Large silver-pelted foxes do not exist in the Mundane world, and the craftsmanship of the cape was far more exquisite than what one can usually get here in the United States. Truthfully, I've never been much of a fur-loving girl, as my sympathy lies with the poor animal, but I decided to keep my opinions to myself so as to not spoil the festive evening.

That decision must have been goddess sent as it so happened that the gift came with a story of exceptional importance to my loving husband. According to Declan's tale, the fox that supplied its pelt for this cape was a very rare, very aggressive beast that had been terrorizing the local Otherworld population near the *Nuada* ancestral home for months. My then sixteen-year-old husband bravely tracked it down and killed the vicious animal on his own despite being explicitly told by his *athair* not to do so. In the aftermath, my Lord *Mac Nuada* was severely scolded by both his parents for his disobedience and sentenced to three weeks of mucking out horse stalls, but his father secretly had the hide cleaned and preserved which he proudly presented to his son when Declan had completed his punishment.

My *Mo Shiorghra* had saved the pelt all these years, waiting for the perfect use for an Otherworld treasure of this magnitude. It was hard not to hear the genuine pride and delight in his voice when he expressed his hope that it would, "forever keep ma 'One and Only' warm of heart and body." I can't tell you how relieved I was that I hadn't gone ahead and rained on the Tax Man's parade with a lecture about the evils of wearing animal fur. It surely would have deeply hurt his feelings, something I certainly didn't wish to do. Plus, it truly was a stunning piece of outer wear, the silver gray of the fur catching the light and shimmering like moon beams on a watery surface.

"It's lovely, Declan, really beautiful, made even more special because of the story attached to it." I gush. "I can't wait to wear it out," I add, secretly hoping I don't run into any animal activists with inclinations to throw red paint on me and my fox fur coat.

"I'm so happy you like it, Love. I've ben' lookin' forward to given' it ta' ya' for months. I decided on a cape rather than a coat so that it will fit over both ya' and our little Peanut," he says shyly. He pauses and then quickly adds, "I am hopin' ya' will want to wear it to The Morrigan's Solstice celebration on the 20th, Love."

Solstice celebration? The Morrigan? What the hell was this all about?

BABY 40

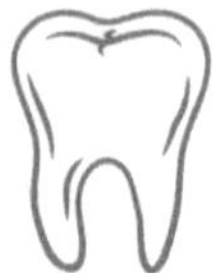

DECLAN THE DRESSMAKER

I CAN SAY, unequivocally, that I adore my husband. There's not a shred of untruth in that statement. I'm head over heels in love with the man, but in the seven months I've known Declan Phineas Fitzpatrick, I found that he has a handful of very annoying habits, one of them being his propensity for holding back on giving me unwelcome news he knows I will continually stress over. In his mind, his not telling me in advance keeps me from what he calls, "obsessin' over things than ken' not be changed." What he doesn't seem to understand is that the obsessin' helps me eventually come to terms with whatever angst the news will cause me.

I've personally never enjoyed holiday office parties. Not when I was an employee during my high school and college days, nor as an employer of a staff of eight. When I first started my practice, I went the usual route of hosting an evening Christmas soiree, but I always felt that no one really enjoyed this forced festivity, especially so close to the holiday. The majority of my staff members are working moms with enough already on their plates during the Yule season without me adding another obligation to their busy Christmas calendar. Five years ago, I changed my night out to a day at a local spa during the week following Christmas. With the office closed, all of us spend the day enjoying a respite of complete pampering that leaves everyone feeling rejuvenated and ready for New Year's Eve. It's an alternative that my staff one hundred percent loves.

To my mind, attending a Solstice party given by Her Majesty, at the home of the *Baphrionsa* (Princess) of *I Idir* and her Black Knight husband is the stuff nightmares are made of. Though The Morrigan has so far been nothing but pleasant and generous, the Queen goddess scares the living crap out of me. Just being in her presence is enough to make me sweat. Plus, I've never actually spoken to the *Banphrionsa.* What would I ever have in common with Fae royalty? I explain all of this to my husband, who as usual, just tells me that he will be right by my side and that I have nothing to worry about. Grrrrr.

During the days leading up to the celebration, I refuse to give up on my litany of reasons why we should send regrets: I can't drink. Rich food gives me indigestion. My feet swell when I stand too long. I don't know what to say to royalty folk. I look like a whale. I don't have anything appropriate to wear.

"I understan' that ya' don' wanna' attend this event, Love. I get that, and I sympathize. I really do," he counters. "I do not especially enjoy large gatherins' either. But I ken' not refuse an invitation from Her Majesty. This party is har' way of showin' her appreciation to har' intelligence staff. As ma' handfasted *Mo Shiorghra*, ya' will be expected ta' be at ma' side. Anything else would be an …embarrassment…ta' me as well as ta' House *Nuada*. I know ya' wouldna' want ta' unintentionally shame me, Love, so I'm askin' far' yar' patience. I promise we'll not stay long, and I am sure the *Baphrionsa* will offer a variety of refreshments so that ya' ken' find somethin' ta' yar' likin'. She is known ta' be an excellent hostess."

I hate when the Tax Man sounds so sweet and sensible. It makes it harder for me to refuse him. Still, I give it one more ambitious try, "Sweetie…if you would have just given me more notice, I could have bought something more in line for a royal summons," I say as I point to my closet and bat my eyes innocently. "I have nothing nice enough in there to wear and by now all the stores are picked clean for the holiday. Especially in pregnant-lady-barrel-sizes."

I sometimes forget about my husband's magical skill. He raises that one damn eyebrow like only he and his *mathair* seem able to do. "Have ya' checked yar closet recently, Lass?"

I narrow my eyes and open the door. There, hanging on a hook, is a chic cocktail-style maternity dress in a soft emerald green velvet, thoroughly Mundane except for the Celtic embroidery at the cuff of the sleeves. It's understated, but classically beautiful with a rather revealing neckline to highlight my most noticeable…assets. On the floor underneath the dress is a pair of satin slippers in the same emerald green color, perfect for someone whose feet have recently taken to swelling.

Part of me is annoyed that the Tax Man has taken it upon himself to select my attire for a party I don't even want to attend. I'm a grown woman, perfectly capable of dressing myself. But the other half of me is genuinely relieved. When it comes to fashion and proper apparel in both worlds, my husband is a master of good taste and is himself always impeccably dressed. The frock he's chosen for me is perfect for hobnobbing with the Otherworld upper crust while still here in the Mundane world.

I run a hand over the sleeve. "It's so soft," I admit. "But what if it doesn't fit? I'm shaped like a beach ball with short legs and no waistline," I grumble. "I'm not even sure what size I wear anymore."

"I know every curve on yar body, Love. It will fit. I can guarantee it," Lord *Mac Nuada* says with a wicked grin. He pulls me closer to him. "Let me show ya' how I do ma' own personal measurin'..."

BABY 41

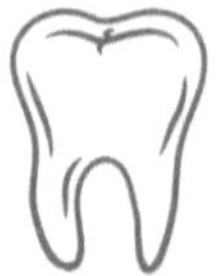

BE OUR GUEST

MR. AND MRS. THEODORE BECKETT, aka The Black Knight, Hand of Her Majesty, and his wife, the *Banphrionsa* of *I Idir*, live in a mansion-sized Victorian home in the most expensive area of Swampscott, Massachusetts. Despite abominable December New England weather, I admit that I am cozy, warm, and dry in my gifted silver fox cape, though I wish my dress were several inches longer so it could cover my knocking knees. The trek from Salem on icy roads takes much longer than we had anticipated and now we are nearly twenty minutes late which only serves to make my husband especially cranky and doesn't help much with my overall social anxiety.

We are met by a valet, who thankfully takes the keys to Declan's car to park it, though who knows where, since the streets lining the house are packed solid with automobiles bumper to bumper for several blocks. The Tax Man grabs me tightly around the waist to prevent me from slipping on any ice, but that's only because I have refused to let him carry me all the way to the front door. I am a nervous wreck which makes Declan more anxious than he normally is when mixing with the Otherworld upper crust, and together, our auras are undoubtedly giving our true feelings away.

In keeping with the valet service, I expect a butler to answer the door, so I am surprised and thrown off guard when it is The Black Knight and his Lady who welcome us to their home. I briefly met the *Banphrionsa* at our handfast ceremony, but I still am amazed at how much she resembles her Great Grandmother the Queen despite being several generations down The Morrigan's line. Genetics are a funny thing and it makes me wonder what my own son will look like. Honestly, I secretly hope he's as handsome as my husband.

Both of our hosts greet us warmly, and the Princess compliments me on my fox fur, which allows Declan to once again tell the story of how he came to owning the pelt. This gets several people within hearing distance interested in the tale, thus taking the focus off Lady *Mac Nuada* and allowing me to take a deep breath and look around. Despite its large size, the house seems cozy and inviting, gaily decorated for the Solstice and Christmas celebrations. People are milling about all over the place, helping themselves to drinks and hor d'oeuvres from the trays of circling waitstaff. I don't see Her Majesty in the crowd, and feel a sense of relief. Unfortunately, the momentary pause in anxiety is short lived. What I do feel is a pair of eyes boring into my back. I turn around slowly and catch my senior-pain-in-the-ass-tooth-fairy-nemesis staring straight at me with a nasty, smug, little smile on her face. Declan must sense my sudden increase of dread because he looks up, first catching my eye, then that of Marcy Kilcrabtree. *"What the hell is she doing here?"* I mentally ask my husband. *"I thought you said this gathering was only for members of the Queen's intelligence service."*

Lord *Mac Nuada* frowns which earns him a stink eye from the tooth fairy lawyer. *"I have no idea why she would be included in this celebration,"* Declan admits. *"I was not aware she'd been invited. The man she's with is Ronin Peirson. He works far' a cyber security company here in the Mundane world and spies far' Her Majesty in that capacity. Perhaps the Kilcrabtree woman is his date, poor soul, though I know the Black Knight usually frowns upon anyone bringin' 'outsiders' ta' intelligence meetings or events. Most citizens of I Idir don' even know this task force exists. It's why The Morrigan hosts this gatherin' here in the Mundane world rather than at Crann Bethadh. Less pryin' eyes that way. I'm afraid that if that connivin', vicious woman is openly welcome here she has somehow managed ta' worm har' way onto our team."*

BABY 42

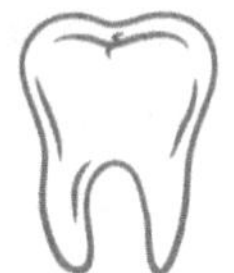

PUTTIN' ON THE RITZ

THIS NEW REVELATION that Marcy Kilcrabtree is not only a guest at this holiday event, but a possible member of the Queen's network leaves me queasy. For a second, I consider the benefits of not having to see her condescending looks and constant eye-rolling in my position at the Corps, but the idea that she's now possibly become my husband's problem is a bigger worry considering their past history. I can tell the Tax Man is also none too pleased with this ugly turn of events. I can hear him swearing in some language or another in my head.

The sneaky bitch whispers something to her date who then looks up and wanders towards us. I can see by the look on Ronin Peirson's face that he is apprehensive about attempting an uninvited meet and greet. Despite this evening being sold to its guests as a celebration, there's no denying that this is an Otherworld function hosted by Her Royal Highness with strict court protocol expected. Lord *Mac Nuada* is a high-ranking member of *I Idir's* social hierarchy as well as the young man's Superior within the Black Knight's spy network, and therefore, not someone to treat as a casual acquaintance.

Peirson gives a short waist bow, and my nemesis is forced to drop what's obviously a half-ass curtsy so as not to look as if she's being outrightly disrespectful. Her date is flustered, his cheeks flushed a pale pink and he stumbles over his words. "Solstice Breastings, Lord and Lady *Mac Nuada*." He catches himself, stares at my low-cut neckline, and corrects his original words. "I mean blessings, not breastings."

I can't help but feel sorry for the young man who has had the misfortune to be hoodwinked into accompanying this mean girl to an event like this. There's no denying that Marcy Kilcrabtree is an attractive *Sidhe* woman in her prime, and her allure would be difficult for any Fae male to ignore. She smiles sweetly at my husband and ignores me altogether. *"Beannacht Shona agus griastad geal, a Thiarna Mac Nuada* (A happy Yule and bright Solstice, Lord *Mac Nuada*)." My hubby doesn't answer, instead pressing his lips together in a thin line and narrowing his eyes. Ronin Peirson colors again and nudges his date in the side. Marcy gives me a half smile and adds, "And to you as well, my Lady."

I can feel cranky Declan vibes crawling all over me. In most situations, my husband is as staid as they come, donning his Mundane accountant personae; cool, collected and maddingly neutral. I suppose it's been his way of keeping the quick temper he's obviously inherited from his mother, along with her good looks, at bay over the years. It's why when we first met, I had no idea of the feelings he claims to have had for me during that initial awkward meeting. Declan Fitzpatrick keeps his feelings close to the vest until he feels comfortable enough to share them with you. Right at this moment, he's not doing a really great job at keeping his annoyance under wraps. "I must say I am extremely curious as to why you are in attendance this evening, Miss Kilcrabtree. The Black Knight usually doesn't include tooth fairies in his social circle," his Lordship replies, not bothering to hide the haughty tone in his voice.

I inwardly cringe at his comment. Not only is it rude and elitist, my husband has inadvertently insulted me as well. I know this is not the way the Declan I know and love truly feels. He is the least title-conscious person I know and his statement here leaves me stunned. I hear him in my head. *"I am sorry, Love. You know I don't truly mean what I've just said. But I'm afraid I ken not let this bold 'calleach' (witch) believe she can act towards me with such blatant familiarity. I have made that mistake with har' before. I will not make it again. If I have hurt ya' with ma' words, then I offer ma' truest apology. I would die befar' I would knowingly wound ya'."*

"I'm not fond of this side of you, Declan. It reminds me too much of your mathair's behavior, though I'm not much of a Marcy Kilcrabtree fan myself."

There is a long moment of incredibly awkward silence. Lord *Mac's* undeniably rude comment has stunned even its thick-skinned recipient. The attractive *Sidhe* attorney blushes a deep red and looks away. I wish I could say I feel sorry for her, but I'd be lying, and I accept whatever that says about me.

Out of the corner of my eye, I see my husband's cousin, Duncan, cross the room in three large steps, a man on a mission if ever I saw one. Duncan is a *gancanagh*, the Otherworld version of an incubus. Even on his worst days, a few of which I've personally been witness to, Duncan Fitzpatrick is unbelievably handsome. He is by far the most attractive and seductive man in the room, although in all honesty, the Black Knight would be a very close second. (I often wondered if there wasn't a bit of *gancanagh* DNA in the young Merlin's bloodline.) This is not to take anything away from my own husband. I still go all mushy every time the Tax Man looks at me with those heavenly green eyes. It's just a fact that my husband's righthand exudes sex appeal from every pore.

Duncan joins our group, immediately greeting Declan with a bow. "Good evening, my Lord. How fare thee on this festive evening?"

My husband greets his cousin with a nod of his head and an open smile, then slaps him on the back in easy familiarity. "I am well content, Cousin. 'Tis all because of my Lady that I am so blessed with the joy few men share." It's my turn to make a face. The Tax Man is laying it on pretty thick.

Duncan takes my hand and kisses it, afforded such public affection because we are considered family. "Lady Rosalinda, you are a sight to behold. The goddess Danu surely shines through you. You bring a touch of the divine to this humble gathering."

I am very fond of my husband's cousin. We've been

through a lot together. He's also my BFF's main squeeze, and the four of us spend lots of time in each other's company. However, I'm not naively stupid. I know when I'm being included in a full-on line of Otherworldly bull-shit. Something is at play here. I can just feel it.

BABY 43

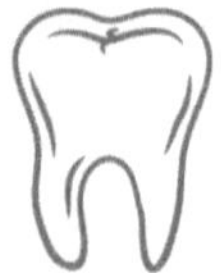

A TOAST TO TITLES

OUR *GANCANAGH* COUSIN abruptly turns his honed-in attention to the two other members of the group. "And who might this gorgeous nymph be, Peirson?" Duncan asks. "Ya've been holdin' out on yar' fellow comrades." He smiles at Marcy with that sexy, boy-like charm that's undoubtedly fluttered an abundance of female hearts, my dear friend's included. I can't help but feel a pinch of annoyance that he's flirting so outrageously while he and Mel are living together. He takes the mean girl's hand, and I see her flinch. I know exactly what she's feeling; that tingling shot of electricity that comes from touching an Otherworld incubus.

Marcy doesn't wait for her date to introduce her. She actually giggles. "I'm Marcy Kilcrabtree. And who might you be, Lord...?"

Duncan laughs and even I can't help but feel the air around us buzz with the *gancanagh's* seduction. On one hand, it makes me want to smack him for attempting to cheat on Mel, right in front of my nose! On the other hand, his magical libido vibes hit home and what I really want to do is find a hidden closet somewhere and drag my husband into it.

In my mind, I hear Declan snicker. *"Hold that thought until later, Lass. And don't get yar' feathers all ruffled over ma' cousin's charade. Duncan is doin' what he does best at ma' personal request. If anyone can get information about what that siren-wanna-be is up to, 'tis ma' cousin."*

I'm a trifle miffed at being caught up in Duncan's games, so I'm probably a little more careless with my choice of words than I ought to be considering the situation. *"Well, isn't that just dandy, Lord Mac. Do you often 'pimp out' your friends?"* I regret the comment the moment my husband receives it. I can literally feel his annoyance with me as if it were a bucket of ice-cold water thrown on my *gancanagh*-induced libido. I immediately try to apologize but get stony silence in return, and I know I've gone and hurt the Tax Man's feelings, which will no doubt require a lot of honey-dipped apologizing and some extra ass-kissing on my part.

At this point, all I desire is to go home. I can feel my feet swelling, and inside the house with its abundance of guests, I am overly warm in my velvet dress. As I contemplate the myriad of excuses I can use on my husband to convince him that we should leave early, there begins loud clapping and the sound of music coming from the house's foyer. It's obvious from the rush of Otherworld magic and the sense of urgent pomp that Her Majesty, Queen Maeve of *I Idir*, has made her appearance.

From where we are standing, I can't actually see The Morrigan. For all the magnitude of her magical presence, the goddess of war and destruction is physically quite petite, a mere 4' 8" or so in stocking feet. I can tell she is officially being greeted by the host and hostess only by the presence of the Black Knight whose head bobs above the crowd, because, like my husband, he is well over six feet. I assume the Lady Dear Heart is with her Knight, though I can't see her either, as her tiny self is also lost to the crowd.

The waitstaff comes around with a tray of champagne in preparation for what I know will be a long series of toasts in the Queen's honor. I start to take a glass to hold just to be polite, but the young waiter stops me. "The *Banphrionsa* has seen to your non-alcoholic needs, my Lady. Someone will be by shortly with a glass of cider for you to drink in place of the champagne."

It's a very thoughtful thing to do, proving that the Princess of *I Idir* is a very gracious hostess. A few moments later, another waiter brings me a single glass on a tray. "Sparkling Cider, my Lady. Alcohol free."

My husband's icy mood thaws a bit, not because of anything I've done, but because the *Banphrionsa* has noted my pregnancy and has taken the time to accommodate me. In my husband's eyes, this is a sign of respect for his title and the work he provides The Throne, which reminds me of just how feudal and foreign the hierarchy of *I Idir* really is compared to what I've known during my whole lifetime in the Mundane world. And just like that, Lady *Mac Nuada* is back to feeling every bit a lowly tooth fairy.

BABY 44

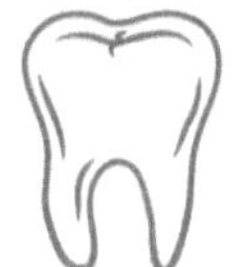

WINDOWS TO THE SOUL

THE TOASTS GO on for what seems like forever and then Her Highness gives her own speech thanking the people gathered here for their loyal service. Her gratitude seems wholly sincere, but the theme is nonetheless seriously alarming. "Never in our history has *I Idir* and the other kingdoms of the Otherworld faced such a serious threat from the Mundane world and its leaders," The Morrigan preaches. "Our enemies of today are like the ancient dire wolves of the dark days, threatening us not with magical teeth and claws, but with the unholy altering of the Universe, using their twisted weapons of technology and genetic manipulation to attack and destroy the sacred gift of life."

I've been standing in this spot for over an hour now and my back and feet are in full-ache mode. Even when I'm working, I need to take short breaks off my feet to counter the extra, off-balance weight of our Peanut. I shift from one foot to another, doing my best not to seem fidgety or distracted while the Queen is speaking. Nothing gets by the Tax Man. *"Do ya' need to sit down, Lass. I will find ya' a chair."*

I'll be damned if I will look like an invalid or a weakling. Everyone else is standing. I plan on doing the same. *No, thank you. I'm fine. I'm thinking dinner should be served soon. I'll sit then."*

I get a single eyebrow raise in return. Apparently, I am still on the shit list. I am, however, right about dinner. I smell hot food being set out so it's easy to deduce we'll shortly be done with all this formality. The end of The Morrigan's sermon is greeted with applause and cheers, and people begin dispersing towards the dining room. The splendid repast is served buffet style with small cafe tables set up in areas all over the first floor. Lord *Mac* takes my arm, leads me to a table and chairs nearest where we were standing, and suggests I sit while he brings me a plate.

Under any other circumstance, I would have preferred to peruse the offerings myself and select what appealed to me in the moment, but I get the distinct feeling my evening will be a lot more pleasant if I refrain from disagreeing. I smile sweetly and say, "As my Lord wishes. I'm sure you will pick out the perfect pairings for me."

The tiniest bit of a smile crosses the Tax Man's face, and it's clear that he understands that I'm trying to be on my best behavior. He disappears into the crowd and I am left to entertain myself until he returns. I watch as Duncan leads Marcy Kilcrabtree toward the buffet table as her obviously disgruntled escort follows behind them. I can tell Ronin Peirson would like nothing better than to take my husband's cousin outside and discuss a few things with him, but Duncan's reputation has grown to mythical proportions since his triumph over *McBadh's* man. In addition, my husband is also the *gancanagh's* Liege Lord, and the *Nuada* name carries a lot of weight.

I watch as Her Highness makes the rounds of the room, her infant great granddaughter in her arms with the Lord Warrior at her side. It's not hard to observe that she is making a point to speak to everyone, careful to show equal attention to members of each and every House. I count myself lucky that Declan is busy at the buffet table and I'm here alone. The Queen of *I Idir* has no reason to notice me.

You would have thought I'd already learned my lesson about underestimating The Morrigan's ability to know everyone's business. Apparently not. Before I can even react, I hear what sounds like the tinkling of bells in my head. I look up and see that Her Highness has excused her royal self from the group she'd been conversing with and is heading directly toward me. I try not to look like a deer in the headlights, but I'm suddenly very, very warm and I can feel a red flush climb up my ample cleavage. As she nears, I struggle to rise from my chair to curtsy but she motions to me to remain seated.

Her Majesty shifts the baby to one arm and smiles at me with utter amusement. "So little tooth fairy *mathair*, why are you not enjoying the delights of my sumptuous buffet?" she asks while the baby in her arms giggles as if she too understands my embarrassment. "Surely you are eating for two?"

Somehow, I make the words come out louder than a squeak. "I look forward to a fine sampling, Your Highness. I have let my Lord select for me this evening."

She grins wider, and for a mere second, I swear I see the head of a raven where her face should be. "You are a fast learner, Lady *Mac Nuada.* The Universe has made an excellent match." The infant princess squirms in her grandmother's arms, and reaches her hands out to me. "The wee *Banphrionsa* wishes to touch your belly, Lady *Mac.* Is that alright with you?" The Morrigan asks.

It's not like I can say no, plus Princess Mairead is an absolutely beautiful child. Not for the first time do I have a pang of regret that our Peanut is a boy and not a lovely little girl. The Morrigan looks directly at me and says, "Your wish will come, little tooth fairy. In time. For now, things are as they should be." Her words do funny things to me and I can't think of a proper response. The Queen lifts the baby towards me and I take the little princess into my lap. She has the coloring of House Morrigan but her little face mirrors that of her handsome father. Her eyes are the most brilliant shade of teal I've ever seen, highly unusual and simply stunning.

The infant places her chubby little hands on my belly, moving them across my rounded baby bump. She looks up at me with a smile and then turns to her grandmother. The Morrigan tilts her head and speaks out loud, seemingly to the baby "*An amhlaidh, a stor beag. Ansin is docha go bhfeicfimid cad ata ar intinn ag na Cruinne* (Is that so, Little Treasure? Then I suppose we shall see what the Universe intends).

Noting my quizzical expression and sudden flash of

anxiety, Her Royal Highness tells me, "'Tis no need to fret, little tooth fairy. All is well. The wee princess has informed me she and your boy child shall be great friends someday."

Relief washes over me like summer rain. Ever since that awful nightmare I had while under the influence of the *Dream Weaver*, I've been hinky about anything that reeks of prophecy. "That is a very sweet thought, Your Majesty. I hope to witness that someday," I stutter, not sure if I should address the Queen or the baby in her arms. Luckily, my husband arrives with two plates of food which he gracefully places on the cafe table before greeting Her Majesty in the proper manner. Bowing deeply, he says, "Solstice Blessings upon you and your House, Your Highness." Declan places his hand over his heart in a sign of fealty. The Morrigan and baby stare at him for an uncomfortably long time, until the Raven Queen touches his cheek with her hand. Even I, as non-magical as they come, feel the vibration of her magical transfer. "You are the future of *I Idir*, Lord *Mac Nuada*," The Morrigan pronounces. "Have faith in your path." Then, without another word, the Queen turns around and walks away, with Princess Mairead looking over her grandmother's shoulder at us with those haunting teal-colored eyes.

BABY 45

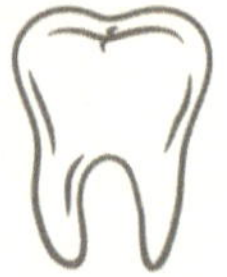

WORDS

DECLAN and I wait patiently until after dessert is served to say our goodbyes. I'm so tired, I sway on my feet and cover a yawn as we don our coats for the ride home. The ice pellets that accompanied us on the ride to Swampscott have turned to thick snowflakes, camouflaging the slippery sidewalk underneath. The Tax Man doesn't even ask permission. He hoists me up as if I weigh next to nothing and gingerly makes his way down the icy path to where the valet has our car waiting.

My husband is unusually quiet on the ride home. I'm not sure whether it's because he's still aggravated with me about my snarky pimp comment, or whether he's as troubled by The Morrigan's prophetic comments as I am. I put a hand on his thigh and rake my fingers along the inside of his leg. "I truly am sorry, you know…about what I said earlier."

A half smile turns up his lips. "Ya don' fight fair, do ya

Lass." He abruptly puts on his indicators and turns into the brightly lit parking lot of a big box store, still heavy with shoppers looking for bargains at this late hour.

"Why did you pull in here?" I ask. "Do you have naughty plans to ravish me here in the car," I tease, "or are you just hoping to catch up on your last-minute holiday shopping?"

He laughs and I'm glad not to see cranky Declan. "A good ravigin' isn't a bad plan, but alas, we'd have far too much of an audience for ma' likin', and the energy of this snow storm will make veilin' difficult. Best we wait until we get home for that. I do wish, however, ta' discuss yar' comments from earlier this evenin' and I ken' not drive distracted on these types of roads. 'Tis best we stop and say what needs ta' be said."

My stomach sinks as I prep for a scolding that's so bad it requires the Tax Man's full attention. I feel myself getting a bit defensive. It's not like I wanted to go to this stupid party to begin with. I just went to please him and now I'm getting reprimanded as if I was a child.

His Jr. Lordship must read my annoyance. Taking my hands in his, he says, "It will not help matters if ya' get defensive evera' time I wish to say something ya' don't wan' ta' hear, Lass. It is sure to cause resentment far' us both."

He's right, of course. I try not to pout. "Look, I said I was sorry. It was a stupid, rude thing to say, but I didn't mean anything by it. Seeing that damn woman there put me on edge. I was just being cranky."

"I understand that, Love, and I fully accept yar' apology. I know ya 'well enough to know that sometimes yar' feelins' and yar' tongue move faster than yar' thoughts, and most of the time the things ya' say make me laugh. But this evenin' ya' crossed the line. To compare yar' beloved husband to a trader of flesh and ta' describe our good and loyal cousin as ma' whore is both disrespectful and hurtful. I realize that words dona' carry the same weight or value in the Mundane world, but they are everythin' amongst the Fae. It is vitally important for ya' ta' remember that goin' forward."

I open my mouth to say something, but he cuts me off. "Imagine if yar' words had somehow leaked from yar' head and Duncan had heard them? The man holds ya' in the highest regard, Lass. You are family ta' him. Do ya' understand how devastated he would feel ta' think that ya' believe his service to his Liege Lord and ta' The Crown is nothing more than a whore's business?"

I'd never given any thought to the idea that my words would refer to Duncan as well. The Tax Man is right. His cousin would have been cut to the heart by a comment I flippantly threw out in my annoyance and frustration. It could have put a permanent rift between Duncan and the two of us. Now I can't help but panic. "Oh shit! Duncan didn't hear me, did he?" I ask

My husband shakes his head. "No. He was far enough away and thankfully yar' shields were strong this evening." He looks directly at me and adds, "But at times, Lass, they are not vera strong and I greatly fear someday ya' will think something out loud ya' can't take back."

BABY 46

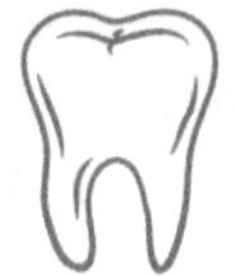

MARCY TALKS

THE LAST THING I want to see when we pull up to our house is Duncan's car parked in front of it. My husband doesn't seem surprised to see him, which annoyingly means that Declan knew his cousin was stopping by and decided not to share this information with me. It's well after 11:00 PM and I'm exhausted. Parties in the middle of the work week are hard enough, but after the stress of Otherworld protocol, along with the shame of being scolded by the Tax Man, all I'm looking forward to are my comfy PJs and shamelessly begging my hubby for one of his magnificent foot rubs before bed. Duncan showing up like this means whatever he has to tell my husband can't wait until morning.

Meeting us at the door, Duncan apologizes to me. "I am sorry to intrude on yar' evening, Rosie. I am aware 'tis late and ya' are most likely wantin' the comfort of yar' bed, but I need to talk to ma' Lord without delay."

The fact that Duncan is using Declan's formal title signals to me that whatever news our *gancanagh* cousin is bringing it's of serious Otherworld nature. My heart sinks with the realization that it no doubt has something to do with Marcy Kilcrabtree, as I am aware that my Tax Man specifically put his cousin to the task of gleaming information from that nasty, little bitch. It appears that this difficult evening has not yet quite come to an end.

Neither man speaks until Declan has removed the wards, and we have formally invited Duncan inside. I find these magical Fae protocols tiresome despite my mate's lectures about how it is necessary for the safety of the home's resident. As far as I'm concerned, Duncan is family, and I don't hold any apprehension about letting him into my house. A yawn escapes me and Declan notes it. "'Tis no reason I can think of far' ya' ta' stay awake, Love. Feel free ta' retire far' the evening. I will join ya' upstairs shortly. Duncan and I will not be long in conversation."

I may not yet know all of my husband's idiosyncrasies, but I can definitely tell when the Tax Man is being cagey. I settle myself on the sofa instead, adding, "I'm curious as well about what our dear cousin has come to tell you, Sweetie. Don't forget that I'm now an official member of 'the team.' Besides, I was desperately hoping you would favor me with one of your rejuvenating foot massages. Standing so long this evening has got them super ache-y."

I also know he won't refuse me, though I do get a look that indicates he would have much preferred if I'd been a good little Fae mate and done as I was told. *Fat chance. That's not my style, Tax Man.* He plops himself on the other end of the sofa, takes my feet in his lap, and removes my holiday flats. Duncan settles himself in the recliner across from us. His current terse body language, so unlike his usually breezy attitude, makes me think that the news he'll impart won't be pleasing to either of us. I am correct.

"I did as ya' asked, ma' Lord. I pressed the woman far' information and she willingly complied. I must admit, she is as forward as ya' warned. I had ta politely remove har' wanderin' hands from ma' person several times during the course of the evening, lest I run amok with ma' own lady. I was genuinely embarrassed far' Peirson. I could tell the man was highly annoyed with me, but I swear, I used only the tiniest bit of *gancanagh* 'glamour' on har'. 'Twas she who was the aggressor. I confess ta' findin' it a tad off-putting."

"Aye. She has issues with boundaries, that's far' sure. Still, ya' say she was open about har' reasons far' being at this particular event?" Declan asks.

"Vera open, ma' Lord. The lady expressed that she was personally invited to the Solstice celebration by the Black Knight himself, and t'was he who suggested that Peirson be har' escort far' the evening. At first, she was hesitant about revealin' the 'hows and whys' of the whole thing, but by the time dinner was served and she had consumed several glasses of champagne, she was all too willin' ta' share her thoughts." Duncan leans forward, clearly not happy to be the one sharing the bad news. He looks up at me and then down at the floor. "It seems that on one of har' recent tooth fairy retrievals, she found evidence that a North Korean group of scientists were falsely posin' as a family, complete with fake *bairns*, and had tried to set a trap far' her when she went ta' track a supposedly lost tooth…a tooth belonging to someone by the name of Ha-Yoon Jeong in the South Gateway neighborhood."

"I remember that assignment," I interject. "I distinctly recall that evening because Marcy complained bitterly to me that it was too far for a last-minute pick-up. Unfortunately, she was the next cadet in the rotation, so I had no choice but to send her. Corps rules." I can feel myself getting agitated. "She never said a single word to me about any trap being set, only that there was no tooth to be found! I marked it as 'an incomplete retrieval' and that was that!" I pull my feet from Declan's lap and sit straight up on the sofa, suddenly wide awake with adrenaline flowing. "I can't imagine why I was never told about this."

The *gancanagh* looks away, obviously uncomfortable about the answer to my question. "Just spit it out, Duncan," I say. "I'm a big girl. Whatever you're going to say…I can handle it."

BABY 47

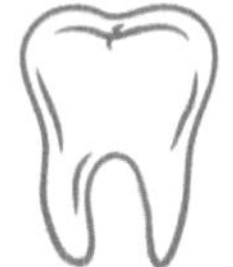

WHEN A FAVOR IS ASKED

"I HATE REPEATIN' what I know ta' be complete garbage, Cousin Rosie. Ya' know how much I care far ya'. Yar' like blood family to me, and I am sure this woman is nothin' but a *breagadoir* (liar)," Duncan explains.

"You're making it worse, Duncan. Just tell us already," I beg.

"Aye, cousin. 'Tis not like I don't already know the true nature of that woman," the Tax Man adds.

Duncan makes a sour face. "She told me that the reason she went directly ta' the Black Knight with this information rather than followin' the normal chain of command is because she is absolutely sure that har' commandin' officer holds a 'deep grudge' against har' far' the 'past relationship' she had with the officer's husband."

"Feckin' hell, cousin! There was no damn relationship!" Declan argued. "She was not much more than an adolescent girl when I met her...she was ma' damn intern, for feckin' sake! I swear I never laid a hand on har', nor did I lead her on ta' believe such actions were desired on ma' part!"

"I absolutely believe you, ma' Lord! I recall when that whole ridiculous nonsense went down. Despite all the gossip and rumor mongering, I thought ya' handled it with more diplomacy than the little minx deserved. It was all I could do not ta' call out her falsehoods right then and there. Of course, if I had shown where ma' true loyalties lie, then she probably would not have gone on ta' tell me how she had further manipulated the situation ta' har' benefit," Duncan said.

"Shit! There's more?" I ask.

"Aye, my Lady. The little *breagadoir* (liar) has used this information about the North Koreans ta' claim the ancient rite of *Chabhair* (boon)."

"What the hell is *Chabhair?*" I question.

It's my Tax Man who goes on to explain. "'Tis a vera old law that states when a subject of an Otherworld Kingdom has provided The Throne with secret information that is of great importance, they are entitled ta' claim a boon or token of their choice as a sign of gratitude from The Crown far' their loyalty. It goes back ta' the Dark Days when kingdoms battled against kingdoms over minor, petty disagreements. Now our biggest threats come from the Mundane world and the idea of getting paid far' one's natural duty is considered bad form. However, the law still remains in *I Idir's* tenets, and being a barrister herself, that she-devil would surely be aware of it."

"You are correct, ma' Lord. Sadly, it doesn't surprise

me that the Kilcrabtree woman would be willing to use such a thing far' her own gain. Har' personal aura is highly unpleasant," the *gancanagh* replies with a frown of disgust.

"So…what has she asked the Black Knight far' as her *Chabhair*?" my husband asks.

"The minx has requested that har' tooth fairy requirements be suspended and replaced with active duty within the Intelligence network, specifically as a member of yar' team, cousin," Duncan says. "As ya' are aware, the Black Knight has no choice but ta' grant her request, which means that Rosie will no longer have ta' deal with har' within the Corps. Unfortunately, this also means that she will now become yar' problem, ma Lord."

"Oh hell, Sweetie, I'm so sorry! I never meant for my inability to get along with her to end up being your problem," I say.

"There is no need far' ya' ta' apologize, Love. Marcy Kilcrabtree was ma' problem long before she ever became yars'," Declan admits. "She undoubtedly took her anger at me out on ya', and for that, I am the one who should be apologizin'."

"There is still the mandate of basic requirements that she must meet before she is allowed ta do field work, cousin. Perhaps she will be unable ta' meet them," Duncan suggests. "The physical and magical prerequisites are extremely demandin'. I have my doubts that as a tooth fairy she will be able to perform at a high enough level ta' ever leave a desk." Realizing that he had inadvertently insulted me as well as Marcy, Duncan quickly adds, "I mean no disrespect ta' tooth fairies, Lady *Mac Nuada*. We all know that yar many other talents and skills far exceed those of most of us on ma' Lord's team."

"I take no offense, Duncan," I laugh. "It's no secret I lack status in the magical department."

"Even without exceptional magical skill, I am forever bewitched by ya, ma' Love," my husband states as he kisses the top of my head and then my rounded belly. "There are things far more important than the sense of self-satisfaction and power sought out by our Miss Kilcrabtree."

Lord *Mac Nuada*, is, of course, absolutely correct in his statement. It was just too bad that the woman at the heart of this whole matter didn't come to the same conclusion before it was too late.

BABY 48

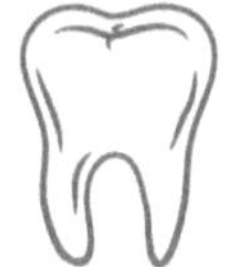

STEWING

REMODELING one's home is always hell on earth. It doesn't matter whether it's a small job like adding a designer closet or fixing up the laundry room, or a more challenging endeavor like a complete overhaul to a kitchen or a bathroom; the fact remains that remodeling your personal space simply sucks. In our case, the home improvement was all of these things in addition to the overwhelming project of putting on a whole new addition to the existing structure. The comings and goings of strangers in your private family sanctuary is off-putting, not to mention the ongoing noise, the forever presence of construction mess, and the constant inconveniences of having your actual living space seriously curtailed. Add to this stress the demanding schedules of two working professionals, the multiple little physical joys of late term pregnancy, and a husband with a dangerous secret side job, and you have all the ingredients for a real shit show of an argument.

When, a few months back, the Tax Man suggested we could expand our present home to accommodate our growing family rather than buying a new house, I was thrilled. I love my little domicile. I've always found its New England style architecture charming, its neighboring streets and businesses perfectly quaint, and the easy drive to my office a genuine blessing for someone who isn't a morning person. In my defense, I obviously didn't realize my husband's plans were going to be...well...so extensive.

I suppose I'm partly to blame for this. The Tax Man did try his best to explain the architect's drawings to me. However, being a numbers guy like he is, his descriptions tend to get a little...long winded. My mind obviously must have wandered off when he got to the part about completely taking out the entire back wall of the house. Now, here it was...early February, complete with frigid, sloppy weather, five weeks away from my due date, and a project that was nowhere near being finished. Granted, it would have been much easier and definitely faster having Declan use his magical skill to make the changes to the house, but a lot harder to explain a new addition to one's neighbors when they haven't seen it being built. Calling attention to one's magical self while living Mundane style is a big Otherworld no-no, and breaking this tenet can likely get you exiled to *I Idir* on a permanent basis. That's not a risk I'm willing to take.

Maybe all of this explains why Lord *Mac Nuada's* bombshell news set me off as much as it did. During the previous months of my pregnancy, my husband had taken somewhat of a hiatus from his spy "shet" activities, handing away-from-home assignments to Duncan and other members of his team so that he could stay close to me. That might also explain why his announcement caught me so completely off guard. We were having a quiet dinner of crockpot stew, my kitchen stove not yet delivered, when he casually announces between mouthfuls, "I ken' imagine yar' not gonna be pleased, Rosie Lass, but I'm afraid I need ta' take care of some business far' the Black Knight." Then, rather sheepishly, he adds, "Out of the country."

I put my fork down and give him my best wifely stink-eye. "You're going on a mission? Now? With the baby due in less than six weeks and the house a complete disaster?"

He takes his time buttering a slice of bread before answering. It's his way of letting me wrap my head around his statement, as if I'm a child who needs time to process negative information. It's a husband ploy that drives me crazy, even when I'm in a tip-top mood. Which today I am surely not. My back is killing me and my ankles look like those pig's knuckles in the butcher shop window on Abbott Street. "Where 'out of the country' are we talking about?" I question.

The way he pretends to examine his stew clues me in that he knows I'm not going to like the answer. "North Korea," he says.

The Tax Man is right. I absolutely don't like the answer. "Seriously?" I ask. "You're going to a global hotspot on some cranked-up, dumb-ass mission for the Black Knight? Now? Really?"

"I swear, Love, I would not go if it weren't necessary. I donna' have much of a choice this time," he explains.

"Why? What's so freakin' important that you'd leave your wife and soon-to-be-born son in a mess of a house without any running water and electricity in half of it?"

Declan looks extremely uncomfortable and my anxiety level rises several notches. "I wish ya would just let this go, Love. Knowin' all the details won' make it any easier ta' swallow."

His vague request makes the situation worse. "You tell me what's going on right this minute, Tax Man! I am your *Mo Shiorghra.* I deserve to know." I demand.

He pushes his plate away, his face registering obvious distaste. I'm pretty sure it's not my stew at fault. "That Kilcrabtree woman has gone missin'," he explains. "Took off ta' North Korea on har' own ta' investigate some supposed threat. No one's heard from har' in three days. She needs ta' be found and extracted."

The stew rises up in my stomach and I feel like I'm going to be sick. This is a bad thing because the only currently working toilet is upstairs and it's doubtful I can waddle up there fast enough. "Why do you personally have to go? Can't someone else do it?" I beg.

"I am har' team leader, so she's ma' responsibility. Plus, ya' are well aware, Love, that I am exceptionally skilled at glamour disguises and linguistics. I am the only one likely ta' get into places no other Fae could go in North Korea." He tries to hold my hand but I pull it away. "If it makes ya' feel any better, I am takin' Duncan with me. The plan is ta' be in and out in no more than forty-eight hours... Universe willin'.""

I feel bile rise in my throat and I can't help but mumble an especially horrendous curse on that wretched Marcy Kilcrabtree. My very superstitious Fae husband looks up at me in alarm. "'Tis bad luck ta' call a curse on someone, Lass. They have a tendency ta' bounce right back at ya!"

I ignore the scolding. "When are you leaving?" I ask, hoping against hope I'll have time to change his mind.

Declan rises from the table. "I'm afraid I am ta meet Duncan in *I Idir* later this Mundane evening. We will cross the Veil into I Idir, then jump to North Korea from there." I do the only thing I can do at that very moment. I swivel around and throw up in the garbage can behind me.

BABY 49

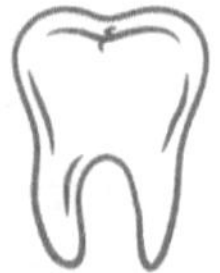

WHEN THINGS GO BAD

I'M NOT proud of how I behaved when Declan left for North Korea. I may have been slightly… disagreeable. I railed on and on about how I couldn't believe he was putting the needs of Marcy Kilcrabtree ahead of his *Mo Shiorghra* and unborn child. My husband calmly tried to explain that The Throne was not only concerned over the tooth-fairy-turned-spy's personal safety but also her inexperience and inability to withstand pressure, aka torture, from the North Koreans, leading her to possibly reveal important information about the workings of *I Idir's* intelligence network.

The rational, medical professional in me understood all of that. The anxiety-ridden wife and mommy-to-be did not. Within minutes of Declan informing me of his new mission, flashbacks of that horrible nightmare I had under the influence of the Dream Weaver started running in my head. I reminded the Tax Man of that, but his reaction was to sigh dramatically and bring up the fact that even the current reigning Merlin, as well as several of House *Nuada's* best mages, concurred that what I had experienced that night was not a true prophecy and that I had nothing to worry about regarding his safety.

I simply could not be convinced that this damned mission was his own personal duty and when my beloved *Mo Shiorghra* left, it was without my blessing. Unable to convince me to give it to him, Declan kissed me and my belly and left me while watching me scowl at him. I felt terribly guilty afterward, but by the time I tried to reach out to him mentally, there was only an echo in my head, a sign that he was most likely already crossing between dimensions.

The first day he was gone, I filled my day with an extremely busy schedule at the office, so by the time I came home that evening, I was exhausted and my feet ached beyond belief. I warmed up some leftover stew, and took it upstairs to eat in bed while watching hours of endless, mind-numbing TV. When I woke up with a start at around 3:00 AM, the television still blaring, I half expected to see Declan on the other side of the bed, home again and snoring loudly, but the space next to me remained cold and empty. I tried reaching out to him mentally, but again there was only an echo. This raised a few alarm bells in my head, but he had said, after all, that he could be away for at least forty-eight hours. I rolled over and tried to go back to sleep, but my anxiety must have somehow seeped into our Peanut's psyche, because the little guy kept me awake for hours with his kicking and rolling.

The following morning, I awoke groggy and tired, but glad that by evening, my husband would likely be home. The day passed quickly, and despite a few attempts when I could find a handful of private minutes to empty my head and concentrate, I was still unable to reach Declan via our personal mental link. My fears about that were starting to build. I questioned Mel if she had heard from Duncan, and I could see the worry and strain on her face as well. My BFF hadn't heard from her live-in lover either and agreed with me that though it was a bit unusual, it was not an unheard of scenario when Declan and Duncan were engrossed in a mission.

Trying to keep a positive attitude, I stopped at my husband's favorite Thai restaurant and brought home a curry and noodle feast in anticipation of his homecoming. By 10:30 PM, I rewarmed a plate for myself and ate alone. By 4:00 AM the following morning, still alone and unable to make any type of mental connection, I began to panic.

Wednesday is my day off, and since I have taken a late pregnancy hiatus from my work at the free clinic, the hours stretch long and empty in front of me. I attempt to try and begin work on building the baby's changing table, but I can't find the required Allen wrench and instead sit in the middle of the unpainted nursery and cry. I give Mel a call on her cell, but there's no answer. I considered reaching out to her mentally like we sometimes did as children, but decide I don't want to unwittingly share my rising fears with her.

I putter a bit, wash some clothes, and then head downstairs to wait for the crew of carpenters that are supposed to finish putting in my kitchen cabinets today. When the front doorbell rings, I assume it's the workmen. Having left my cell phone upstairs, and without the doorbell's video feed, I'm required to peer through the front windows to see who's out there before opening the door. I push aside the curtains, and what I see in front of me sucks every bit of air from my lungs. There on my front porch stands the Black Knight and his Lady, along with Mel and Duncan. I don't need the somber expressions on their faces to know something is terribly wrong. If they're all here, and my husband is not, the news they are here to bring me is bad. Very bad.

BABY 50

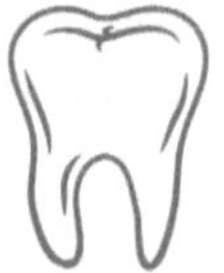

HOPE

I LEAN against the front door, unable to make myself open it. The sensible part of my Lady *Mac* brain screams to me that keeping the *Banphrionsa* of *I Idir* and the Black Knight waiting on the porch in this frigid February weather is extremely rude and absolutely against proper Otherworld protocol. However, the real Rosie Parker Fitzpatrick, eight months along and totally freaking out, wants them to take their bad news and go away.

I consider what my Tax Man would expect me to do in this situation and thus the sensible *Lady Mac Nuada* wins out. I take a deep breath and, with shaking hands, punch in the security code and open the door. Thank goodness his Jr. Lordship didn't insist on leaving any complicated warding on the house before he left. I'm not sure how I would have handled that. I drop a quick curtsy, made awkward by my protruding belly. "Good evening, Lady Dear Heart...Lord Knight. And to you as well, Mel and

Duncan." I am sure my voice has a noticeable tremor. "Won't you please come in."

I lead them to the parlor and offer them seats. Everyone sits except the Black Knight. He's obviously been chosen as the bearer of bad news. "Can I offer anyone some refreshments? Coffee or tea?" I ask. "Something stronger, perhaps? I know my Lord keeps Irish whiskey in the house but I'm not sure…" My words trail off in a whisper.

"Please don't fuss on our account, Lady Rosalinda," The Knight replies for the group. He gestures toward a seat on the sofa next to his own Lady. "May I suggest that you take a seat yourself? I'm afraid the news I bring is difficult to hear."

My brain, along with the rest of my body, seems to shift into slow motion; every part of me comes to an almost complete stand-still, except for our little Peanut, who must feel my fear and adrenaline and has decided to do fetus gymnastics in response. I sit next to the *Banphrionsa* who takes my hand in hers, making me want to run screaming out of that room. Instead of fleeing, I look at my feet in front of me on the floor, unable to view any of their plainly held sympathetic expressions. I fully expect the Black Knight to tell me that my husband is dead, though for the life of me, I can't understand how, if Declan and I are as connected as he promised, why I wouldn't feel his loss before having to be told of it.

"I'm afraid, Lady *Mac Nuada*, that your husband has been taken captive by the North Koreans. Despite a very thorough search, both magical and physical, we have so far been unable to locate him for extraction. We assume that the North Koreans are constantly moving him to different locations and are using something to buffer our attempts at getting a magical read on his whereabouts. We've been aware of this Mundane shielding ability by several countries for two years now, though we were unaware that North Korea had also advanced to the stage of being able to block our magical surveillance. You have my word...and that of Her Majesty...that we will do everything in our power to locate your husband and bring him home."

All I can focus on is that tiny strand of hope. *He's not dead. He's not dead. He's not dead.* I need to hear the Black Knight say it out loud. "So...you believe that Declan is still alive, Lord Knight?"

"The Merlin has confirmed that he is," the Knight states. "He is still able to pick up Lord *Mac Nuada's* aura even if he is magically unable to get a solid read on where they've taken him. I trust my father's skill, Lady Rosalinda. If he says Fitz is still alive, then I believe him. Of course, you yourself would have the best connection to your *Mo Shiorghra,* dear Lady. Do you still feel a living connection to him?"

BABY 51

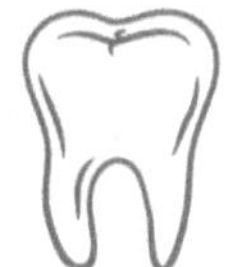

PROMISES MADE

THE BLACK KNIGHT'S question is a difficult one to answer. There's no doubt I still feel the presence of the telepathic connection the Tax Man and I have shared from the moment his ink found a home on my shoulder, but where it had always been like a clear and direct feed to my brain, it now feels more like a radio wave full of static and echoes. "I can still feel his connection to me, Lord Knight," I admit, "but I'm afraid it's not at all as clear as it was before my Lord left for this assignment."

"The fact that there is still somewhat of an open channel between the two of you is a very good sign, Lady Rosalinda. It means that Fitz still has enough magical energy available to him to keep your connection open. That's a positive sign to his state of well-being. As I said, we are doing everything possible to locate him. As soon as I leave here, I'll be making arrangements to go to North Korea myself."

Still holding my hand, I can feel the *Banphrionsa* tense up next to me. I can't blame her. No wife wants to see her husband put himself in harm's way, and these "spy shet" missions are known to almost always involve some type of danger. On that note, a thought instantly pops into my head. "How did it happen that my husband was captured? I was under the impression he and Duncan were only being sent to retrieve Marcy Kilcrabtree. Do the North Koreans have her as well?"

I catch the sideways glance the Black Knight gives Declan's cousin, who has been unusually quiet while basically not meeting my eyes since his arrival. With a nod from his boss, my husband's cousin relates his story with a shaky voice. "I take complete responsibility far' ma' Lord's capture, Lady *Mac Nuada*. 'Tis entirely ma' fault that I sit here unharmed while ma' Liege suffers at the hands of the North Koreans. Ya' have every right ta' forever hate the sight of me."

Apparently, the Lady Dear Heart has had enough of the protocol posturing. She drops my hand and tisks loudly, ignoring her husband's disapproving look. "That's a ridiculous statement, Duncan Fitzpatrick! And an absolute rewrite of the truth! I want you to tell Dr. Parker what really happened. She deserves at least that."

Duncan looked for permission from his superior, but the Black Knight just shrugged. "Do as the *Banphrionsa* has asked, Dunc," he says, with a twinge of annoyance. "My Lady can be quite... fierce over the 'spinning' of truth."

Duncan leaves his spot next to Mel, and sits down on the other side of me. "As you may be aware, sweet Lady, that damn Kilcrabtree woman went to North Korea of har' own accord. For what reason, we can't fathom, though knowing har' sly ways, we assume it was ta' gather important intelligence and thus curry additional favor with The Crown. She was hell bent on movin' up the ranks faster than protocol deemed fair. As her superior, my Lord was responsible far' har' actions, and he insisted on retrievin' har himself before she could do any irreversible damage ta' our Asian intelligence network. Once in North Korea, it didna' take long far' us ta' verify that she indeed had been captured, but when we arrived at the place she was bein' held, it became vera obvious that har' abductors had expected us ta' come try and rescue har'. She was little more than bait ta' them, a way ta' reel in a … bigger fish. We managed ta' free the Kilcrabtree woman, but ma' cousin and I found ourselves quickly overwhelmed by sheer numbers."

Duncan looks away, regret and pain clearly framing his expression. "Ma' Lord insisted I take the woman and return ta' *I Idir* while he held them off. I refused ta' leave him, but he then outrightly ordered me ta' do it, dearest Cousin Rosie…as ma' Liege Lord! He has never, in all the time I've known him, 'ordered' me ta' do anything. I could tell he meant far' me ta' obey him without hesitation. And thus, I obeyed. I took the damn woman and jumped ta' *I Idir*, leaving ma' own cousin…ma' own flesh and blood… ta' fight alone."

The *gancanagh* drops to the floor at my knees and takes both of my hands in his. His grief-stricken face tears at my heart, and I can feel the ache of my own pain in his. "There has not been a single moment since it happened,

Rosie, that I have not regretted ma' actions. I should have disregarded ma' responsibility ta' his title and replaced it with the love I hold far' the man I view as ma' dearest brother. I swear ta' ya, on ma' own life, that I will find him and bring him home, or die in ma' attempt."

Across the room, I can hear Mel's intake of breath at her lover's statement. I stand and pull Duncan up from his knees. I don't need or desire his public display of remorse. I already understand what Declan means to his cousin. His despair is in the same realm as mine. "You don't need to offer penance for something that you didn't cause, Duncan. I know how demanding Declan can be in his 'Lordship mode.' He's hard to disobey. If anyone is to blame for this horrible situation it's that wretched woman." I look up at the Black Knight. "Where is the nasty bitch now?"

No one even flinches at my vulgar comment. And too bad if they do. Marcy Kilcrabtree is the reason my beloved Tax Man is not home where he belongs, and I'm in no mood to sugarcoat it, protocol be damned. "Cadet Crabtree is being treated for some minor injuries. Once she's released from doctor's care, she'll be debriefed on the whole matter," the Lord Knight explains.

"And then what? I ask, not hiding my venom. "She's free to go on her merry way? Life as usual for her while my husband languishes in some North Korean prison?"

I can tell that despite his sympathy for me, the Queen's Hand does not like to be put on the spot. He answers my angry interrogation with a tight jaw and a ring of terseness. "The repercussions regarding the Cadet's actions will, as always, be subject to *I Idir*'s law and the discretion of Her Majesty. I'm afraid I'm not at liberty to discuss them."

"No…of course you can't," I mumble under my breath. I fully realize that I should be embarrassed by my bold rudeness to The Crown's representative. Since our handfast, Declan has reminded me on a daily basis that when it comes to Otherworld politics and policies, my behavior as his *Mo Shiorghra* directly reflects on him, but my emotions are running far too hot to worry about the Black Knight's feelings. Right now, I just want them all to leave. Even Mel and Duncan. All I desire is a modicum of privacy…to cry, and scream, and rant without the benefit of an audience.

I start heading toward the front door, hoping they'll take the hint. "I am grateful for all of your support, truly I am. But I feel as if I need some time to myself to fully… absorb this news. I hope you'll update me with any new information, Lord Knight?" I ask.

"I'll be sure to stay in close contact, Lady *Mac Nuada*," he replies.

It's the *Banphrionsa* who adds, "If there's absolutely anything I can do for you, Dr. Parker, please don't hesitate to ask." She opens her small clutch purse, and pulls out a white card, blank except for a phone number, which she hands to me. "This is my personal cell phone number. You can call me anytime…about anything."

I take the business card, pretty sure that I'll never dial that number. The Princess of *I Idir* and I don't move in the same circles. "Thank you, Lady Dear Heart. I appreciate the offer," I express.

The group moves toward the exit. Mel opens her

mouth to speak, but I put up a hand to stop her. I know if my BFF starts me crying, I'll fall apart in front of everyone. That's something I don't want to do. The Black Knight is the last one out the door. Before leaving, he stops and places something in my hand, laying it flat in my palm and then curling my fingers around it. What's this?" I ask.

"A token from Her Majesty. She's asked me to relay her regret that you have had to relinquish the company of your mate so close to the arrival of your first child," he explains.

I open my hand to discover a large opal on a gold chain. I'm not sure what I'm supposed to do with the gift. If it's some kind of payment for my husband's sacrifice and my personal angst, I surely don't want it, but even in the midst of my grief, I have enough sense to keep that thought to myself. Or at least I thought I was keeping it to myself.

The Black Knight looks me straight in the eye and says, "It's more than a gift, Lady Rosalinda. It's a sacred promise from The Morrigan, Herself, that she will do everything in her power to return Lord *Mac Nuada* to his family. Still, if during the time your mate is gone, you should find yourself in a position where The Crown's aid is needed, this stone is your line of communication. Grasp it and mentally call for Her. She will immediately answer your summons."

Me? Calling the living Goddess of War and Destruction with a request? It simply wasn't going to happen. Nope. Not ever.

BABY 52

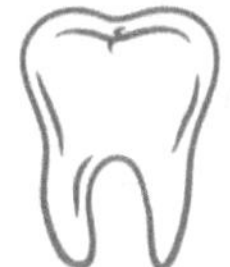

BLAME IT ON THE CHOCOLATE CHIPS

I SUPPOSE you could say I spent the following two days and nights in complete pity party stasis. I rarely left the bedroom, preferring the comfort of our shared marital bed and sheets that still smell of my husband's Otherworldy herbal soap. Forgoing any thought of regular meals, sleep, or even basic hygiene, I volley between complete despair about the hand dealt to me and gut-wrenching guilt over the way I behaved on the day Declan left for his mission. I make deals and promises to every god and goddess I can remember and literally beg, on my knees, for the Universe not to take my *Mo Shiorghra* from me and our baby.

It isn't as if my friends and family don't offer me their support and companionship. Mel calls me five times a day, begging for the chance to come over and stay with me while the Tax Man is away. I tell her she's doing enough by staying at the office and handling the consequences of my canceled appointments. Duncan offers his companionship as well, but even when he tires of me not answering his phone calls and shows up on my front porch unannounced and uninvited, I refuse to let him inside, not even pretending to play the game of polite socializing. I realize that he takes my refusal to see him as a sign that I personally blame him for Declan's capture. It isn't true, and at some point in the future, I will have to explain this reality to him in person. However, right now I want no intrusion into my self-inflicted solitary confinement, especially from someone who has his own guilt issues over the situation.

On the third day, a miserable, wind-howling, snow-swirling, wintery, Saturday morning, I awake from a few hours of snatched sleep to find myself ravenously hungry. I rouse myself from tangled sheets and pad down the stairs to the half torn apart kitchen. Before I can rummage through the fridge, I catch my sorry-ass reflection in the stainless steel of the door. The image staring back at me is both shocking and more than a little embarrassing. My hair hangs in a tangled nest, greasy and lank, the dark circles under my eyes have friends of their own, and there's a deep groove embedded across my cheek from falling asleep on top of the TV remote. I'll have to do something about the mess I've become, but at the moment, breakfast is the problem at hand.

Of course, in the mood I'm in, nothing in my larder appeals to me. The notion crosses my mind that what I truly want are homemade chocolate chip pancakes, handily made on an electric skillet in leu of my still-missing stove.

This presents a problem as I am fresh out of chocolate chips. Between the lousy weather and my slovenly state, I should have just been a mature adult and settled for regular pancakes, but I couldn't make myself do it. Maybe it was a late pregnancy craving, or perhaps just the simple need to control the outcome of something in my life that makes me decide to throw on a coat and some boots over my rumpled, smelly sweats and head to the nearby convenience store.

Observing the state of the back steps with their layers of snow should be the final straw that forces me back inside. But the chocolate chip pancakes have become a goal that desperately needs achieving, so I gingerly make my way down the steps toward the garage and my car. As careful as I am, the fresh snow is nothing more than camouflage for a slick layer of hidden ice, and as I put my foot down on the second step, my boot slides across the glassy edge, causing me to lose my balance and forcing me all the way down to the bottom of the stairs on my ass.

I hit the ground with a thump, the wind completely knocked from my lungs, my butt and back aching from the rough ride down. My thoughts immediately go to Peanut, and putting both hands on my belly, I'm relieved that I can still feel him kicking around in there like a little bronco rider. My plan is to push myself up using the bottom step and then crawl carefully back upstairs to the house. That's when I first became aware of it; a warm sticky feeling running down the length of my pant leg, followed by an ugly red puddle rapidly growing beneath me.

BABY 53

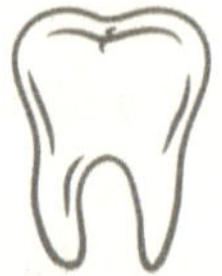

ROSIE NAILS THE LANDING

IF THERE IS anything to be grateful about regarding this awful incident, it's the fact that before leaving the house, I'd oddly tucked my cell phone in the zip up pocket of my parka instead of its usual location in my purse. This was lucky foresight, as said purse ended up flying off my shoulder as I went zippity-do-da-ing down the backstairs, ending up several feet away from where I landed, its contents spread across the back yard. As it was, though the glass on the screen was smashed to smithereens by my falling on it, the phone part still worked and I was able to call 911 without having to move.

While waiting for the ambulance to arrive, I find myself in orderly panic mode. Not being one hundred percent sure where all that blood is coming from, I know better than to try and stand or change my immediate position in an attempt to discover its cause. In some situations, changing positions after a trauma can worsen whatever injury might be going on. I fight the urge to do my own examination and instead wait for the paramedics to arrive and carry out their triage so that they can determine the safest way to move me.

My biggest concern is that the fall has caused a placental abruption, a situation that is critical for both mother and baby. I hurt all over, but none of my pain feels like contractions which I rule as a good sign. Then, good 'ole Doomsday Rosie reminds me of the fact that I've never had a baby before and therefore have no frickin' idea what labor contractions feel like so I wouldn't know if I was having them anyway.

It seems in my mind that it's taking an enormously long amount of time for the ambulance to arrive and for the first responders to slip and slide their way to the back of the house. In truth, the cracked cell phone shows that less than seven minutes has passed since I first dialed. Apparently, time moves a lot slower when you're freezing your ass off and watching your entire life about to fall to pieces.

When the paramedics arrive, they are calm and professional, and it isn't long before they shift my position and determine that the bleeding is not vaginal, but coming from a deep puncture wound and tear running from my lower right butt cheek and down the back of my right thigh. They find the culprit, a bloody, four-inch framing nail obviously left by one of the carpenters working on our addition, sticking out from the back of my sweatpants. The nail must have been hidden under a layer of snow, just waiting there for my ass to find it as I skated down the stairs.

However, because of the advanced stage of my pregnancy, the response team insists on taking me to the hospital for further evaluation and the long line of stitches I am undoubtedly going to need. I am relieved to my very core, but angry with myself for taking such a stupid risk, an opinion shared by my obstetrician when I finally arrive at the hospital. Erring on the side of caution, Dr. Brannigan admits me overnight for observation and fetal monitoring, shaking his head in disbelief while scolding me. "I can't imagine, Dr. Parker, why with all you hold dear, you would think going out in weather like this was a responsible action! I realize things are very stressful for you with Fitz…away, but it's unlike you to be so entirely reckless. I'm keeping you overnight. We'll see what the fetal monitoring shows in the next several hours and take it from there. You do understand that placenta abruption is a possibility after a fall like this, correct? We'll know better if that's what's going on here in the next six to eight hours."

I'm not a big fan of being scolded and I want to give my fellow physician an indignant, snarky response, but I stop myself. Robyn is one hundred percent correct. It was a truly bad decision on my part. One that still might have dire consequences. Though I want to mentally beat myself up for it, I already hurt like crazy from the fall, and the puncture wound from the nail I didn't even save for posterity is re-introducing itself in a big way. Even with the monitors strapped to my belly, the glare of the hospital room lights, and the constant traffic of the nursing staff, I find it difficult to keep heavy eyelids open. As I watch the little blips of Peanut's unborn heartbeat on the fetal monitoring screen to the right of my bed, I find myself eventually dozing off and dreaming about our son's missing father.

BABY 54

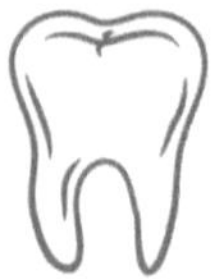

AT THE END OF MY ROPE

Like all dreams, this one is a kaleidoscope version of places, people and visuals my brain has thrown together; a movie of tilting and turning colored memory tiles reflecting back on a mentally mirrored surface. In my dream, the house of my childhood is now an old pirate galleon, my mother at its helm, a tiny Fae captain, steering the way across dark waters under a moonless sky. I call to her, but she doesn't answer, silently pointing to the port side of the boat to where a rope is hanging across the ship's rail and dangling over the side.

I try to get to the rope but I discover the deck is covered in ice, and my fear of falling keeps me glued to the spot. Then I hear a male voice calling my name. At first, I believe the voice to be my father's, desperately pleading for my help. In a panic, I drop to my hands and knees and begin to crawl toward the ship's rail and the rope hanging over it. When I finally reach it, I use the rope to pull myself upward. As I stand, the ship suddenly turns into my back porch...the way it looked before the remodel, with the same rope hanging off the handrail. I am afraid to look over that damned rail...afraid to know who or what is on the other side. Now the voice sounds different. I hear the sound of rolling r's...the lilt of an accent. No...it's not my father's voice. It's Declan's.

I gather my courage and peer down over the side. Instead of the snowy covered lawn I expect to see, the space beneath my porch is filled with churning water, with my husband hanging on to the rope's end for dear life. He looks up at me with desperate eyes and begs, "Hang on tight, Rosie, Love! Don' let go! Whatever ya' do, don' let go of me, Rosie Parker...Rosie Parker" I open my mouth to call to him but no sounds come out. Then, somewhere in the distance I hear an angry beeping sound..."Dr. Parker...

"Dr. Parker...Dr. Parker," the voice calls out. "I need for you to wake up, Ma'am. You've dislodged the fetal monitor. We need to get you hooked up again."

I open my eyes with a start and sit up. A male nurse stands over my bed, the end of the fetal monitor's cord in his hand. I'm covered in a sheen of sweat and my heavy breathing matches the dramatic jumping lines of my heart monitor. "You were obviously having a nightmare, Dr. Parker. The tossing and turning knocked the cord out. We need to reattach everything."

I'm still half out of it, but my thoughts immediately jump to Peanut. "My baby...is he okay?"

"Your baby seems fine, Dr. Parker. Everything looks normal. But Dr. Brannigan wants the fetal monitor on for twenty-four hours, just to be safe. If you could shift to your right side, we'll get you all set again."

I roll over to my right side. The pressure on my

recently torn skin knocks any drowsiness straight out of me. The ripped skin and puncture wound hurts like a sonofabitch and I gasp, now completely wide awake. "What time is it?" I ask the nurse.

"Quarter to five, Dr. Parker. I'm guessing they'll be around with your dinner soon. Would you like me to turn the lights back off so you can rest?"

"No. I've slept enough, thank you," I answer. "I think I'll just watch some TV until my dinner comes."

* * *

After that nightmare, I don't sleep another minute, afraid that if I doze off, I'll have that terrible dream again, a visual I can now only remember in bits and pieces. I recall a rope being involved with my husband hanging off of it, but little else. I chalk off the dream as a normal reaction to the stress and trauma of the past few days, but I sure as hell don't want a repeat viewing. By dawn, I am chomping at the bit waiting for Robyn to come and release me. The monitors tracking both baby and mom show normal readings, so I assume I will be heading home by late morning.

When my doctor finally makes an appearance, he looks anything but pleased. He shoos the nurse out of the room so that we can speak privately. "The fetal monitor readings look normal, Dr. Parker," he begins, "but I'm concerned with your vitals and blood work. You show signs of edging towards preeclampsia; your blood pressure is higher than normal and you have protein in your urine. Let's take a look at your ankles, shall we?"

I already know what he'll see when he pulls back the blanket covering my feet. I've had "preggo cankles" for the past week or so, my normally slender feet appearing swollen and grotesque. I can tell from Robyn's expression he's concerned. "I'd rather not induce you, Dr. Parker, if I can help it. I prefer that nature take its course, especially with Fae babies."

The thought that I might have my baby a month early...without Declan at my side...panics me. "I one hundred percent agree, Dr. Brannigan. Is there anything else we can try?" I stammer.

He makes a face. "Frankly, I'd much rather have you here in the hospital where I could keep an eye on you, but I'm guessing you'd fight me on that."

"I'm a medical professional, Doc. I know how serious preeclampsia can be. If I promise to take it easy, watch my diet and take the meds for hypertension, can I please go home? I know I'd feel better there. I have too much time here to think with nothing to distract me from...." I let the words trail off. I don't have to explain the situation to Robyn. There's no doubt he's concerned for Declan as well.

The doctor thinks for a moment, then says, "I'll let you go home, Dr. Parker...under one condition."

I'm relieved, but the one condition part worries me. "What's that, Doctor?" I ask with an air of complete innocence.

"My condition is that you strictly adhere to my orders for bed rest, and that you have someone with you at all times. Day and night. You got lucky that this recent fall didn't do any serious damage to you or your baby. Let's not push our luck, shall we?"

I had originally planned to work as long into my pregnancy as I possibly could, especially now that I need to keep my mind busy. Hoping against hope I ask, "Can I at least work a few hours a day? Maybe only in the mornings?"

The man sighs in exasperation. "When I order bed rest, Dr. Parker, I mean complete bed rest. No standing on your feet for hours at a time. The goal is to reduce your blood pressure and get more blood flow to the placenta."

"Oh," I say with more meekness than I feel. "I suppose I can take maternity leave earlier than I planned. I'll have to call my replacement and see if he can start a few weeks earlier than we arranged."

"If he can't, then you'll have to shut down your practice until he's able. I mean what I say, Dr. Parker…absolute bed rest. If Fitz were here, he'd expect you to do as I recommend. There's no reason to take unnecessary risks. If I find out you're not adhering to my orders, you will find yourself right back here at the hospital. Do you understand what I'm saying?"

This is the most forceful I've ever seen Robyn. Usually, he's the calmest, most unimposing figure in the Black Knight's network. In this moment, his commanding "Lord *Spideog*" (Robyn) personae is fully apparent.

"I understand, Dr. Brannigan. If you let me go home, I promise I'll follow your orders to the letter of the law."

"I'm glad to hear that, Dr. Parker. I'm holding you to that promise."

Promises are a big ass deal among the Fae. They are

not given lightly, and failure to keep your word is a major mark against your character. I groan inwardly over the thought of being stuck in bed for the next three or four weeks, bored out of my mind with too much time to think. Plus, there's the issue that the nursery, along with most of the new addition, still remains unfinished. I'm afraid to even dwell on that, lest somehow my thoughts leak out. I change the subject instead. "So, do you think I can go home soon? Maybe in the next few hours?" I plead.

With a nod of his head, the Doc agrees. "I think we can arrange that. As long as you have someone coming to pick you up, and someone set to stay with you at home. Do you have someone already in mind?" he questions.

I can't think of anyone besides my husband that I'd want to live with for the next few weeks. Nor do I want to impose the dumb ass job of being my personal nursemaid on anyone I know. Therefore, I'm less than truthful when I give him my answer, a fake smile pasted on my face. "I know just the person for the job, Doc. Don't you worry about me. I got it covered."

BABY 55

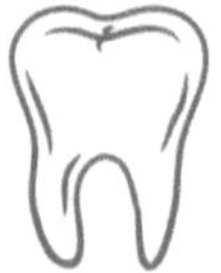

FORGET THE TEA... JUST GO AWAY

THERE ARE APPROXIMATELY three people I feel like I can call in a situation like this; my older sister Claire, my BFF Mel, and Declan's cousin, Duncan. I get the same lecture from all three of them about the stupidity of my taking unnecessary risks as well as my totally ridiculous need to self-isolate while Declan is missing. They're not entirely wrong. I very much regret my bad decision to venture out yesterday morning in lousy weather, and I fully understand that it's only by the grace of the Universe that I have not made a bad situation even worse. When my husband returns home (and he WILL return home...I don't let myself think otherwise) and hears this story (and he WILL hear it from some Otherworldly blabbermouth...guaranteed) I expect he will read me the riot act in true cranky Declan form.

I plead temporary insanity and beg forgiveness for not notifying any of them sooner. I humbly ask my sister to pick up a few necessary groceries for me (yes…chocolate chips are on that list; I still have a deep craving for those damn pancakes.) and meet me at my house. Mel and Duncan offer to pick me up from the hospital and I agree. Once at home, I hope we can all sit down and try to work out a schedule where no one is stuck baby-sitting bad girl Rosie around the clock.

Dressed and impatiently waiting, it takes several tedious hours before all the paperwork for my release is procured and a wheelchair arrives to take me to the lobby. As planned, my best friend and her beau are there waiting, though getting into Duncan's tiny Jaguar takes some special maneuvering. By the time we arrive home, I am not afraid to admit that I'm exhausted, and the stitches on the back of my leg are burning like a day in Hades. I'm half tempted to take my husband's cousin up on his offer to carry me into the house, but the little bit of self-pride I still retain keeps me from agreeing. All I can think of as I cautiously make my way up the newly shoveled steps, is the anticipation of a hot shower and a mega-hour nap wrapped up in the quilt that was a wedding gift from *Magda*, Declan's childhood nanny. Perhaps that's the reason I slip up and use a cranky Declan phrase when I open my front door and see my husband's parents sitting on my sofa.

"Oh feckin' hell!" I mumble, just loud enough for everyone in the room to perfectly hear. I feel Duncan and Mel tense next to me, and my sister turns a deep shade of pink. My in-laws look extremely put-out, but they don't say a word. Lord *Nuada* coughs and clears his throat. My swearing at them is a huge protocol faux pas. Not only are they Declan's mother and father, they are Lord and Lady of House *Nuada*. If I had been anyone other than their missing son's mate, the mother of their House's soon-to-be-born anticipated heir, I would surely have faced some serious damn consequences. As it is, I immediately burst into tears, not because I'm at all sorry for what I just said, but rather because I can't believe my luck has gone from extremely bad to frickin' unbelievable. Of all the people in the entire Universe, Callum and *Siobhan* Fitzpatrick are the last people I want to spend time with now.

My preggo lady tears puts everyone on instant pause. My sister comes over to embrace me. "Oh Rosie, you poor thing! This is too much for any expectant mother to bear." Claire helps me off with my coat and boots, and then settles me into a chair, pushing an ottoman under my legs and putting my swollen feet on top of it. "How 'bout a nice cup of warm chamomile tea? Would you like that Rosie Posie? Perhaps with a bit of honey?" she asks.

Lord *Nuada* nods and adds, "Yes…get the girl a cup of tea. That's what she needs in this foul weather."

My husband's *athair* is dead wrong. I don't need any damn tea. What this girl wants…no, not wants…what this girl needs…is for everyone to just go away and leave her alone in her misery.

BABY 56

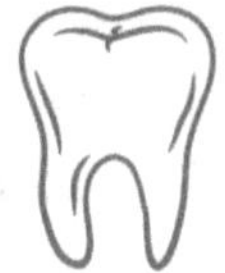

CALLING IN THE CHIPS

CLAIRE SCUTTLES OFF TO get the tea, relieved to be out of House *Nuada* range. It's no secret my father-in-law makes my sister feel uncomfortable because Claire is the spitting image of my mom at that age. I suppose one should feel sorry for the old guy. It appears he was truly, crazy, in love with our deceased Fae mother. Still, the way he stares at my big sister with those hound-dog eyes drives me crazy and I've told my husband as much.

The rest of us sit in silence until Lord *Nuada* leans forward, hands clasped together and asks, "How do you feel, Lady Rosalinda? From what Robyn has described to me, you've had yourself quite the ordeal."

His statement annoys the hell out of me. Why is Doc Brannigan speaking to my father-in-law about my personal medical issues? It's wrong on a multitude of levels. Then I remember that we're all playing by a different set of rules here. As Lord of House *Nuada*, it would be considered within my father-in-law's rights to inquire after my personal welfare, especially with Declan away. "I'm a little sore, my Lord, but otherwise baby and I are fine."

He grunts and stares at me for a bit before addressing my comrades as Claire returns with my tea. "I will speak to Lady Rosalinda alone. The three of you may go," he orders with a dismissive wave of his hand. Steeped in Otherworld tradition, Mel and Duncan make faces but reluctantly head toward the door. One simply does not disobey a Ruling House Lord. It's a hill you don't want to die on.

Claire, however, is firmly rooted in the here and now of the Mundane world. She folds her arms across her chest. "I think I'd prefer to stay. Rosie is my little sister. Her welfare is my concern," she argues.

The patriarch of House *Nuada* glowers at her, and I can tell her being here isn't helping my cause...or the level of her safety. "It's okay, Claire. I'll be fine. Why don't you go along with Duncan and Mel. Have some lunch. We'll talk later." My big sister hesitates, unwilling to leave me alone with my Otherworldly in-laws, whom she knows I don't much care for. "Honest...it'll be fine," I insist.

She grabs her coat from the hook in the hall and follows Mel and Duncan out the front door, loudly tisking her annoyance the entire time. "If you would please go ahead and say what you need to say to me, my Lord," I begin, doing my darndest to sound polite and non-confrontational. "I find myself exceedingly weary after these events. I had hoped to wash up and then settle myself in for a much-needed nap."

"As you wish, dear Lady." His face looks grim and determined, every inch *Tuatha de Danann*, while a glimmer of anxiety begins to pool inside of me. "It has become quite obvious that you are far too distraught over the demise of my son to properly care for yourself here in the Mundane world," my father-in-law matter-of-factly states

His use of the word demise shakes me to my core. "Declan is not dead, your Lordship. He's been taken prisoner. I have every confidence that the Black Knight will be able to find him and bring him home."

Himself shakes his head in a condescending manner. "Hope is a gift the Universe gives in abundance to women, dear Lady. Especially to females under the spell of love. Common sense and an eye toward the black and white of reality say otherwise," my father-in-law lectures. "I have spoken to a great number of people in the know, Rosalinda. In all likelihood, my son no longer walks among the living."

His damning words are like a sucker punch to the gut. I feel sick, the few sips of that damn chamomile tea churning in the pit of my stomach like burning acid, making my next words come out strangled, "With all due respect, Lord *Nuada*, Declan is not dead. I would know if he were. I'm his *Mo Shiorghra*. I can still feel his presence."

The man shakes his head as if I were an addled child. "I admire your tenacious faith in the goodness of the Universe, little tooth fairy. But someone in my position must face the facts as they are presented and thus, make plans according to that reality. My mages cannot guarantee that my son...my heir...will return home someday to take his place as House *Nuada's* Lord. Therefore, I must take matters into my own hands. I must first and foremost see to the future of my House. You will return to *Dun Siorai* with my Lady wife and I, and have your baby there. I will officially make your son our reigning heir."

I've had about all that I can take from this pompous ass. Protocol be damned, I struggle up from the chair and say, "I'm afraid that's a hard no, your Lordship. My husband is not dead and I have no intention of leaving our home, the home Declan and I have created together. I will have my baby here in the Mundane world like my Lord and I have planned. I feel it is the safest, and most reasonable option for my family. As for your plan to make our son your current heir, you do a great disrespect to my husband, your Lordship. That title still belongs to him."

"That title must belong to a living soul, girl," He growls, now standing as well. "Though it pains me to say, there is no proof that my son is still alive. He has given his life to The Crown and will be honored for his sacrifice. But time waits for no man's grief. House *Nuada* must have a living heir." He turns to my mother-in-law, who, up until this moment, hasn't said a single word, staring straight ahead and making little eye contact, which for the woman I've nicknamed, Dragon Mama, is incredibly out of character. "Talk some sense into this girl, Lady Wife. Explain to her what her duty involves."

Dragon Mama finally reacts…but not in the manner I expected. She turns to her husband and looks at him with such pure disgust it spills from her aura and into the space of the room. I've known for a while that there is no love lost between these two, but up until now, I have never seen her so obvious regarding her feelings toward him. As for the two of us, our relationship has slightly shifted since that horrible day on the cliff, though by no means does this include comradery. Lady *Siobhan* leans forward in her chair and looks up at me. "Do not let him bully you into having this baby in *I Idir*, tooth fairy! He will snatch your son and browbeat you into believing that you are unfit...as he did to me." She then addressed her husband. "Our son is not dead. I have repeatedly told you this over and over again, but for whatever reason, you refuse to believe me. Declan is still alive...I, as well, feel his life force. You cannot name a new heir when the current heir is still among the living."

Her admission sucks the air from the room. His Lordship turns red in the face, spittle flying off his lips as he scolds her. "There is no reason for me to trust your 'feelings,' *Siobhan*. You are the last person our son would turn to in time of need. He hates the very sight of you!"

Now the old guy has gone and pissed me off to no end! How dare he say something so hurtful and untrue to my beloved's mother, especially in this situation. Sure, Declan and his mom have their issues, but I have never once heard my husband say that he hates her. My Tax Man is devoted to his family, all of them, as screwed up as they are. The mini Dragon Mama in me gets her own courage up. "Don't you dare say that to her, Lord *Nuada*! It's one hundred percent not true! Despite countless reasons to do otherwise, Declan loves both of you! He has shared his feelings with me on many occasions. And your wife is correct...Lord *Mac Nuada* is absolutely not dead!"

The red, angry face is gone. In its place is a colder,

more determined Fae Lord. "I have heard enough. I am Lord and you will both obey me as the law demands or I will have you locked away, as is my right. Lady Rosalinda, you have approximately ten minutes to gather whatever things you wish to take with you to *Dun Siorai.* You will not be returning here for quite some time." He then addressed Lady *Siobhan.* "You, Lady wife, will be dealt with when we return home."

I am forced into a corner with every fiber of my being telling me that I shouldn't go along with Lord *Nuada's* plan to take me from the Mundane world. My mother-in-law's expression mirrors the angst of my own. With little recourse, I do the only thing I can do in an extreme position like this one. I walk over to the fireplace mantle and pick up the little wooden box I put there just a few days before. Opening it, I pull out the large opal hanging on a gold chain, and before my nasty father-in-law can stop me from doing it, I call for The Morrigan.

BABY 57

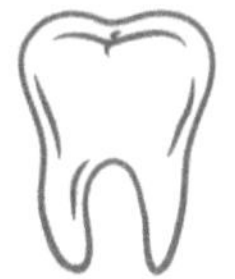

THE QUEEN'S GAMBIT

IN A MATTER OF MERE SECONDS, there is an odd feel to the atmosphere inside my house, as if the oxygen were being sucked out and replaced with some kind of vacuum. It's not unlike the feeling I experience when I first cross over into the Otherworld, but on a much grander scale. Before any of us can comment, the Celtic goddess of war and destruction appears in the center of my living room, dressed in traditional fencing attire, her thick red hair pulled back into a bun and the classic sabre mask pulled to the top of her head, cluing me in that I had undoubtedly called upon her at an inopportune moment. Though The Morrigan is petite in stature, physically smaller than any of us in the room, the way her magical aura fills the space leaves little doubt of her overwhelming wealth of power.

The three of us instantly drop our curtsies and bow, with myself teetering as I come up, my sense of balance completely thrown off by a protruding belly. The Queen sighs loudly and looks at me with an emotionless expression. "I am here as promised, little tooth fairy. What concern weighs so heavily on you that you feel the need to call upon me? Should you not be surrounding yourself with quiet peace and harmony as you await the birth of your son?"

I don't get the opportunity to answer, as my father-in-law beats me to it. "I offer my sincere apologies, Your Highness. My son's *Mo Shiorghra* has spent too much of her life in the Mundane world and is ignorant of royal protocol. She should never have taken it upon herself to seek your counsel, especially regarding what is nothing more than a family issue...one House *Nuada* is perfectly capable of handling on its own." I don't have to read any auras to know he's totally pissed off at me for calling The Morrigan in my defense. The little muscle over his left eye is twitching like a flea on a dog. My mother-in-law, however, looks remarkably smug, as if she's secretly amused over the idea of her husband being put on the spot. Seeing these two together always makes me wonder how in the hell they stopped bickering long enough to have six children together.

A red velvet chair appears out of nowhere, and The Morrigan settles herself in it before answering Declan's *athair.* "I have given Lady Rosalinda a promise of assistance while her husband is away in the service of The Crown," the goddess remarks. "You don't expect I would ignore my promises, do you, Lord *Nuada?* Especially while your son makes such an important sacrifice for the future of *I Idir.*"

"Of course not, Your Majesty. Rather I am embarrassed that this silly girl has used such a generous offer for such a minor family disagreement," his Lordship blustered.

The Queen tapped a red painted fingernail against her chin, then took a sip from a china tea cup that appeared in her hand out of thin air, reminding me that I am a terrible hostess not to have offered her something sooner. The Queen looks up at me in response to what I believed was a private thought, reminding me that nothing is private from The Morrigan. "You must stop fussing, little *Mathair*, lest your wee one enter the world in the same state. 'Tis not a good way to begin a life. Now suppose you yourself tell me what has caused you the need to call upon me."

I feel three sets of eyes boring holes in me. I've no doubt that Declan's father wants me to keep silent on his threats to cart me off to *Dun Siorai* against my will, while I sense that Dragon Mama is calling my bluff to do so. As far as I'm concerned, the two of them can go sit on a tack. I'm not getting in the middle of their raging war against each other and there's no way in hell I'm not going to fight for the right to have my baby where I want... with my husband beside me. I stand to address The Morrigan, which I remember from Declan's countless lectures is the proper protocol when seeking The Crown's counsel. "I am most grateful foor Your Majesty's ear regarding my concerns. My Lord *Nuada* has demanded I return with him to *Dun Siorai* to await the birth of my son. As much as I understand and appreciate his concern for my welfare, my beloved *Mo Shiorghra* and I have already made the decision to have our son born here in the Mundane world under the care of Lord *Spideog* (Robyn). This decision is as important to Lord *Mac Nuada* as it is to me, as I have family members here, including my own father and sister, who are unable to cross the Veil. I realize, Your Highness, that by my handfast I owe fealty to his Lordship and House *Nuada*, but I feel very strongly about holding true to a sacred matrimonial decision jointly made. I am hoping you will intercede on my behalf."

"I see," The Morrigan replied. "You may be seated, Lady Rosalinda." I curtsy again and return to my chair, but not before I get a good whiff of myself. After all that's happened, it's been two days since I've showered or washed my hair, and I'm wearing a stretched-out pair of sweatpants that I asked Mel to bring to the hospital, as they are the loosest thing I own that doesn't rub against my stitches. I realize my appearance doesn't help my cause and a tendril of fear begins to wrap itself around my thoughts. *Oh hell, Tax Man! I'm losing this battle...*

The Queen switches her attention to my father-in-law. "And you, Lord *Nuada*...what reasons do you have for wanting your Lady Daughter to return to *I Idir?*"

It's Lord *Nuada's* turn to stand and make his case. "Isn't it obvious, Your Majesty? One look at Lady Rosalinda's present condition proves that she is so overwhelmed with grief at the loss of my son that she has been unable to properly care for herself. She has just returned from a hospital stay after a very careless fall down some icy steps, a situation that could have been dire for the life of my unborn grandson. In addition, Lord *Spideog* has shared with me that her blood pressure is far too high and that he has ordered complete bed rest until the Lady goes into labor. I fear that in her current state and left to her own devices, my son's mate will not heed the good doctor's advice which could possibly cost my House its only heir. You of all people understand how important this child is to the future of House *Nuada*. I would be lacking in my duties as Lord not to assure a safe delivery of this child."

"I take from your words that you do not believe your son still walks among the living, Lord *Nuada*?" questioned The Morrigan, her expression giving no clues as to what she personally believes.

"As much as it pains me to say, Your Highness, I believe the Universe has taken *Deaglan* from us. I no longer feel his life source, and my House mages have been unable to make any contact with him. I must put aside my grief and do what is best for my House. *Deaglan*'s son will be House *Nuada*'s heir and I must put the *bairn*'s safety above the heightened emotions of my deceased son's mate," his Lordship states.

The heartless bastard couldn't have hurt me more if he had taken one of the Tax Man's nasty-looking knives and stabbed me straight through the heart with it. My hands are shaking so badly that I tuck them under my butt so no one will notice. In the process, I put pressure on the puncture wound from the errant nail, but it doesn't cause me nearly as much pain as Lord *Nuada*'s determination to dash any last hope I'm hanging on to over the belief that Declan is still alive.

Across from me, I note that Dragon Mama's aura has switched to a reddish black. If I can see it, so can everyone else in the room. Thus, The Morrigan notes it immediately. "You do not share your Lord's views, Lady *Nuada*?"

I don't know everything about the traditions and protocol of the Ruling Council, but even I know enough from the short time I've been handfasted to one of its heirs that one does not question one's Lord in public, especially in the presence of The Throne. Nor does one air the House's dirty laundry to any outsiders. My mother-in-law is swimming in dangerous waters, and Declan's father is not hiding his thinly veiled looks of warning. Still, from my past experiences with Lady *Siobhan,* it doesn't surprise me in the least when she stands, curtsies, and says, "I do not, Your Majesty. My son is not dead. As his mother, I would know if he were." Her husband gives a derisive snort, which earns him an annoyed look from The Morrigan, but it doesn't intimidate Dragon Mama. "I respectfully believe that my Lord is being far too quick in giving away my son's title. I also do not share his opinion that my son's mate is unable to make decisions regarding her health or the birth of her *bairn,*" says my mother-in-law. "While I do not condone the Lady's recent choices, I do not think they point to her being in any way…unfit."

"I appreciate your honesty, Lady *Nuada,*" said the Queen. "You may be seated as well." The goddess takes another long sip from her tea cup, examining the three of us as if we were chess pieces on a board she was looking to move. After a dramatic pause, the cup disappears from her hands. "I believe I have the perfect solution," The Morrigan says with a cryptic smile. "One that entirely suits this particular situation."

BABY 58

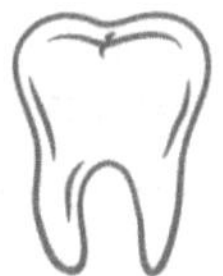

MOTHER KNOWS BEST

MY POMPOUS ASS of a father-in-law looks over and gives his wife and me a glimmer of a smug smile. "As you can imagine, Your Majesty, we are appreciative of your keen wisdom on this subject. What do you suggest we do?" he asks in a voice that sounds rather condescending to my female ear.

In return, The Morrigan gives him a look that would freeze a regular, mortal soul. "I never 'suggest' anything, Lord *Nuada*. In *I Idir*, my word is law," she icily comments.

"As it should be, Your Highness," my father-in-law says, though personally, I see little sincerity in his hooded eyes. "My words are only meant as... a figure of speech. Of course, House *Nuada* shall abide with any and all... decisions...Your Majesty puts forward regarding this tragic event."

The Queen steeples her fingertips. "You are correct on one part, Lord *Nuada*. This situation is tragic. I am grieved that your young Lord is made to suffer for the careless actions of another, though I am impressed by his show of leadership and valor. However, you are incorrect in assuming that your son is dead. He is not, and therefore, there will be no transferring of rightful titles while he remains among the living. Do I make myself clear, *Nuada?*"

I would have expected my father-in-law's response over Declan's fate to be more in line with mine and Lady *Siobhan's*. Our relief at The Morrigan's pronouncement is physically audible. If anything, Declan's father seems more embarrassed over being called to task by his superior than giddy with relief over the knowledge that his only son is still alive. "That is wonderful news, Your Majesty," he stammers. "My own mages have been unable to give me a definitive answer."

"The enemy has taken great pains to rein in his magical energy," The Morrigan says. "Rest assured, I have no doubt that the heir of House *Nuada* is alive and fighting with his whole being to stay with us on this plane, though time is not our friend. The Black Knight is working around the clock to locate him. Once we ascertain his whereabouts, we will retrieve him." The Queen of *I Idir* then turns her attention to me. "It is my hope that this will happen before the arrival of your wee *bairn*, Lady Rosalinda, but the Universe moves as it wishes, so this I cannot guarantee."

Just having the goddess verify that Declan is truly alive is enough for me at the moment. My due date is not for another four weeks, and I'm holding out hope that this is plenty of time for the Black Knight to bring my husband home to me. "I understand, Your Highness," I say. "I am grateful for your verification of what I know to be true in my heart. As long as my Lord is alive, I hold onto my faith that I will see him home soon."

The Morrigan nods her approval, but then adds, "That does not mean, little tooth fairy, that I do not have my own concerns over your being alone in these final weeks. Lord *Nuada* is correct in his comments regarding your somewhat reckless behavior of these past few days. Though I completely sympathize with your anxiety and grief over the sacrifices your *Mo Shiorghra* is making on behalf of *I Idir*, I would also be remiss in my duty not to see to it that his mate and unborn child are properly cared for in his absence."

I feel my freedom slowly slipping through my fingers and I start to panic. "I fully understand your concerns, Your Highness. I am ashamed that I haven't been as strong in spirit these past few days as my House and my husband would expect of me, and I take full responsibility for the trouble and concern my carelessness has caused everyone. But I've now arranged for my sister and my dear friend to stay with me and you have my undying word that I will follow all of Dr. Brannigan's mandates for the remaining days of my pregnancy. I beg of you to let me stay here in the Mundane world. It is where..." I choke up on these last few words..."I feel closest to my missing *Mo Shiorghra.*"

"I feel for you, dear Lady. Bringing a new life into the world is no easy task, and these final days should be spent in peaceful anticipation despite the unusual circumstances," The Morrigan says, her sympathy apparent. "In addition, it is imperative that you keep the line of communication and soul spirit between you and your mate open and clear, and if being in this location helps you do this, so much the better. Therefore, I will grant you your request to stay here in the Mundane world to deliver your *bairn*." I start to stand up to curtsy and offer my gratitude, but before I can do so, The Morrigan holds up a finger, and then signals that I should sit back down. "However," she adds, "I don't have confidence that your kin or your friend will be able to keep your feisty spirit in line. Despite your sweetness of character, little tooth fairy, you have a will of steel. You will surely walk all over their attempts to rein you in for your own safety."

I feel my face getting hot, unsure if I should take the monarch's words as criticism or as a complement. "I don't mean to be this way, Your Majesty," I mumble.

"Do not apologize for your strength of character, Rosalinda. It is a trait I am counting on seeing in your offspring, though in this case, I believe an equally strong will is required. What you need, as you move toward the end of your waiting period, is a skilled maternal force, one who has had experience in this phase of woman-hood," the goddess explains. "As your own *mathair* is no longer with you, I am placing your mate's *mathair* in that role. I am leaving you here in the Mundane world under the care and guardianship of Lady *Nuada*."

BABY 59

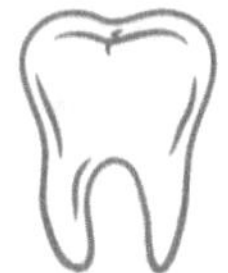

LET THE GAMES BEGIN

WE ALL STAND and express our united displeasure over The Morrigan's decision at the same time. Apparently, the goddess is tired of negotiating. With a wave of her hand, we all find ourselves thrown back into our respective seats, though I'd like to think she was a little gentler with me than the other two. Lord *Nuada* is not holding back on his feelings of anger. His aura shimmers with the fiery red of his hostility and he works hard to desperately rein in the outward sign of his displeasure. She is, after all, his Queen, and The Morrigan has the power to make his life miserable.

Strangely enough, Dragon Mama's aura is orange, a mix of red anger and yellow anxiety. She too is struggling not to give away her true feelings. I understand the anger part. The stress and anxiety mix in her aura is puzzling to me. Is she worried about spending too much time on this side of the Veil? Is it the fear of reprisals from her Lord that has her spooked? Or is it the thought of being forced to spend time with a lowly tooth fairy in the Mundane world a blow to her social-climbing ego?

It's a mystery I'll have to try and solve another time. The Morrigan stands, her petite stature replaced by the physical form of a woman who now stands at least six feet, ten inches tall. "I see that my decision has caused some consternation. You may speak, Lord *Nuada*."

My father-in-law stands stiffly, bowing from the waist before speaking. "Your Majesty is asking me to do without the companionship of my Lady Wife. You must be aware that she is my *Mo Shiorghra* as well. 'Tis not a fair solution on my part."

Her Majesty raises her eyebrow, and her voice holds a measure of threat. "These are troubling times, Lord *Nuada*. The Mundane world breathes down our necks in an attempt to take what is not theirs. As a member of the Ruling Council, should you not be first in line to make deep sacrifices for *I Idir* in the same manner as your heir? In addition, I do not believe you will find the absence of Lady *Siobhan* a great hardship. If the rumors I hear at court are true, you will not lack female companionship."

This last little nugget of information causes both my husband's parents to turn equal shades of embarrassed pink. On a personal level, it blows my mind, though, considering what I've witnessed between them since meeting Declan, it probably shouldn't. Infidelity among fated mates is extremely rare, though good ole Callum and *Siobhan* are in a special category of their own when it comes to being *Mo Shiorghras*.

"And you, Lady *Nuada*?" the Queen asks, now turning

her annoyance toward the Tax Man's mother. "What concerns do you hold onto? I should think a respite from your Lord would be a welcome situation for you."

My mother-in-law seems unsure of herself, a state that is utterly foreign to me judging from my past experiences with her. The Lady stands, curtsies, and says in a voice much softer than I'm used to, "For the past twenty years, I have not spent much time in the Mundane world, Your Majesty. I'm not sure I will be able to assimilate…especially without staff to help me." She pauses, wringing her hands in obvious anxiety. "As to my experience with motherhood…my youngest child is nearly sixteen years of age. It has been too long since I've been an expectant mother. I'm not sure I am the right person to…guide Lady Rosalinda through any of this. None of my own daughters have yet been gifted with a child. I worry I will not know what to do."

"Nonsense," The Morrigan states. "You have birthed six living children. Despite the feelings you hold for your mate, the union has been exceptionally fruitful, a blessing you should be extremely grateful for. Children are a treasure, Lady *Nuada*, especially among the Fae. To be here for the birth of your first grandchild, a male child, no less, is a gift beyond measure. I have every confidence you are just what our little tooth fairy needs. Still, in deference to your title, I will not require scullery work of you. I will send you a small, hand-picked staff from *Crann Bethadh* to add ease to your directive. This should be all you require. I want your focus to be on your role as a comforting guide to this first time *mathair*. Do you understand what I expect of you?"

Lady *Siobhan* nods her agreement but her voice doesn't hold a lot of confidence. "Yes, Your Highness." She drops another curtsy and sits back down without another word.

It's my turn in the hot seat. The Morrigan crosses her arms against her chest, and I swear she's grown another two inches in height. "And now to you, Lady *Mac Nuada*. If you have any further concerns, I will hear them now."

I may be a lot of things, but stupid isn't one of them. I stand, get the whole protocol curtsy thing over, and say in a voice I hope doesn't crack, "I've reconsidered your decision, Your Majesty, and find it to be most satisfactory. I have no complaints and look forward to sharing these last weeks of pregnancy with my *Mo Shiorghra*'s *mathair*. I hope it will allow me to get to know her better. I am most grateful for The Crown's wise counsel over my little problem."

The Morrigan eyes me for a moment and then breaks into laughter. "Well played, little tooth fairy! You are a constant delight! 'Tis no wonder your mate is so enchanted by you." The chair the Queen was sitting in disappears. "I am glad this is all settled so easily. Now we must turn our attention to the safe recovery of Lord *Mac Nuada* as we await the birth of his son." A fencing sword suddenly appears in The Morrigan's right hand which she points at my father-in-law. "I should not like to hear that you have been badgering your Lady Wife or your son's mate over my decisions, Lord *Nuada*." She then points the sword toward Dragon Mama. "I have granted you a golden opportunity for a new beginning, Lady *Siobhan*. I hope you will not squander it." Finally, taking a few small steps toward me, the goddess leans down and whispers in my ear, loud enough for only me to hear. "Hang onto that rope, little tooth fairy. Do not let go of your *Mo Shiorghra.* His connection to you is the only thing keeping him in the land of the living." Then, she pulled the *sabre* mask down over her face, and in the blink of an eye, was gone.

BABY 60

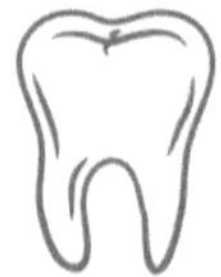

FUN AT ROSIE'S HOUSE

WITH THE MORRIGAN GONE, Lord *Nuada* lets loose his anger toward us. He stands and shakes a finger in the direction of Declan's *mathair* and myself. "I do not understand what you think you have accomplished here, but know this…I promise that you will regret your actions of today…both of you. The Queen fills your head with empty hope. If my son is alive, then why did she not show proof? No. She only leads you on with empty promises so that we will continue to help her fight a battle she cannot win. We should be peacefully negotiating with the Mundanes…not angering them with petty skirmishes. You will one day see that I am right. But by then, it will be too late for the both of you. I have a long memory and I will not forget your treachery today."

Truthfully, I may not be privy to all of the political volleying and discord between the Ruling Houses and The Throne, but it doesn't take a genius to realize that the words my father-in-law are spewing are akin to treason. Before I can think of a proper response that won't get me deeper in shit with my husband's father, the man disappears. (On a side note, have I ever mentioned how I find the way these *Sidhe* types pop back and forth between dimensions, without any warning and completely in silence, more than a little creepy? I say this with not an ounce of jealousy. Honest.)

This leaves Lady *Siobhan* and I alone together in my house which is...well...awkward. I try to lighten the mood. "Gee...someone's not a happy camper. He didn't even say goodbye."

My mother-in-law glares at me. "You stupid, stupid girl! You don't even have enough sense to be alarmed at the trouble you've gotten yourself into! On top of it all, you've dragged me into your mess as well. You don't have the slightest idea how terrible his Lordship can be when he doesn't get his way. You better beg the Universe that my son's feelings towards you are stronger than his *athair's* influence over him. I have no doubt that when *Deaglain* returns, his Lordship will work at poisoning our son's opinion of you before the 357 days of your handfast are up."

Her comment both alarms and infuriates me at the same time. "Declan loves me...and I love him. What we have together is unbreakable," I protest.

"Hmmm...for your sake, I hope you are right," Lady *Nuada* says, "because you will have your hands full enough with The Morrigan's hooks in you."

Okay. Now this woman is just being a complete Debbie Downer. This is not the way I want to start the next four weeks together. This forced proximity is bad enough. "Look, Lady *Nuada*, I realize you're not happy with the 'assignment' you've been roped into. I'm not exactly doing handstands over it myself. But there's no way I was going to let his Lordship cart me off to *Dun Siorai*. That would have been a bad deal all around. You said so yourself. My hand was forced so I turned to the only resource I had. I didn't ask for The Morrigan's help. Her Majesty offered it to me. I think she's a lot kinder and more sympathetic than people give her credit for."

At this, Dragon Mama leans back into the sofa and laughs, though the sound of it doesn't seem to carry an ounce of joy. "So sure of yourself, tooth fairy, and so wholly naive. You have no idea of the debt you'll owe."

"What debt?" I ask, thoroughly confused.

"We need to have a serious talk, mother of my grandson. A long, hard talk." Lady *Siobhan* states. "But not before you take care of your personal hygiene. You smell like a goat, tooth fairy girl, and should my son miraculously return this very minute, he'd most likely take one look at the sight of his unattractive *Mo Shiorghra* and offer himself back up to his captors."

I don't want it to, but her insults hurt my feelings. "That's just mean, Lady *Nuada*. I've been to hell and back this past week. I realize I may have let myself go a bit, but with my husband missing and in absolute danger, my thoughts are focused on more important things than my personal appearance."

Her response is to have a full-length mirror appear in front of me. I stare at the mess looking back. Dragon Mama isn't altogether wrong. I'm a disaster, from my greasy hair, to my stained, smelly sweatpants, and finally down to the giant hole in my sock exposing two of my un-pedicured toes. Embarrassment creeps over me as I remember that I appeared in front of the goddess of war and destruction, the Queen of *I Idir*, looking more like a careless slob than the professional woman I am. "You can get rid of that damn mirror," I say. "You're right. I need a shower. A nice long one. When I'm done, I'll make us some afternoon tea and we'll talk."

"Yes, Lady Rosalinda...talk we must," she answers. "And use the shower bench. No standing in the shower, you stupid girl."

BABY 61

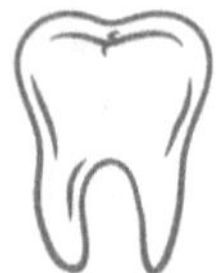

THINGS TO THINK ABOUT

As I pass through my bedroom on the way to the shower, I realize I need to do something about the state of this space before Lady *Nuada* makes her way up here. The bed is unmade, the sheets themselves none too clean. There are plates and cups stacked on the nightstand on my side of the bed, and little piles of dirty clothes decorate the floor. I have no doubt that if my obsessively neat Tax Man were here, he'd have a complete apoplexy over the condition of this room we share. I put straightening it up as number one on my list of "things to-do" after my shower.

For the next thirty minutes, I let the hot water spray over me as I sit on that shower bench, alternating between thinking, fretting, and crying. I carry on a running conversation in my head with Declan, mostly begging him to stay strong and come back to me and Peanut because we absolutely cannot do without him. I work hard at shielding my concerns over this latest run-in with his parents and the appearance of The Morrigan. Those are things better left to discuss in person when he returns.

When I'm finally prune-y enough and all cried out, I step out of the shower, dry off and reach for my favorite terry cloth robe. I find it missing, and in its place is a lovely white cotton eyelet nightgown and matching robe that I've never seen before. Unless I want to try and streak across the bedroom to find something else to wear, I have no choice but to dry off better and don the new apparel. I'm not surprised when I slide it over my head and it fits perfectly. It's obviously been magically produced and perfect in every way. I want to feel annoyed over my mother-in-law's interference regarding my choice of clothing, but honestly, the gown is soft and comfortable and makes me look prettier than I feel.

A bigger surprise waits outside the bathroom. My bedroom is now perfectly neat; the bed made with all new linens, the furniture clean and dusted, and the laundry gone from sight. A young *Sidhe* woman with her back to me is busily arranging flowers in a vase that sits on the nightstand recently cleared of its collection of dirty dishes. She senses my arrival and turns to drop a curtsy. "*Trathnona maith* (Good Afternoon), Lady *Mac Nuada*. I am Freza. My mate, Tobias, and I have been sent by Her Highness to attend to you and Lady *Nuada*. We are very sorry to hear that your Lord has been forced away in service to *I Idir*. Tobias and I are both asking the Universe to bring him home as quickly as possible, good Lady. If there is anything you wish us to attend to while we are here, please do not hesitate to ask."

At that moment, my mother-in-law appears in the

doorway. Seeing her, Freza drops another curtsy and heads toward the door to leave. "We will want high tea served up here at early eventide, Freza," the Lady in Charge orders.

"Aye, Lady *Nuada*. Tobias is working on something special for your tray as we speak," the young fairy says.

"Very good," Lady *Siobhan* comments. "I will let you know our needs regarding the evening meal a bit later."

The fairy drops another curtsy and I think that I'm surely going to get very tired of all this overblown protocol before the first week is out, but I leave that discussion for another time. When the woman leaves, Dragon Mama appraises my appearance. "A much-needed improvement," she says, then points to the bedside chair. "Sit."

The clean sheets look terribly inviting and I'm more than dead on my feet, but I just don't have the energy for another go-around, so I do as she asks. She picks up a comb and brush from my dressing table and begins detangling my mop of wet hair without speaking a single word. Lady *Siobhan* is gentler than I expect, and in the exhausted state I'm in, her attention to my hair puts me into a drowsy stupor. When she finishes combing the strands into some kind of order, she braids my hair in a classic fishtail style. With my hair now dry and neatly arranged, Declan's *mathair* pulls back the covers and orders me into bed as if I were a child. "I hope I can trust you to stay put, Rosalinda. I'd rather not stand guard over you."

"I'll stay put," I promise. "Honestly, I'm exhausted. I

hardly slept a wink in the hospital and I've been looking forward to this cat nap since I walked through the door."

She nods, then closes the window blinds and leaves me to rest.

I have that damn rope dream again, although this time, instead of a ship or my back porch, I'm standing on a cliff with one end of the cord in both of my hands and the other dangling over the side of jutting rocks. I don't look over the edge to see who or what is on the other end. If it's Declan hanging on for dear life, I don't want to know. The wind suddenly picks up and my hair begins whipping around in front of my face. I want to brush it away, but I'm afraid to loosen my grip on the rope. Suddenly, a large black bird lands on a rock next to me and begins to furiously caw. Somehow, I seem to know what the bird is saying. The ugly, menacing thing is scolding me, telling me to hold on tighter...

I awake to a semi-dark room with just a faint glimmer of late afternoon light coming through the closed slats of the blinds. I grab for my phone on the nightstand. It shows the time as 3:37 PM, meaning I've been napping for two solid hours. As if on cue, there's a single knock on my bedroom door. "Come in," I say, as I struggle to sit upright. My husband's *mathair* enters the room. She's no longer wearing Otherworldly garb. Instead, she's donned a Mundane-style emerald green silk pants suit of sorts, designer quality by the look of the cut and the fabric. There's no denying that despite having a son who is 36 years old, *Siobhan* Donnely Fitzpatrick is still a very attractive woman. My father-in-law must be crazy to look for love somewhere else.

"It's nearly time for tea. I would guess that you might be hungry," she says. "I'm glad to see you have rested as promised."

Freza enters the room carrying a tea tray, followed by a male *Sidhe* I presume to be her husband, Tobias. He totes an even larger tray loaded with tea sandwiches, scones, clotted cream and...joy of joys...tiny chocolate chip pancakes. A table suddenly appears next to my bed, which startles me and makes me jump. I'm not used to all this outward magic. Declan uses his own so subtly that I hardly notice when it happens. I always supposed he didn't want to make me feel self-conscious about my own lack of magical abilities, but I doubt my current house guests will consider my feelings regarding something that comes so naturally to them.

The two staff members lay out the delightful spread, then quietly see themselves out. Dragon Mama makes herself comfortable in a chair next to the tea table, and after pouring tea for the both of us, and fixing me a small plate of assorted treats, she takes a sip of the Darjeeling before speaking. "There is much you don't understand about life within *Crann Bethadh* and your ignorance is likely to cause you a great deal of unhappiness. There is always a constant jockeying among the Ruling Council Houses for a spot within the Queen's inner circle. To the average citizen of *I Idir*, The Morrigan is considered a hero...a savior to her people. There is truth to that belief. It was she alone who gathered the different clan leaders into some semblance of an orderly ruling class. What most Fae forget, however, is that The Morrigan is an ancient force of power not to be thought of lightly. When it comes to her demands, she is ruthless and without moral conscience. My own *Mathair* served in her entourage for a number of years while I was growing up. As her only daughter, I often accompanied her to *Crann Bethadh* where I saw first-hand what it meant to be a pawn of the Raven. It is a difficult path to walk. She can be extremely demanding."

Her mention of a raven makes me think of the big ugly bird in my dream and a shiver runs down my spine. "You needn't worry about me becoming any kind of pawn, Lady *Nuada*," I say. "Every time Her Majesty sees me, she calls me 'little tooth fairy.' That doesn't sound like someone she'd want as part of her personal tribe. I know she seems genuinely fond of Declan, so I can rightfully assume her interest in me only goes as far as being polite to his *Mo Shiorghra*. Beyond that, I can't for the life of me believe there's any more to it."

Lady *Nuada* shakes her head and tisks in disgust. "Surely you are not as naive as that, silly girl? For someone with a career requiring a high level of intelligence you sometimes seem to be not very bright."

I'm growing increasingly tired of being insulted in my own home, so the words just sort of roll off my tongue without much thought. "And YOUR constant insults and name calling makes YOU appear rude and bitchy," I complain.

The tea cup rests mid-air in the Dragon Mama's hands, and then she raises one perfectly arched eyebrow in annoyance. It reminds me so much of my husband that it squeezes at my heart and makes tears well up in my eyes. Seeing this, my mother-in-law sniffs and says, "You needn't cry about it, silly girl. We are casually speaking as adults. You have too thin a skin."

"I'm sorry," I admit, "it's not your words making me emotional. It's just that Declan looks exactly the same way when he's annoyed with me. That whole single arched eyebrow thing. He resembles you so very much that sometimes when I look at you..." My voice fades off. In my hormonal state, something like this easily sets me off, and I don't need Lady *Siobhan* to see me ugly cry.

"Yes. I've been told *Deaglain* resembles me. I, however, don't see the likeness," she says. I just roll my eyes over that comment. One would have to be blind not to see that acute family resemblance. Dragon Mama changes the subject from her son and returns to her Morrigan lecture. "You, for whatever reason, Rosalinda, have caught The Morrigan's attention. First, it was the gift of your hand-fast dress, which, if you remember correctly, I vehemently suggested you not accept."

"When you said that, I just thought..."

She cuts me off. "I know what you thought, girl. But I had my concerns...even back then. After the dress boon, she bestowed on you that over-blown awards ceremony, followed by a festive ball in your honor, and then finished her gifts with your big promotion within the Tooth Fairy Corps. Now, today, she appears and intercedes on your behalf in a family matter that would traditionally be handled privately. Do you not see a pattern here? The Morrigan has completely set you up to be in her debt, tooth fairy. The real question at hand is why?"

BABY 62

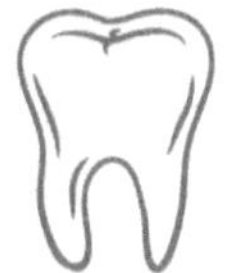

THE NURSERY TALE

THE FIRST FEW days of cohabitation with Declan's *mathair* are relatively calm simply because the two of us agree upon an unspoken, mutual cease fire of hostilities. We both understand that The Morrigan's generous offer of household help is little more than a method for the Queen of *I Idir* to keep tabs on us, and we are careful not to give Freza and Tobias any fodder to take back to Her Majesty's ear. In truth, Lady *Siobhan's* earlier dissertation regarding the goddess's interest in me does the job it is intended to do. What the Lady of House *Nuada* had insinuated wasn't completely untrue and it now left me wondering if I hadn't been played from the very start. For the life of me, though, I can't figure out why. My husband is one hundred percent loyal to The Crown, this latest sacrifice obvious proof that he is the Queen's man. Did The Morrigan somehow think I was not?

I have a lot of time to think, stuck in bed as I am.

Firmly set in her role as Lady of the Manor, Dragon Mama runs a tight ship even here in the Mundane world. A healthy, low-sodium breakfast is served promptly at eight whether I want it or not, and is followed by *am ullmhuchain* (preparation time) which was nothing more than a big, fancy name for the normal routine of getting washed and dressed in the morning. In truth, if I took as much effort and attention in real life as I am being forced to do now, I'd never make it to work on time. Once I am dressed in yet another exquisite, perfectly-fitting dressing gown, hair traditionally braided and put up by the Lady herself, it's back to bed to await my lesson with the Gaelic language tutor.

I'll admit I haven't been as dedicated in becoming fluent in the Otherworld language as perhaps I should have been in these past eight months. Knowing this older version of Gaelic would not only make my visits to *I Idir* easier, it is necessary in my role as a parent. Tradition expects that our Peanut, as my husband's heir, will be bilingual, fluent in both English and Otherworldly Gaelic, as well as a number of other Mundane world languages as is deemed necessary for his standing and occupation. Me not being able to speak the language of my husband's native country would make that goal nearly impossible.

Annoyed with my lack of progress, my mother-in-law orders that during afternoon tea, the two of us will converse entirely in the Old Language, which makes the usually anticipated respite less than enjoyable. However, I quickly discover that speaking and listening to the spoken words does help me better grasp them, and I keep reminding myself of how surprised and pleased the Tax

Man will be when I welcome him home in his native tongue.

Overall, since our pow-wow with The Morrigan, life in my Mill Hills homes is surprisingly calm, if a bit over-organized. This isn't what I had anticipated, given what I'd already witnessed of Lady *Nuada*'s personality. That's why when the first big disagreement pops up between us, I am not altogether surprised, though the consequences of it will undoubtedly linger. The dissent begins over the state of my unfinished remodeling job. I try to explain to my mother-in-law that Mundane tradesmen, especially American ones, are traditionally inconsistent about completing jobs, and long delays in finishing their work are not uncommon. Dragon Mama brushes off my concerns, lecturing that the problem is entirely my fault, and blaming my weak leadership qualities when it comes to handling the help. In annoyance, I offer her the job, expecting she'll be met with the same tired excuses and no-shows that I've been plagued with for months, while I look forward to smugly saying "I told you so" when she fails.

This problem is solved in an entirely different manner than I had presumed. Lady *Siobhan* is naturally bossy. She handles those contractors like a Marine Drill Sergeant. I'm not sure if it is out of respect and fear of her tongue-lashing, cringy attitude, or if she's used some Otherworld magic on them, but more work gets done in three days than Declan or I had been able to procure from the contractor in two months. One of my biggest concerns has been the completion of Peanut's nursery, which is across and down the hall from our bedroom and part of the new addition. This morning, I was given a short reprieve from my mandated bed rest in order to tour the newly completed work.

The idea of seeing the nursery finally built raises a tidal wave of emotions in me. On one hand, I am relieved to know that the room will likely be ready for our son's arrival. On the other hand, it is a stark reminder that Peanut might be born any day now, while his father was still missing, and thus might not be in attendance when that big day comes. In hindsight, I suppose my highly charged emotions are only partly to blame for the brouhaha that ensues, though I take full responsibility for the terrible way I handled the situation.

No doubt Dragon Mama expected me to gush with gratitude that so much progress had been made in so little time, but standing there, all I could focus on was the shock of seeing a room that was completely different from the nursery I had planned. The pale, yellow walls with the baby duck border I'd so carefully picked out were now a shade of dusty blue. The large back wall was completely blank with some pencil lines drawn in. The few pieces of furniture in the room were heavy and old fashioned, and entirely different from the modern, stream-lined, convertible pieces my husband and I had been strongly leaning toward. Worst of all, Peanut's crib, the crib Declan had himself built a few days before he'd left for North Korea, was completely gone.

"Are you pleased, Rosalinda? As you can see, quite a lot of progress has been made in just three days. It should offer you some peace of mind," Lady *Nuada* remarked.

"Obviously, there is much left to be done, but it is a good start."

My tongue feels twice its normal size. I can't tell whether it is a physical reaction caused by justifiable anger, an Otherworldly curse, or a just deep sense of loss. "Where's the crib that was here?" I ask, my voice echoing in the nearly empty room.

"You mean that hideous thing with bars?" Dragon Mama questions. "'Twas more like a dog kennel than a bed for a wee sleeping *bairn*. I packed it up and sent it away. I have something very special in mind instead."

The logical and mature thing to do would have been to calmly explain to my husband's mother why I was so upset over the missing crib and politely ask her to return it, along with the room's intended decor. Using her level of magic, it would not have been a difficult assignment. She would have been disgruntled, of course, maybe even insulted, but perhaps I wouldn't have said the awful words I'm not able to take back. Unfortunately, it wasn't a day for thinking rationally, nor apparently, for considering anyone's pain but my own. I look at my husband's mother, at a face that resembles the one I hold so dearly in my heart, and spit out the words. "How dare you! How could you do something so callous? So evil and mean-spirited? It's little wonder your own family can't stand the sight of you, *Siobhan* Fitzpatrick!

Then, I turn abruptly around and stamp off to my bedroom, locking the door behind me.

BABY 63

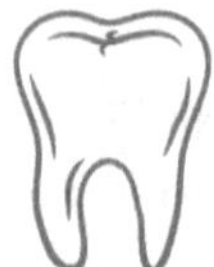

A PICTURE PAINTS A THOUSAND WORDS

It's hard to imagine that I could find a way to be any more miserable. Leave it to me to find a way to go above and beyond my new role as pity party planner. In addition to the usually uncomfortable physical symptoms of late pregnancy, (chronic heartburn, hemorrhoids, constant urination, sleepless nights) I've gone ahead and managed to alienate my only source of companionship. My husband's mother may not have been a ray of sunshine in this dismal situation, but I believed somewhere in her heart that she was truly concerned about her missing son and her unborn grandson. We shared a constant level of anxiety over things beyond our control. How she felt about me personally was still a mystery, but until our little disagreement over the nursery, and my subsequent wretched comment, we had managed a workable truce.

Currently, Lady *Siobhan* and I are embroiled in what can only be considered a standoff of who will blink first.

She has given up tending to my hair in the morning, passing the job off to Freza, and no longer joins me for tea or the evening meal. I hate eating alone, but I'll be damned if I'll apologize for something I don't feel is entirely my fault. Occasionally, she'll check in on my welfare, but her conversation is limited to specific questions about my physical well-being, and her tone is brisk and business-like.

This whole situation sucks. I've never been very good at holding grudges. In my opinion, they take far too much energy to maintain. In addition, I'm going absolutely stir-crazy sitting in this room hour after hour, day after day. I can't seem to concentrate long enough to read, and I've watched enough inane television to last me a lifetime. Though I fully understand Dr. Brannigan's orders are meant to keep my blood pressure down, it might be all for naught if Peanut's Mama ends up in the loony bin on account of all this anxiety and isolation.

On top of everything else, I can't ignore that today is Valentine's Day...the first one for Declan and me as a couple. This Mundane celebration focused on love has only the barest roots in the Otherworld, where some of the older Houses still follow the traditions of *Lupercalia*, a festival focused on the act of purging and the hope for increased fertility. Flowers and chocolates don't make a single appearance in *I Idir*, but I'd rather had my heart set on celebrating with my *Mo Shiorghra* in the Mundane tradition. Now, I'd gratefully skip every year of the commercial Valentine's Day trappings if only I could have my husband back home with me for this one.

At a mental breaking point, I can't take another

minute of sitting and stewing. I roll myself out of bed and waddle to the hallway where I meet Freza on her way to my room with an armful of clean laundry. "You should be in bed, Lady *Mac Nuada.* Her Ladyship will be quite cross if she finds you wandering about," the young woman warns.

"Where is her Ladyship?" I ask

"She has made a short trip home for more supplies, my Lady."

"Supplies?" I ask, curiosity getting the better of me. "For what?"

"Lady *Nuada* prefers her special brushes and her own palette, Ma'am. For her nursery project," Freza clarifies.

I don't reply. Instead, I make the trek down the hallway to the nursery. Opening the door, I stand dumbfounded in the entryway. Despite the big go around about the nursery decor Lady *Nuada* and I had two days ago, the damn woman has gone ahead and continued doing exactly as she pleased, making unexpected progress on the most whimsical wall mural I've ever seen. I'm not sure whether to laugh or cry, so I do both. I instantly recognize the subject matter. It's a landscape painting of the countryside surrounding *Dun Siorai,* but it's been painted in a charming, child-like style, the flowers, trees, and woodland animals all sporting sweet little faces. It's altogether charming, but it's the scene painted under the branches of a willow in the far-right corner of the wall that takes my breath away. In that spot, Lady *Siobhan* has painted Declan and I as we appeared on our handfast day, perfectly detailed down to the four cords that bind our hands together. Looking at the painted images of us, so full of love and hope on that remarkable day, my laugh-ing-crying combo turns to strictly weeping. In the midst of yet another good cry, I feel the artist behind me before I actually see her. "It's amazing," I sniffle.

"I would have preferred for you to see it finished," Lady *Nuada* says. "As of yet, the sky is not quite the right shade, and the wee *coinin* (rabbits) appear more skittish than joyful."

"I think it's perfect," I reply. "Utterly perfect."

"Hmmm…and so much more fitting for House *Nuada*'s heir than a room full of silly waterfowl, don't you agree?" Dragon Mama asks, her response dripping with sarcasm.

I should be appalled at her attitude. After all was said and done, my mother-in-law still won't admit she rudely crossed household boundaries and was completely out of line. When I turn around to tell her so, she looks so much like cranky Declan, leaning in the doorway, her hands crossed in front of her chest, chin out, with that Donnely family look of determination settled on her face, I end up smiling instead. That stubborn personality trait must run hard in both of their ancient bloodlines. Goddesses help me if our Peanut falls strongly to his *seanmhathair's* (grandmother's) and father's side of the genetic fence.

"Are you laughing at me, girl," she asks, getting her dander up.

"Not at all, Lady *Nuada*. I was just pondering how life will be for me if your grandson takes after his father and grandmother. I will surely have to get more sleep and grow a thicker skin to keep up with the three of you."

There's the slightest upturn to her lips so I know my

remark pleases her. Maybe a slight thaw in our frosty relationship is possible after all. There's no chance, however, for the two of us to explore that possibility any further. Freza comes to the nursery in full hand-wringing mode. With both of us there together, the young staff member tries to decide which of us to address first. Going the safer route of traditional protocol, she speaks to my mother-in-law even though this happens to be MY house. "Excuse the interruption, Lady *Nuada*, but there is a young Lord at the front door wearing the colors of House *Badh*. He says he's come to pay his respects to Lady Rosalinda."

"Did you explain to him that the Lady is indisposed and not seeing any visitors, Freza?" Lady *Siobhan* asks.

"Aye, your Ladyship. But he's quite insistent. Says he's come with a special request that cannot wait. Being that he wears House *Badh's* colors, I thought it best to check with you."

Lady *Siobhan* sports a face that shows her obvious annoyance at being bothered. "Show him into the parlor, Freza, and offer him the usual late morning hospitality. The Lady Rosalinda and I will be down shortly," she orders the woman. Once Freza leaves, I hear Dragon Mama mutter under her breath, "What is now afoot that House *Badh* comes to our door uninvited?"

BABY 64

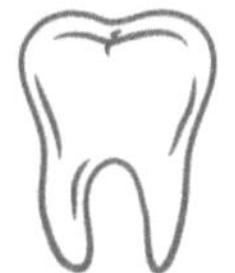

TELLING TALES

ACCORDING to the Lady of House *Nuada*, neither she nor I are dressed appropriately to receive visitors of this type. Not knowing the business that draws him here, it seems prudent to not keep a Jr. Lord of a prestigious Ruling House cooling his heels for too long in my parlor. Therefore, my mother-in-law uses magic to speed up what I sarcastically call our costume change. The comfy, granny-gown style nightdress and robe in a soft cotton that Dragon Mama has gotten me so accustomed to wearing is replaced with a simple snap of her slender fingers. Before I can blink, I'm outfitted in a maroon silk gown, Empire-waisted, and cut in the bodice to accent my abundant cleavage. It glides over but does little to hide the huge baby bump. In fact, the dress seems to accentuate my all over…roundness. Freza's simple French braid is replaced with a more complicated up-do, with a Celtic woven comb holding it in place.

Lady *Siobhan* has traded in the free-flowing, Mundane-style pant suit she's favored while living here for a traditional Otherworldly day gown with matching chemise in pale gold and with the sigil of House *Nuada* embroidered in glittering, burgundy thread on the skirt portion.

"Is this performance art really necessary?" I complain to her.

"What you so crudely call a performance is the way the game of politics is played in *I Idir*. I do not lose games of any kind, girl. You should already know this of me," Dragon Mama scolds.

"Great. Another competitive Fitzpatrick to contend with," I murmur under my breath. Speaking louder I add, "Why do you think he's here?"

Lady *Siobhan* shrugs, a gesture not in keeping with her usual formality. "I admit that I am not in the know regarding his unseemly intrusion. My son's capture and the fact that you are close to ending your 'waiting time' is no secret across the kingdom. Friends and associates are well versed in the polite protocol regarding how situations of this type should be approached. Thus, I am puzzled as to why young *Badh* has decided to break with tradition. If he only seeks to express his sympathy and concern, he would have done it as custom requires."

I understand what my mother-in-law means by "custom requires". Since this whole nightmare began a week ago, I have been bombarded with raven grams, small tokens, and carefully-worded expressions of hope and good wishes. I haven't been able to make myself open a single one of them, instead leaving my mother-in-law to go through them and respond in my place. "I suppose the only way of finding out is to go downstairs," I comment.

"Aye. You are correct, though once we have carefully traversed the stairs, I expect you to select the divan as your spot and to be sure you put your feet up. Your ankles are already as thick as tree trunks."

Yes, indeed. Lady *Nuada* always knows just the right thing to set your teeth on edge. "Thanks for the boost of confidence, Lady *Mathair*," I reply, throwing caution to the wind and addressing her as such. I can't turn around on the stairs, afraid I'll lose my balance, so I just have to imagine the sour look on her face.

The young Lord *Badh* is not what I expect. Frankly, he looks as if he's still of high school age. The earlier years of high school at that…like a freshman or a sophomore. He's tall and lithe like all Fae males, and once he gains a few years and grows into his ears, he will undoubtedly sport the handsome features of his ancient *Tuatha de Danann* heritage. Currently however, he has a scattering of acne across his forehead and a whisper of facial hair above his lip which reminds me of a ginger-colored baby caterpillar. His long auburn hair is haphazardly braided down his back in the typical Otherworld fashion. Upon seeing us, he executes an awkward bow, obviously uncomfortable in his newly acquired, taller frame. "Greetings, Lady *Nuada*…and to you Lady Rosalinda. I bring good wishes from House *Badh*."

I detect a flinch from my mother-in-law when the kid uses my first name instead of my proper title as Declan's mate. I'm not sure if this is just a faux pas of protocol on his part, possibly brought on by nervousness, or if he actually meant any type of slight in ignoring the *Mac Nuada* part. Still, it definitely annoys the Dragon Mama's sensibilities. Her voice has a decidedly sharp edge when she addresses the boy. "Greetings to you as well young Lord," Lady *Siobhan* replies, strongly stressing the word young. "What brings you to Lady *Mac Nuada's* home at such an…inappropriate time."

The kid's slightly pointed ears turn a deep shade of pink over the obvious reprimand, but he doesn't back down. "I come on an important mission, your Ladyship, one I was led to believe would be a welcome one."

"Allow my daughter-in-law to get properly settled, Lord *Badh* and then we will hear your missive. As you can see, my son's *Mo Shiorghra* is heavy with child and common social formalities are a burden at this time."

"Of course," the young man stammers, his adolescent eyes firmly planted on my over-full cleavage. I doubt he even notices that I have a face.

Declan's *mathair* is not wrong. Getting up and down off this sofa won't be easy, and I plan in advance to have Tobias come and help pull me up when our visitor leaves. As of yet, I still don't have any idea what Lady *Nuada's* "game" is here. I'm sure she's more than aware that House *Badh* has family ties to The Throne, and even though its representative is just a mere teenager, he's owed a level of respect simply because of his family connections.

Once I'm settled on the sofa with my feet up (my disgusting tree trunk ankles covered by the hem of my gown), and Freza has poured all three of us some tea, my Lady *Mathair* continues her interrogation. "Now, my young Lord, tell us why you have come here to the

Mundane world with what I assume is your wise sire's permission. I am aware that his Lordship does not much care for spending time with humans. I cannot imagine what would need to be said in person during such a difficult time as this?"

"There are some matters that must be handled face to face, Lady *Nuada*…or so I've been told." The kid fidgets in his seat, and I can sense he's very nervous by the rattle of the cup on his saucer. "You see…I've come to offer for Lady Rosalinda," he states, his voice cracking.

Lady *Siobhan's* tea cup hangs on her lip in disbelief as she looks at the Fae boy as if he had two heads sprouting from his shoulders. I think I understand what the kid is implying, but the idea is so far-out crazy, I figure I must be mistaken.

"Lord *Badh,* are you suggesting that Lady Rosalinda consider…handfasting you?" Dragon Mama asks.

"Aye, your Ladyship. As you are aware, I am not my House's heir. That honor belongs to my older brother, Cillian."

I know the kid's brother. He and my Tax Man are not friends, and it was Cillian's man who lost to Duncan in a challenge orchestrated by Lord *Mac Badh* himself. I smell a rat here, and I must be leaking some thoughts because I get the stink eye from my Lady *Mathair*. As a result, I gather focus and shield my thoughts as best I can. "I am aware of your status, Lord *Badh.* Connor is your first name, is it not?" Dragon Mama asks.

"Yes, your Ladyship. After my mother's father."

"Well then, young Connor, I am still at a loss to understand why you are here. Lady *Mac Badh* is lawfully fasted to my son, and expecting his heir any day now. Why in the goddess's name would you come to offer for her?"

"As I said before, Lady *Nuada,* I am not my House's heir, and therefore not held to the mandates of The Ritual. I can select my mate at will. Though I do not wish to be the bearer of sad tales, 'tis no secret throughout all of *I Idir* that Lord *Mac Nuada* has been sacrificed in service to The Crown. If he should not return home, as many believe, then I should like my offer to be considered first before any other."

I get that the Fae are big on protocol and all that shit, but the modern adult woman in me can keep still no longer. "*Cac* (Shit)…are you saying that you're here to ask me to become your wife? Are you out of your frickin' mind? First of all, my husband isn't dead, so stop talking like he is. Secondly…how the hell old are you anyway?"

His tone becomes defensive. "I will be sixteen this coming Beltane, Lady Rosalinda. I am no child. I have lain with several females."

"Well goody for you, Connor! I'm sure that was very exciting for all parties involved, but do you have any idea how old I am? Hell…I'm twice your age! In truth, I could be your *mathair.* Even if I were single…which I'm absolutely not…you're much too young for me. What you're suggesting is…well…unseemly."

Like any typical Fae male, the kid gets his testosterone up. "I am aware that you are much older than me…as well as only a tooth fairy, good Lady…but as you've already proved to be fertile, my House and I are willing to overlook your advanced years and your weak bloodline in the hopes that you and I together will bear offspring. House

Badh has wealth and power, and a direct connection to The Throne. What we lack, however, is an abundance of progeny. I see this as a win-win situation for us both. Surely you cannot disagree? I have been assured that my House can offer you a very competitive handfast contract."

Now it's my hands that are shaking, and not because I'm nervous. I'm so angry…so insulted and hurt…that I want to grab the kid by the collar and toss his skinny ass right out my front door. I suppose it's a very good thing that Dragon Mama reads the room right and puts the proverbial magical whammy on me, preventing actions that might have eventually proved disastrous. Had I gone ahead with my plan, we might have never known who was truly behind this absolutely ridiculous and mean-spirited notion.

I find myself glued to my chair, unable to move, and hear my husband's mother in my head. *"Keep silent, girl, and let me handle this, lest you make things worse."*

Lady *Nuada* begins to laugh, as if the whole conversation has been some hilarious prank. "You are most amusing, Lord Connor. 'Tis fine mischief you bring to our anxious minds. We are grateful for your jolly respite."

The young Fae flushed with embarrassment. "I'm afraid I do not understand, Lady *Nuada*. 'Tis no joke. I meant every word I said. I was led to believe that both you…and especially Lady Rosalinda…would welcome my offer," the boy stammered.

"And just who led you to make this…unusual offer, young Lord?" Dragon Mama asks.

"'Twas your own Lord, good Lady. Lord *Nuada*

insisted that Lady Rosalinda would welcome the opportunity to marry within the same station, since her own mate has tragically left this life. He said House *Nuada* would consider my offer a 'blessing that wouldn't be forgotten.'"

Lady *Siobhan* pulled a lace handkerchief from her sleeve, and dabbed at her dry eyes. "Oh, dear goddesses… my Lord Husband has taken up drinking again! He has been so heavily burdened by the thought of our son being captured that he has resorted to full drunkenness. I beg you to excuse his weakness, good Connor. It is not easy to worry over one's child, especially his only son."

The boy looked at her oddly. "Lord *Nuada* did not seem overtaken by drink, good Lady. He spoke as if he were perfectly sober."

"Yes… 'tis a sure sign of someone so deep in the bottle that he himself no longer knows fact from fancy. I apologize for my husband's escape into drink, Lord *Badh,* and any nonsense he might have imparted to you. I hope you will keep his little indiscretion to yourself as a great favor to me. I can be a most grateful ally, young Lord," my mother-in-law says, with a raised eyebrow.

The kid was astute enough to know a favor from someone like Lady *Nuada* was a worthy token. He shook his head in agreement and stood to take his leave. "I am sorry to hear of his Lordship's attachment to drink, Lady *Nuada,* and deeply apologize for the…misunderstanding regarding today's visit. I will ask the Universe to deliver Lord *Mac Nuada* safely home to you."

"Thank you, kind Lord. Give my best to your lovely *mathair,* won't you?"

"I surely will, good Lady. The best to you both," he said with a bow.

My mother-in-law walks him to the foyer where the kid ups and disappears from our view. "*Mallacht ar an sean-sionnach sin* (Curses on that old fox)!" Lady *Siobhan* swore.

Now free to speak, I ask, "That was well played, Lady *Nuada*. Do you think the kid will keep quiet?"

Dragon Mama laughed under her breath. "He certainly will not. There's nothing the Ruling Council likes more than a juicy piece of gossip. By evening tide, everyone in *I Idir* will believe my husband has a serious drinking problem. In fact...I'm counting on it. Serves him right...the dirty bastard."

BABY 65

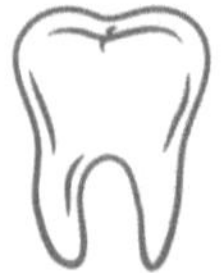

WATER WORKS

THE HOURS TURN into days and the days turn into weeks. Each morning that I wake alone becomes a battle not to fall deeper and darker into hopeless desperation. I don't sleep at night, too physically uncomfortable to relax and too afraid of the dreams that haunt my mind when I close my eyes. The rope nightmare now shares space with a recurring dream of an intimately erotic nature, the Tax Man and I naked and sweaty, locked in the throes of passion while a large dark bird squawks at us from a nearby perch. It doesn't matter that one dream is less a nightmare than the other. In their own way, both make me weep.

If it weren't for Lady *Siobhan's* constant poking, pushing and prodding, I have no doubt I'd readily forgo hot showers, clean clothes, regular meals and conversation of any kind. I can physically tell that the baby has dropped lower in anticipation of his impending birth, and the Braxton-Hicks contractions that roll across my belly signals Peanut's impatience to join us on the outside. I whisper to him over and over again, "Hold tight, little guy. Stay put," begging our son to hang on a little longer to give his daddy a chance to come home. His answer comes in the form of a barrage of kicks to my bladder, which, unfortunately, I can't determine to be either a yes or a no.

Oddly enough, since Lord *Nuada's* attempt to marry me off to some half-pint, pimply kid (which Lady *Nuada* explained would give his Lordship a loophole to avoid paying out on the handfasting contract I negotiated), we have become allies. The old saying, "my enemy's enemy is my friend," couldn't be any truer in this case. I find it extremely ironic that I once thought my husband's *athair* was the lesser of Declan's evil parents. It's become increasingly clear over the course of the past month that his Lordship is a certified creep.

That's not to say that, overnight, my husband's *mathair* has become a living version of the mother goddess, *Danu.* She's still the same sarcastic, prickly and stubbornly opinionated pain in my ass she's always been. However, there's been small glimmers of concern and thoughtfulness towards me, moments where I can actually sense her excitement over the idea of being a *seanmhathair* (grandmother). One afternoon, a few days back, I accidentally caught her weeping over a photo of Declan on our Mundane wedding day. She viciously scolded me for sneaking up on her, and made me swear I would never tell a single soul that I caught her being less dignified than her title required. I agreed, but it made me realize that despite her hard exterior, Lady *Nuada* was still the mother of a missing child.

Not a single day of the past month has been easy on either of us, but today I seem to be having an especially rough time of it. Everything bothers me. I'm overly warm despite the thermostat registering the house's normal temperature of 72 degrees. My stomach is queasy and I have zero appetite even when Tobias tempts me with all my known favorites. Plus, no matter how I sit, stand or lie, I can't escape the grinding pain in my back.

I'm not stupid. I've had enough medical training to realize that I am most likely in the early stages of labor, but I desperately will my body and our little Peanut to slow the hell down. I don't want to have this baby without Declan beside me. I take deep cleansing breaths and use all my Druid-inspired lessons to manifest my desires to the Universe. "Not yet, not yet, not yet" becomes my daily mantra.

It's probably why when my husband's mother insists that I need to join her in the nursery, I become a Dragon Mama myself, swearing a blue streak of every Gaelic obscenity I know at being bothered. When I'm finally red-faced and sweating from the exertion of my tirade, Lady *Siobhan* tersely replies, "If you're done fecking everyone and everything, I need you to come to the nursery. Walking is good for you. It will take some of the pressure off your back."

I grumble my way down the hall, expecting that she'll yet again show me something cute or amusing she's added to the mural. I've already caught on that this is her sneaky way of making me get out of bed and move a little. Yesterday, she surprised me by adding a big, fat pig on his way to market, with a face that bears a great resemblance to that of her husband. I will admit...that one made me laugh. Today, however, all bets are off. Nothing will help my morose mood.

But it's not the mural she wants to show me. Next to the crib, aka "the dog kennel," that magically appeared back in the nursery, is an absolutely gorgeous baby cradle, covered in rows and rows of hand-wrought lace, and accented with a canopy decorated with Celtic embroidery. Upon seeing it, I begin to cry, because...well...that's all I do anymore is cry. "It's beautiful," I hiccup in between sobs. "Did it come from *I Idir*?"

"Aye," Lady *Nuada* answers. I hear the catch in her voice. "I had it freshened up and sent from *Dun Siorai*. 'Twas Declan's infant cradle. I am guessing it will have a new occupant very soon."

No sooner do the words leave her mouth when a lightning bolt of painful tension rounds its way from across my lower back to the pit of my belly, while something warm and wet runs down my legs and puddles at my feet.

BABY 66

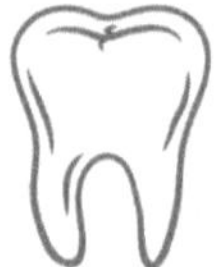

TIMING IS EVERYTHING

I SUPPOSE I should have had a plan for this moment. A week before he'd left for North Korea, Declan had partially joked about making a spreadsheet with all the things we needed to do when I went into labor. I say partially because if you know the Tax Man well enough, you know he makes lists and spreadsheets for EVERY-THING, and I personally think he was dead serious. In hindsight, I wish I would have gone ahead and encouraged him to make that list because as it stood now, not only did I not have a comprehensive go-to-guide, I didn't have my husband either. I'd spent all my time leading up to this moment willing him home in time for the birth of his son, and no time creating a Plan B in case the Universe had other plans.

In complete contrast to my own apprehension and confusion, my mother-in-law is all business and efficiency. She has Freza pack my small overnight bag, instructing her on what should go in it, while she contacts Dr. Brannigan. (And no…she doesn't use a cell phone. She reaches out to him the Fae way…telepathically. Truth be told, I've never witnessed that woman ever touching any piece of modern technology.) I can't drive in this condition, and Lady *Siobhan* has never learned how, so she leaves it to me to arrange our transportation to the hospital. I call Claire first, and when that call goes to voicemail, I leave a message and try Mel instead, knowing full well she's at the office. My best friend hears only the first seven words, "Hey Mel…I think I'm in labor," before telling me she's on her way and hanging up.

As it goes, both my sister and Mel arrive at the same time. After some discussion, it's decided we'll take Claire's larger SUV, but that both ladies will accompany Dragon Mama and I to the hospital. I sense my mother-in-law tense when my sister arrives. I understand her emotions, but I can't change the past any more than I can change the fact that Claire physically favors our deceased mother and therefore is a walking reminder of Lord *Nuada's* long past betrayal. From my vantage point, Declan's father is the villain at the heart of this whole mess.

We all pile into Claire's SUV, my sister driving with Mel in the front seat, and me and Dragon Mama in the back. The idea that I have this cabal of female sisterhood surrounding me at this central point of my womanhood makes me smile, and I offhandedly make a joke about them all dancing naked in a circle around me while I give birth. Under a full moon, of course. This earns me a look from my mother-in-law that would peel paint, and silence from the rest of the cabal. Jeesh. Tough audience.

The hospital is just a short drive away, thus quickly ending my short career as a car comedian. My mild contractions appear every 20 minutes, and I can still easily breathe my way through them. Claire drops us off at the main entrance and goes to park the car while Mel scouts out a wheelchair. We are met in the lobby by Nurse Amy from Doctor B's office, who helps expedite my admission, and gets me settled into my birthing room on the maternity floor. Amy is one of Dr. Brannigan's two *Sidhe* staff members, and apparently used to dealing with Fae pregnancies and hoity-toity Otherworld types. She does a fine job of handling Lady *Nuada* with the correct amount of respect without handing over her nurse's control of the situation. I understand why she was exclusively chosen for this particular delivery. She exudes a unique sense of cool, calm confidence in the face of Dragon Mama's demanding personality.

The expanded maternity floor of the hospital was recently updated and remodeled perhaps a year or so ago, thanks largely to a huge donation from the Beckett Foundation in anticipation of the birth of Sheriff and Mrs. Theodore Beckett's daughter, Mairead. (Have I mentioned before that the Black Knight is incredibly wealthy? Of course he is! Just another feather in the cap of The Morrigan's right hand man!) I am grateful that all of the birthing rooms are spacious and cheerfully decorated, but are also supplied with all the medical emergency necessities, discreetly camouflaged for if and when they are needed. To the left of the bed, I note a small wardrobe marked Mommy meant to hold my things next to a matching one labeled Daddy. Knowing that the Daddy closet, as well the set of clean scrubs inside, will most likely remain unused hurts me a hundred times more than any physical discomfort I'm currently experiencing.

I'm not settled in very long when Dr. Brannigan makes his appearance and confirms that, yes, my water has broken, I'm in the early stage of active labor, and with my dilation at nearly 5 cm, I have a bit of a wait ahead of me. Knowing I have a medical background, he doesn't waste time on hand-holding pleasantries and drawn-out explanations. After a few words with me, and then with Lady *Nuada*, Dr. B advises me to relax as much as I can, walk around if I'm able, and to let Nurse Amy know if I need anything. He promises to check back in on me shortly

Because my labor is progressing normally and I feel physically okay, Mel and Claire are allowed to stay and visit. For a few hours, they act as a welcome distraction, keeping the conversation light and breezy and the energy in the room upbeat. But as the time between my contractions grows shorter, and I have to work harder and harder at breathing through the pain, I'm finding any interaction with anyone in the room too difficult to bear, and when they speak to me, I mostly don't answer. As Peanut gets closer to being born, I feel the full absence of my *Mo Shiorghra*, and it's hard to concentrate on little else. The very last thing I need is more uninvited guests vying for my limited attention. Which, of course, is exactly what I get.

BABY 67

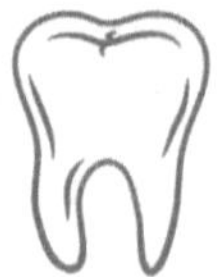

FAMOUS LAST WORDS

CHEWING my way through yet another tasteless ice chip (it being the only thing my fussy stomach can handle at this moment), I hear a light rap on the birthing room door as uninvited guest number #1 steps into my room. If I had not already been thoroughly queasy, the appearance of the infamous, much-cursed, Marcy Kilcrabtree would have undoubtedly brought on a massive case of indigestion. Before I can formulate a response, I feel a cutting pain building across my left side, and I know I'm due for another contraction. All the earlier vows I made to myself...the multiple promises swearing to handle this experience without the support of my husband with the calm rationalization of a mature, professional woman evaporate like wet sidewalk on a hot summer's day. That's how much I detest the woman I personally blame for my husband's disappearance. My grief and rage push aside any attempt at feigned fortitude. "What the 'feck are you doing here, Lieutenant? I can one hundred percent guarantee that no one in this…"

I don't finish the sentence as I pant and puff my way through the waves of pain. Being the thoughtless person she is, Kilcrabtree takes this pause in the conversation as an opportunity to step further into the birthing room. Despite my own physical discomfort, I sense Dragon Mama's flare of anger. Over these past few weeks, I've come to realize that *Siobhan* Donnely Fitzatrick is a certified player in the magical skills department. It's no longer a surprise to me why so many of the *Sidhe* are wary of her. Lady *Nuada* hands me a cool cloth to wipe my sweaty face, but her green cat eyes are narrowed and firmly settled on the room's intruder.

I finish dabbing my perspiration before continuing the conversation. "As I was saying…I'm sure no one in their right mind invited you to this party, so why don't you just turn around and go out the same door you slithered in. I have nothing to say to you."

Any normal person would have already read the hostility in the room and scuttled out of the line of fire. Unfortunately, Marcy isn't like most people. She has an enormous measure of self-importance that makes her determined in all the wrong kinds of ways. "There's no need to get all huffy, Rosalinda. We're all adults here," she said.

"Mind your manners, tooth fairy," my mother-in-law growls. "You are treading on my last nerve. My son's mate deserves the same respect afforded to every member of *I Idir's* Ruling Council."

At least the bitch had the courtesy to go a shade paler

over a scolding by someone of Fae nobility. "My apologies, Lady *Nuada*. I sometimes forget that one of our tooth fairy kind has elevated her position so greatly through a marital joining. It's not something that happens often, you understand," Marcy says. "Anyway…I was here at the hospital to partake in a physical therapy session for my recent injuries when I noted members of The Morrigan's security detail in the elevator. Curiosity got the best of me and upon further investigation…a skill I'm very good at… I learned that 'Lady' Rosalinda was here to deliver her baby, so I thought I should stop by and…well…wish her the best," said the young Fae, over-stressing the word lady for spite.

If I hadn't been so put-off by the conniving snake-in-the-grass standing in front of me, I might have given more thought as to why the Queen would have security detail here at the hospital. As it was, Marcy Kilcrabtree had all my attention, though it was Dragon Mama who took over the conversation. "And now that you have completed your goal, tooth fairy, it's time for you to leave, lest I decide I must help you along."

Marcy's response was to drop a curtsy that reeked of sarcasm. She stood, her chin high in the air as she turned to leave, but not before adding, "Despite what you all believe, I am not to blame for what has happened to Lord *Mac Nuada*. Truthfully, had you been more on your 'Supervisor' game that night, 'Lady' Rosalinda, you would have asked more questions when I returned from my assignment without the tooth and little to no explanation. It was surely an anomaly our Black Knight would have expected you to have investigated…given your recent honor and promotion. But no…you ignored the whole matter. I often wonder if you had taken the time and fortitude to dig a little deeper, would I perhaps not have felt the need to take matters into my own hands. At the time, I assumed you were in too much of a hurry to race home to your lover boy to give any thought to the future of *I Idir*, and thus it is you who are at the core of all the fuss that followed."

The next contraction begins to build again like the scales on a keyboard, rising from the low notes of back pains to a crescendo finish tearing across my middle section. I anticipate that I'm going to lose the ability to get all my words out before I need to start my panting again. "How dare you! You sneaky, lying *soith* (bitch)! You're actually going to stand there…and blame my husband's capture on me? It was you…your own selfish need…" I say in a breathy voice, "to be the feckin' center of attention… the hero. That's what…sent you to North Korea." The rest of the words slip away as I grit my teeth with cramping sensations that render me silent.

The wretched girl simply shrugs. "Believe what you wish, Lady *Mac*. We both know the real truth. And so does Her Majesty."

At this point, I've totally lost any focus and the labor pain takes complete control. I roll to my left side, setting off the fetal monitors while I stammer out the words between clenched teeth. "Get the hell out of here, Kilcrabtree…before I crawl out of this bed and choke you with my bare hands."

I don't receive a response because, right before my eyes, Tooth Fairy Lt. First Class Marcella Alexandra Kilcrabtree simply disappears.

BABY 68

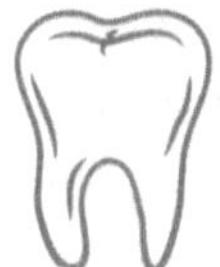

UNDER THE BIG TOP

"WHERE'D SHE GO?" I ask, forever caught off guard with these Fae types popping-in-and-out with no warning.

Lady *Siobhan* gives me a wry smile. "I believe that hideous woman is somewhere on the border between *I Idir* and *Asgard.* And seeing that it is early morning in the Otherworld, the sun already high in the sky, one would guess that as a tooth fairy with no daytime magical ability, she has a long walk ahead of her. Unless, of course, she comes across another traveler…though those roads tend to be deserted this time of the year…the weather being so…unpleasant."

"Can I just say that you rock, Lady *Nuada*?" says my sister, Claire, who has no understanding of proper Otherworld protocol. "Serves her right, the nasty bitch."

"Well done, your Ladyship," adds Mel.

When I finish panting through an especially difficult contraction, I'm able to comment too. "Thank you. I appreciate you getting rid of her, but won't you take some heat for doing that? I know *I Idir* has laws about moving people against their will."

The Lady shrugged. "I suppose I will get a terse scolding by the Black Knight himself, followed by a substantial fine. 'Tis of no concern to me. T'was worth every penny of what it will cost. That low-bred liar is most lucky I used common sense and restraint. I desired to do worse, but thought better of it. As she has no magical power until sunset in the Otherworld, it is a safe bet we will not be bothered by her before your son enters the world."

Our conversation is interrupted by the appearance of Dr. Brannigan, who does a quick exam and pronounces me 8 cm dilated. "It won't be too much longer now, Dr. Parker," he politely tells me. Doc Robyn is old school and uses my formal medical title even when he has his whole damn hand up my lady parts. I would laugh over the irony of that if I wasn't so damn uncomfortable. "How are we holding up?" Dr. B asks, "Have you been able to manage the pain?"

I don't get to answer him because there is a slight popping sound and suddenly another person is in the room. The doctor quickly covers me up for modesty's sake and takes charge of the conversation, his annoyance seeping through his polite phrasing. "Good evening to you, your Lordship. This is a surprise to see you here. Though I can understand your excitement and concern over the birth of your grandson, as Lady Rosalinda's physician I must respectfully ask that you await the good news in the lounge. This is not a place for...

gentlemen, the child's father and medical staff being the exception."

My father-in-law answers him just as tersely. "As the child's father is obviously not in attendance, I claim the right to stand in his place."

Most Otherworldly residents would have backed down from Lord *Nuada's* status. The man is head of one of the most powerful ruling houses in all of the kingdom. However, despite spending most of his life in *I Idir*, Robyn Arthur Brannigan, Lord *Spideog*, is actually a Prince of *Avalon*, the great grandson of The Lady of the Lake, and himself a member of an Otherworldly royal family. Thus, the usually unassuming physician isn't required to take orders from a Lord of *I Idir's* Ruling Council. Still, ever the gentleman, Doctor B tries to get his point across to my father-in-law without being disrespectful. He can obviously feel my absolute panic over having Declan's *athair* in attendance. "I'm afraid I won't be able to accommodate your wishes, Lord *Nuada*. As it is, I have direct orders to leave that position open in anticipation of the *bairn's* father arriving in time for the delivery of his son."

"*Caic tarbh* (bullshit)!" his Lordship mutters. "Who would give such a ridiculous order?"

And just like that, The Morrigan is also standing in my birthing room, toe to toe with my father-in-law. Apparently, I'm not the only one in the room registering shock at seeing the Queen. Several jaws in the room drop, including poor Nurse Amy, whose hands are literally shaking.

Her Majesty is dressed in all-black tactical gear similar to what I saw on Declan and Duncan during the Chechen raid. She, however, is not wearing any head covering. Instead, she has her long auburn hair tightly braided and wound on the top of her head. Her face is marked with magical sigils created in red paint. (At least I hope it's red paint and not blood of some kind. Yikes!) Today, this woman standing before us all is not just the respected ruler of *I Idir.* Her aura shimmers with crackling magical energy, every bit the true goddess of war and destruction she's always been. The goddess smiles at my father-in-law but her expression is not friendly. "I would be the person issuing that ridiculous order, Lord *Nuada.* I assume you disapprove?"

His Lordship shrinks several inches until he is now eye to eye with the shorter Queen. I can't be sure if it's her magic that's lessened his height, or if Declan's father is trying to somehow diffuse the situation by appearing less threatening. Either way, it's mind-blowingly weird, and when another contraction grabs my focus, I work to keep one eye on what's happening on that side of the room while moving through the pain. "Truth say, I approve of whatever Your Highness thinks is necessary," Lord *Nuada* wisely answers. "You are well aware that my House and I have always been loyal to *I Idir's* Throne."

The Morrigan doesn't respond to his statement. Instead, she asks another question. "What brings you to the solemn sanctity of a woman's birthing room, Lord *Nuada?* 'Tis surely no place for a man who is neither the mother's mate or her doctor."

"I was full of worry over my only son's mate and child, Your Majesty. Since my *Mac Nuada* is not here...due, of course, to his service to The Throne, I felt it was my place to be here at their side in his stead," he explains with a perfectly straight face.

"As you are aware, *Nuada,* your own Lady was assigned that role by me several weeks ago, and here she sits…as I ordered. I find it oddly…unseemly for you to be part of the Universe's most intimate and sacred acts of womanhood. You may wait in the lounge as Robyn has asked, or return to *Dun Siorai* until there is news to tell you."

There was no doubt whatsoever that Lord *Nuada* is both embarrassed and angry at being called out so publicly. His face turns a deep shade of red, and the vein in his forehead is throbbing with the intensity of his rage. Still, he has enough control to manage the traditional bow required by protocol before disappearing without another word.

"I will talk to Lady Rosalinda alone now," The Morrigan says to the five people left in this bizarre circus of a birthing room. According to my calculations, I have about three minutes left until the next contraction. I sincerely hope Her Royal Ringmaster will get straight to the point.

BABY 69

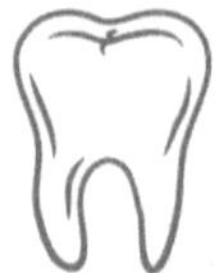

ROLLING OUT THE WELCOME MAT

DOCTOR BRANNIGAN USHERS everyone out of the birthing room, leaving me alone with the Celtic goddess of war and destruction. The Morrigan takes a seat on the right side of my hospital bed and takes my hand in hers. A feeling of cool well-being travels up my arm and throughout the rest of my aching body. "Thank you, Your Majesty. Whatever you just did for me, it's a welcome relief," I admit gratefully.

"You are welcome, little tooth fairy, though 'tis only temporary. The Universe will demand its due for the monumental gift of new life. Right now, however, I need your thoughts to be entirely focused on what I am telling you so there is no chance of a...misunderstanding. 'Tis impossible to concentrate on important matters when your body desires to have its own way. What I need to tell you is grim."

All I can do is nod my understanding, my heart racing

and my stomach rolling over the possibilities of what the goddess has to say to me. She waves a hand over our heads and the air surrounding the bed seems to pull inward, as if the two of us are now sitting in a closed vacuum. "Despite our best efforts, Lady *Mac Nuada*, we have been unable to locate your *Mo Shiorghra*. The terrorists holding him are using a combination of dark magic along with the physical properties of *prais* (alloy of copper and zinc-brass) to conceal his life source. We know the general location but not the specific site. What I can read of him shows a soul nearing its breaking point. If we do not extract him soon, I am afraid this world will lose him for good. That is why I need your help, little tooth fairy. I believe you are our last chance to rescue Lord *Mac Nuada*."

Despite my absolute desire not to look weak in front of Her Royal Highness, the news overwhelms me. My entire body is shaking, and silent tears run down my face. "How can I help, Your Majesty? Please! I'll do anything you need me to do! I can't lose him now. We haven't had nearly enough time together. My son needs his father! I need my mate! Whatever you need I can do it!"

"I believe you can, little *mathair*. It was your sense of hope that has kept him alive this long. Now, perhaps you can find him as well," the goddess says.

"How? Please tell me!"

"I have been told that you experienced a prophecy regarding this event several months ago. That in a dream you saw the location of your husband's imprisonment. Is this true?" The Morrigan asks.

My heart drops. If this was my husband's only

chance…then all is lost. "The mages all determined that what I dreamt couldn't possibly be a true prophecy. Not for someone of my very weak magical energy. They believed it was just my anxious mind in combination with the *Fiodor Aisling* I was taking for my morning sickness. Even the Merlin agreed it was doubtful I had a true vision of the future." I try hard not to dissolve in a complete mess of tears and hopelessness.

"Magic is not an exact science, sweet girl. I have been alive long enough to understand that. The Universe has a strange and fickle sense of irony. I have learned never to discount any of the possibilities."

"But even if what I did experience that evening was a true vision of things to come, I barely remember much about it. It's just a hazy memory, and a troubling one at that. I'm not sure I could even offer you any useful information that would help locate Declan," I counter.

"Our brains are built to store information, little tooth fairy. The details of that dream are there somewhere in your mind. They just have to be located," the goddess says as she taps my forehead.

"How do we do that," I ask, "with such limited time?"

"If you are willing to allow me access to your thoughts, Lady *Mac Nuada*, I believe I can find the information we need. But it must be your decision to allow me inside your head. I will not break the laws I myself set up for the good of my people."

What The Morrigan is offering me is hope…a chance that maybe I can have the love of my life back with me and our son. Truthfully, I would have cut off my hands and feet, or plucked out an eye or two if that's what she had said she needed to save my Tax Man. Allowing her access to my head seems easy in comparison. "Absolutely, yes! You have my permission! Dig around all you like… but please…please find my husband!"

The goddess smiles. "I knew you had heart and spirit the moment I saw you, little tooth fairy. The Universe has been beyond wise in matching you and the young Lord. Still, I need to warn you that once I have gained access to your thoughts, there is no telling how long that freedom will continue on my part. There is a definite chance you will be unable to hold any thoughts private from me for days, months or even years to come. There is no way to know in advance how long this magic will linger within your mind. I want you to be fully aware of the possible consequences."

What the goddess was admitting was downright scary. Giving someone access to all your personal and private thoughts was more than a bit overwhelming. But all I could think of was the fact that my Tax Man was slipping away from me and our family forever. There was no way I was going to allow that to happen. Not if there was even the smallest chance that I could do something to help my One and Only. "I understand," I say with genuine conviction. "I want you to go ahead and find the information that will save my husband. Immediately."

She nods her agreement. "Very well. We will do just that. You may feel an odd, probing sensation, but no real pain from my intrusion. I want you to close your eyes and relax the best you can while still focusing on the words you hear me say."

I nod back and close my eyes. I feel The Morrigan

place her hands on the temples of my head and then press her forehead to mine. Initially, a pleasant sense of euphoria fills my head while I try to do as she asks by focusing on the strange and unusual words she repeats over and over again. They don't sound anything like the old Gaelic I've been studying, and I'm pretty sure I've never heard them spoken aloud before. The euphoric feeling gives way to a sense of movement that reminds me of lifting and tugging. I'm not feeling any type of pain, not from The Morrigan's occupation of my mind nor from my labor. I can best describe it as a feeling of complete stasis. Then suddenly, I'm snapped right back into reality, which actually does hurt. My body feels like it did before the goddess laid her hands on me, achy and tired, and I'm left with a growing contraction and a slight headache.

"I found what I need, little mother! I know where they're keeping *Mac Nuada!* It was right there in your prophecy all the time!" She stands to leave. "You did very well, *Ros Beag* (Little Rose). Your strength of will is impressive for one of such limited magical skill. I will find your *Mo Shiorghra* and bring him back here to you. You have my word on it. Hold onto your son as long as you can, though the little Lord mightily fights for his freedom. Blessed be, sweet girl." And then she was gone.

BABY 70

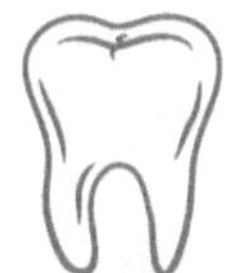

A PROMISE KEPT

ONCE THE QUEEN has left my room, my sisterhood circle makes their way back inside, minus Dr. B who has moved on to check another patient. Lady *Siobhan* is the first to enter, and taking one look at me, says, "What have you gone and done you, stupid, silly girl?"

"I don't know what you mean," I answer sheepishly, though that's a lie. I know exactly what she means.

"You are covered in powerful magical residue...the kind that only the most elite of the Otherworld possess. What in the Universe have you gone and let her do to you, girl?" Dragon Mama asks. I might be over reading the situation, but Declan's *mathair* actually seems concerned about me.

"Her Highness explained to me that Declan is in a very bad way. If they don't find him soon, she's not sure if..." I let the words trail off, unwilling to form them. According to my beliefs, saying those words out loud could make them true. "She said I was his only chance."

"And what was it she required of you?" my mother-in-law probes.

I pause and take a few deep breaths because I know no one in the room is going to like what I say. Plus, whatever spell the goddess placed on my physical self is obviously wearing off and I'm starting to feel like shit again. "The Morrigan believes that the horrible nightmare I had at the Ball last fall was an actual prophecy despite the mages all saying it wasn't. I couldn't remember the details clearly... so I let Her Highness enter my mind to find them herself."

As predicted, no one in the room likes my decision. They all start yapping at once at me about what a huge mistake it was on my part and how I have no idea what I'd let myself in for. Even Nurse Amy, who so far had been nothing but positive and supportive, is shaking her head at me.

I feel that familiar wave of gut-splitting pain wind up for the pitch so I hold up a finger for them to stop their scolding while I pant and puff my way through another contraction. Both Amy and Lady *Siobhan* rub my lower back, while Claire and Mel hold my hands until they turn white from squeezing them so hard. When the pain subsides, I flop back onto the pillows behind me. "Look," I argue, "we were out of options. I would have ripped my heart out of my chest and given it to her if it meant getting my husband home. It wasn't nearly as bad as you're all making it out to be. Plus, she gave me her word that she'd bring Declan home in time to witness Peanut's birth. I believe her."

"Peanut?" Dragon Mama says in horror. "Tell me that is not the name you have chosen for my first grandchild!"

I'm almost tempted to tell her that Peanut will be his actual name just to see her get all up in a huff, but keeping a straight face requires more energy than I have. "No. That's just what Declan named him the first time we saw him on the sonogram…because he was no more than the size of a small nut." It dawns on me that we never did firmly settle on a proper name before he left for North Korea. "We haven't decided on a name yet. That's why I need him here. I'm not naming his son without Lord *Mac's* input, so whatever happens because of The Morrigan's magic…so be it! And…I'd do it all over again in a heartbeat if I had to, so let's knock it off with the lectures, because you're not helping."

Nurse Amy squares up her shoulders. "Her Ladyship is right. The last thing we desire in this room is negative vibes. We need to focus on helping the baby enter this world in a peaceful, positive field of energy, so no more dwelling on the 'what ifs' and 'should haves.' Affirmative thoughts only, ladies."

My contractions are now less than two minutes apart and growing in length and intensity. This cycle of pain with short intermissions seems to go on for an eternity, but which the clock on the wall suggests is really just under an hour. I can no longer speak at all, not even in the brief moments of pain-free intermission. I am thoroughly exhausted, and the last bit of determined hope I had of Declan being with me after The Morrigan's visit is slowly ebbing away.

Dr. Brannigan eventually comes in to check my

progress and finds me to be 10 cms dilated and totally effaced. "It should be anytime now, Dr. Parker. You're going to start to feel the need to push. Let me or Nurse Amy know when that happens because things will usually move quickly after that."

I can't help but wail. "You need to slow this down, Doc! Declan isn't here yet. We have to hold off for a bit."

"I'm afraid babies are very bad at 'holding off,' Dr. Parker. "They enter the world when they are ready."

"Feckin' hell…can you please stop calling me by my title? It's weirding me out. Just call me Rosie, okay," I ask the doc in breathy tones, not caring that I just swore at the Prince of Avalon.

Robyn smiles, taking my foul language in stride. "As you wish…Rosie. We're going to start setting up your room for your delivery now. Just keep doing what you're doing. Things are going perfectly normal. I don't see any complications ahead."

"Great," I murmur under my breath. "No complications except for the fact that my husband isn't here with me."

The words barely leave my mouth when The Morrigan pops back into my room. Her once immaculate tactical apparel is covered in blood splatter, and what looks suspiciously like brain matter and internal organ pieces. I try not to focus on that and instead take in her satisfied expression. "I bear good news, little tooth fairy *mathair*. We have located your husband and extracted him as I promised. Your prophecy was key in locating him."

I start to cry, as do several other people in the room. "Where is he? He needs to hurry. Doctor B says it's any…"

I have to stop talking as a contraction takes over my focus.

"Your *Mo Shiorghra* is changing into something more appropriate for a hospital environment and the Black Knight will bring him to you shortly." She pauses, then adds, "I must warn, you sweet girl. Your mate has suffered greatly in his service to The Crown. His physical appearance and general condition will undoubtedly alarm you. Understand that he will eventually heal himself, though it may take more time than he will be happy about. During this period, he will require your patience and understanding while this comes about, and you will find your resolve and loyalty tested as well. Do you understand what I am telling you?"

The Queen's words fill me with anxiety, but I am so relieved over having the Tax Man home, no less in time for Peanut's birth, that I don't fully register the true impact of her words. It would take a great deal of soul-searching measure to fully understand the prophetic nature of the goddess's words on the day of my son's birth.

BABY 71

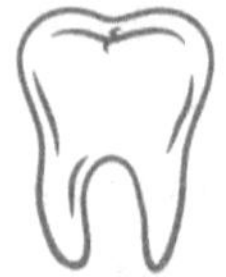

BITTERSWEET

THE CELTIC GODDESS of war and destruction tilts her head and studies me, though I'm not exactly sure what it is she's trying to assess. Then, she steps aside and with a wave of her hand, the Black Knight and Duncan stand behind her holding up my husband between them. At least I think it's my husband. The figure standing between the two men barely resembles my beloved Tax Man. His face is bruised and bloody with one eye completely swollen shut. The long elegant fingers on both hands are mangled and broken, while his glorious head of red hair is shaved to dirty stubble. Borrowed hospital scubs hang on a gaunt frame, with the pants being several inches too short and showcasing deep ligature marks worn into the skin around his ankles.

"Declan?" I say his name but it comes not as a word but a choked sob. I immediately feel The Morrigan's piercing stare on me and hear her words in my head.

"Remember what I advised, Lady Mac Nuada. Look past his current state. 'Tis only a single moment in time. Your Lord needs for you to see him as he was and not how he is now."

I don't trust myself to speak so instead I put out my arms to reach for him. Declan takes a shaky step forward but wobbles, causing Duncan to grab his arm to steady him. My *Mo Shiorghra* shakes him off. "I am most grateful far' yar' concern cousin, but 'tis importan' I greet ma' Lady unaided."

Hearing the familiar voice with its undeniable Otherworldy lilt hits me straight in the heart and I struggle with the tangled linens to get up and go to him. Before I can even swing my legs free, a massive contraction rises up along with a slight breeze to my backside as I remember that my hospital gown is completely open in the back giving everyone in the room a free show. I try breathing through the pain but by now my focus is completely lost. What I'm feeling must be written across my face, because an expression of alarm blooms on the Tax Man's own and he dives to the edge of my bed in one giant step. "Oh ma' par, par, Lassie…'tis breakin' my heart to see ya' sufferin' so. I am so sorry I was not here earlier to halp' ya' through it," he says as he rocks the both of us in a tight embrace.

The irony of this statement coming from someone who, without doubt, has been put through an excruciatingly painful experience makes me start blubbering. Though he makes no sound at all and his face is tucked into my shoulder and hidden from everyone's view, being this close, I can feel the wracking shudders in his chest resulting from his own deep weeping. In the midst of all of this, I can no longer ignore the deep pressure building below along with the need to push. I pull away from Declan's arms. "Uhm...Dr. B?"

The physician pushes his way through the crowd of people surrounding my bed. "I'm guessing it's time... Rosie?" he says, my nickname sticking on his ever-polite tongue.

"Yup. I think our Peanut knows his daddy is here and now he's in an all-fire hurry to make his escape." A thought suddenly pops into my head. "Shit! Declan...we haven't decided on a name yet."

"I've had plenty enough time ta' think on that question, Love. I was hopin' we might name him Dylan *Eamon* (Edward)...after ma' twin brother and yar' father," he replies.

"That's perfect!" I say, squeezing him tight. "Dylan Edward...I love it. Has a lovely sound to it."

Dr. Brannigan interrupts our little name party. "Unfortunately, I think it's time for everyone but Mom and Dad to clear out of this room. You can all wait in the lounge at the end of the corridor. Nurse Amy will let you all know when Baby Dylan is born."

The circus crowd shuffles out of the birthing room. As Lady *Siobhan* stands to leave, Declan calls out, "*Mathair?*" as if noticing her presence for the first time.

"Aye, *Deaglan*. Blessed be, son. I am grateful for your safe return," she says softly.

"Thank you, *Mathair*," says my husband, obviously confused over Dragon Mama's change of character.

An idea comes into my head. "Lady *Mathair*...I would like you to stay for Dylan's birth." I say, looking up at my doctor. "If that's okay with you, Doc."

"If that is what you'd like…Dr. Parker, it's perfectly fine with me. I am sure your Lady *Mathair* is familiar with the next sequence of events," Dr. B answers, reverting to formal protocol with the Queen still in the room.

Still lost about the changing family dynamics, the Tax Man asks me quietly, "Are you sure 'tis what ya' want, Lass?"

I lean over and kiss him, careful not to press too hard on his swollen and split lips. "It's exactly what I want, Sweetie. If it weren't for your *mathair*, I'm not sure I could have made it through these past four weeks. She belongs here with us."

Declan stands and kisses his mother on the cheek. *"Taim an-bhuioch diot ansin go siorai, a a mathair, as aire a thabhairt do mo Mo Shiorghra is mo mhac fad nach raibh me in ann bheith leo. Beannaithe bheith.* (Then I am eternally grateful to you mother, for taking care of my Mo Shiorghra and my son while I was not able to be with them. Blessed be.)"

The Morrigan, who hasn't left with the rest of the group and was certainly not going to be asked by anyone in their right mind to do so, winks at me and speaks again to my mind. *"Well done, little tooth fairy. There can be no peace in the kingdom if there is no peace within its families. I am well pleased with your actions."*

"Thank you, Your Highness…for bringing Declan home and for giving me an opportunity to fix things with my husband's mathair. I believe my son will be forever blessed with a loving grandmother."

"Aye, that he will. Siobhan will be fierce in her love for him."

"Will you stay for his birth, Your Majesty?" I ask.

"'Tis a sweet offer, but one I must refuse. Duty calls in I Idir. In addition, this remarkable moment belongs to the three of you alone. No worries, sweet girl. I will see your new son soon." Without a word of warning, the goddess simply disappears, leaving my beloved Tax Man on my right side, and his Dragon Mama on my left, as I bring Dylan Edward Parker Fitzpatrick *Nuada* into the world.

BABY 72

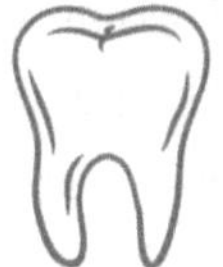

WATCH OUT FOR THOSE FALLING BOULDERS

FIVE DAYS, 120 hours, 7,200 minutes, 432,000 seconds: Five sunrises and five sunsets filled with an abundance of bliss inspiring, bittersweet, emotionally charged and thoroughly exhausting single moments in time. That's exactly how long we had at home together…as a family of three… before the stark reality of Fate was dropped on our doorstep.

Dylan Edward Fitzpatrick was born shortly before 10:00 PM on the same evening of his father's return. At 21 inches long and 7.06 pounds, our son was born with a tuft of ginger colored hair sitting atop of his head along with the high forehead and slightly elongated ears of his Otherworldly heritage. Like most Fae newborns, Dylan came into the world with his eyes wide open and in their natural color, a deep moss green that was a match to his father and paternal grandmother. Thanks to the ways of The Universe and the magical intervention of The Morrigan, my beloved *Mo Shiorghra* was there to hear the first cries and proudly cut the cord of his first- born son and heir.

Since my delivery was normal and without any serious medical issues, Dr. Brannigan was more than happy to let the three of us return home the following evening, with the understanding that I would have access to some extra help, my husband not being one hundred percent his usual robust self. Despite our invitation to stay, Lady *Siobhan* returned home with the excuse that she'd been away from *Dun Siorai* far too long, though I think she was simply not ready to work on mending a life-time of harsh words with her only son. Dragon Mama promised to return in a few days to check on us, while convincing us to allow Freza and Tobias to continue to help out as needed.

Declan was both pleased and surprised at the state of our home, amazed that the bulk of the remodel work had been completely finished, and even more shocked when I explained it was entirely his *mathair's* doing, the Lady herself dealing with the construction workers as effi- ciently as any foreman. My husband just shakes his head over my revelations regarding his mother's apparently changed outlook while muttering something in Gaelic about zebras and their stripes.

Most of these glorious 120 hours are spent cuddled together in bed, Dylan between the two of us, talking about everything that has transpired in the past four weeks. Everything, that is, except for what went on during his weeks of captivity in North Korea. It is the one subject my husband refuses to speak of, going as far as to not allow me to see him completely nude. He showers alone with the door locked, and when he emerges, it is always completely clothed. This is odd behavior from a man who normally feels more comfortable out of his clothes than in them, and the more privacy he demands, the more anxious I become, believing that something terribly horrible has been done to disfigure him. On the third day home, after a barrage of my tears and heartfelt words spoken with the bathroom door between us, he finally allows me to come in and have myself a look-see, but only with the promise that I will not "rain pity on his *granna* (ugly) physical state." In a voice that breaks my heart he says, "I ken' not bear ta' see the reflection of ma' misery in the beautiful eyes of ma' Lady, Lass."

I'm still unsure as to how I managed not to fall on my knees in a weeping mess when I saw, first-hand, the extent of damage done to my Beloved's body. There isn't a single spot, from the top of his head to the soles of his feet, that isn't covered in burns, bruises, welts, and cuts. I gather whatever calm I can muster from the very center of my soul, then undress without a word and join him in the shower where I proceed to gently kiss each and every wound on his battered and mangled form. We stay in that shower a long time, locked in an embrace, ignoring my leaky boobs, letting the water run over us until we begin to turn water-logged. But when we emerge from that experience, I feel like we've turned a major corner in an attempt to move forward from the nightmare of the past month.

We find our daily affirmation and joy in our beautiful son, and like every new parent, take delight in the care of him, not even minding the sleepless nights or the count-less wet diapers. We are blessed to have Freza and Tobias who keep the household going, allowing Declan and I to focus all of our attention and energy on becoming a family. It is exactly the reason why the intrusion into our cozy cocoon feels akin to having a mega-ton boulder dropped on our heads.

In the past few days, we've had more than our fair share of visitors since arriving home with Dylan. Friends and family have been thoughtful about keeping their conversations upbeat and their visits short, and in all truthfulness, we do enjoy showing off our sweet baby boy. So, when the Black Knight shows up at our door one evening, gift in hand, the alarm bells in my head that usually accompany a visit from the long arm of Other-worldly law, are lulled into a false sense of security. "Beck," as my husband calls him, says all the right things, coos appropriately at the baby, and watches as we unwrap a beautiful, knitted baby blanket, a treasure wrought by the very hands of the Princess of *I Idir*. It's not until he asks us if perhaps we could sit down and talk a bit does the bottom fall out of my stomach.

Declan takes my hand in his, obviously concerned as well. "What news da' ya' bring us, Beck? I ken' tell that yar' uneasy about this conversation. I read it in yar' aura. I think it's best ya' just come right out and tell us what has ya' so worried."

The Knight folds his hands in his lap. "I hate to be the bearer of more bad news, especially so soon after the arrival of your son, but I'm afraid that what I have to tell you can't be delayed. It seems there's been a great deal of fall-out over Her Highness's...extraction mission. As you yourself are aware, Fitz, The Morrigan inflicted a decimating massacre on North Korea's key people and their lab facilities in her attempt to pull you out. Reliable intel has them plotting extreme revenge on key targets in our own ranks, yourself included."

I feel my heart-racing. This is like a terrible *deja vu* scene I can't escape. I squeeze my husband's hand tighter and he squeezes back, letting me know he understands my fear. "Their reaction isn't out of the ordinary, Beck," the Tax Man admits. "They all vow vengeance when we take them down, but sayin' it and actually havin' the means ta' wreak havoc are two different things. What makes ya' think we're actually in any real danger?"

"This time is different," Beck states. "This mission coming so close after the failed Chechen plot has our enemies up in arms over the idea that we are completely outmaneuvering them. The North Koreans have put out an 'all call' for any group that wants to join them in their fight against the 'Evil Fae Nation.' It's all over the dark web...this call to action. Our teams located in every part of the Mundane world are hearing lots of chatter on the subject with some intelligence teams already being targeted in the Eastern European block. We need to take this seriously. Her Majesty doesn't wish for a repeat of your capture, and unfortunately your name and photo, as well as that of your Lady, has shown up on these dark web sites. The Queen is asking that you take your Lady and your son and return to *I Idir* as soon as possible...for your own safety."

"For how long," my husband asks more calmly than I can believe.

"Hold on," I interject. "Are you saying we need to leave Salem? Immediately? And move to the Otherworld?"

The Black Knight looks at me with a grim expression. "I'm afraid that's exactly what I mean, Rosie. I'm sorry. I realize the timing is terrible…with Fitz just returned home and a new baby and all. But Her Majesty and I feel that under these circumstances we can't keep your family safe in the Mundane world." He pauses, and then adds, "If it makes you feel any better, Lady *Mac Nuada*, I'm sending my own Lady and daughter to *I Idir* as well. Even with the Royal Troll Guard camped out in my attic 24/7, I still feel that having them stay in the Mundane world is a serious risk. We have no idea the number of players involved in this pursuit."

"And the Lady Dear Heart is okay with this?" I ask, the horror in me growing by the second.

Beck makes a face. "As a matter of fact, she's not speaking to me at the moment so I'm led to believe that she's not okay with me insisting that she leave her home. But the facts remain as they are, and I will not put either my wife or my daughter at risk despite her negative feelings on the subject. I suspect your Lord will do exactly the same," he says as he gives my Tax Man a pointed look.

"Aye. I am walkin' proof of what those bastards are capable of," Declan says. "There is no feckin' chance I will risk even a hair on the head of either ma' *Mo Shiorghra* or ma' son. I will send them to *Dun Siorai* immediately. As far' me, my place is with ma' team. I plan on staying and facing what comes. The heir of House *Nuada* doesn't run and hide."

"The hell you are," I mutter. "I'm not going if you're not coming with us."

I get the "cranky Declan" look along with, "I am yar' husband, Rosalinda. You will do as I ask because ya' love and respect me."

I open my mouth to respond, but the Black Knight cuts me off. "I'm afraid your conversation about staying in the Mundane world is a moot point, Fitz. Not in your current state, anyway. You need time to heal, both physically and magically. In a few months, if Robyn says you're good to go, then you will return as your team's leader. Duncan will take over the team until you are well enough to take command again. I will see that you are kept in the loop about our progress. Until then, I expect you to follow my orders and return to *I Idir*. We are currently without a clear objective. As all this progresses, we'll have a better idea of a time frame, and I will need you back to work... fully healed."

I can tell by his blazing red aura that my husband is all-together embarrassed, upset, and angry over being side-lined from his intelligence work. I, however, am greatly relieved. I don't think I could handle another experience like the one I just had. If my son and I have no choice but to leave our home in the Mundane world, we sure as hell aren't going without our Tax Man.

BABY 73

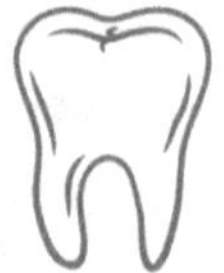

THE MOST EXCELLENT PLACE

THERE IS little time to debate an issue we have no control over. The next 46 hours are spent in a whirlwind frenzy preparing for our temporary move. At least that's the notion I try to convince myself of. This departure from my home is only a temporary situation. In a few months, the Black Knight will take care of all this terrorist shit, and the three of us will be able to go back to our normal lives. Or if not completely normal, at least back to the status quo that reigned before Declan left for North Korea. In the meantime, I tell my aching heart that this is the perfect opportunity for the three of us to bond as a family, and for me to learn more about my son's ancient heritage.

I am, fortunately, still on maternity leave, so preparations have already been put in place for my practice to run without me. If this debacle should run longer than the planned three months, then I may have issues to work out. But I don't even let my mind go that route. I know Mel will keep me in the know if anything out of the ordinary needs my attention. Surprisingly, my BFF has not been mandated to return to *I Idir,* as her relationship with Declan's cousin Duncan is not a well-known fact. She has, however, moved out of his place and back into her own apartment, and has been ordered not to be seen with him in the Mundane world, which undoubtedly means I'll be seeing plenty of her when the two love birds meet up in *I Idir.*

The handling of Declan's financial firm while he's in *I Idir* is a bit more complicated, being that he has clients all over the globe. While he'd been held by the North Koreans, the Black Knight had arranged for a firm within his holdings to cover Declan's clients. Now that the Tax Man was no longer in captivity, my husband wanted control of his company returned to him. Because so much of his work is done online, if D.P. Fitzpatrick had been anywhere else in the entire Mundane world, he could have worked efficiently from his laptop. This is not the case in the Fae Otherworld, where not a single piece of Mundane technology functions as it should and there is no such thing as the internet, thus making working from home far more difficult. Amid much scrambling, it's discovered that Connor Dell, a member of Declan's team and his good friend, has a *Sidhe* nephew who has just passed the bar in Massachusetts, is a whiz with numbers, and has a burning desire to be part of *I Idir's* political inner circle. It is decided that he will meet with the Tax Man in *I Idir* several times a week and handle things in the Mundane world at my husband's instruction. This requires a lot of back and forth between the Veil, which has proved to sometimes not be a good thing for one's health, but Rory Dell is set on making a name for himself at Court and is more than willing to take on the risks. Ah…the blind determination of youth.

Surprisingly, packing was the least complicated part of our move. We took only what we felt we couldn't live without during what might be a long stretch, items that were not available in the Otherworld. For me, that meant an over abundant supply of disposable diapers to use instead of the cloth nappies that were the norm in *I Idir,* several pieces of needlepoint I'd been working on for my dollhouses, and six bags of Swedish Fish, a passion I'd developed while pregnant. Declan's must haves include two pairs of his favorite running shoes and shorts, a stack of paperback crime novels by his favorite Mundane authors, and his favorite faded jeans and white T-shirt, which I imagine are more for me than him, if you get my drift. There is no guarantee all these things will make it unscathed to the other side. Sometimes things break down on a molecular level in the crossing, but we plan on giving it the good old college try anyway. It makes the idea of leaving home less overwhelming.

This evening, we are gathered in the living room of our newly remodeled home. "Beck" has promised to send someone capable of moving all three of us, as well as all of our necessities, safely and efficiently to *I Idir.* The fact that my husband can't move us himself, injuries to his magical energy field being far too extensive to risk it, only makes him more disgruntled and ashamed, thus leaving me with "cranky Declan"…on steroids. Though we expect someone with considerable magical ability, we are not prepared when the Lord Merlin himself, Ambrose James Myrdynn, appears on our stoop.

The presence of someone of such magical esteem doesn't help matters regarding my husband's insecurities over his current physical and magical state. The Tax Man is the sweetest, most loving, most honorable man I know, but like most *Sidhe* males of ancient blood lines, he has a Fae ego that matches his ginormous shoe size. The knowledge that the most powerful mage in all of *I Idir* is here to witness what Lord *Mac Nuada* considers a personal failure, digs heavily at his self-confidence.

The Merlin, himself, is a very unassuming, calm and reflective soul, the complete opposite of his fiery Knight of a son. He is, first and foremost, a sincere practicing Druid, and he always gives me the impression that he is completely in tune with the will of the Universe. I don't believe for one moment that he views my husband in any negative light. In fact, I think it's just the opposite, but of course, my husband is in no mood to consider such deeper thoughts.

"This must be a difficult day for the three of you," the Merlin says. "Leaving home can cause all types of negative energy within your soul. Try and give yourself over to the path you've been set on and trust things are as they are meant to be." When neither of us respond, too lost in our own emotions, the mage draws a large circle around my family, the one large trunk, and the *Nuada* family cradle that I insist we take along. In my arms, our son fusses and squirms in response to the building energy of the magical circle that I'm sure his *Sidhe* blood can feel but not understand.

"Are you ready to go," the wizard asks.

I nod my head in agreement, but my husband speaks up. "I need to get these heavy thoughts off my chest, Lord Merlin, lest I put walls up against your magic."

"Then speak you must, Lord *Mac Nuada*. Say what's in your heart so that you can let it go," Lord Merlin advises.

The Tax Man takes my free hand in his and looks at me with such grief and sorrow that my heart begins beating faster in my chest. Up until now, I've been doing a decent job keeping my anxiety over this turn of events at bay, but now, seeing my husband's face like this, I can't help but be worried about what's going on here. "I am so sorry, ma' Love…so vera, vera sorry that this is the life I've put in front of ya'," my *Mo Shiorghra* confesses. "Since the vera moment I came inta' yar' life, I've done nothin' but cause ya' distress and heartache. I am surely cursed as they say, and I am sorry ya' have joined yourself with such a wretched soul as me. It kills me ta' say this, but I wish for all the love I hold for ya' that the Universe had found ya' someone more deservin' of yar' beautiful soul."

Maybe it's the presence of the Merlin…his calm sense of acceptance…or maybe it's my own Druid beliefs kicking in…but I can clearly see this for what it is; a man, both Fae and human, overwhelmed by all the things that have been thrown in his path these past ten months. The Tax Man is simply having his own pity party. I get it. We are all entitled to them at some point or another. Hell knows…I've had my own share of them, one as recently as a few days ago. But not for one moment do I truly believe that Declan wishes me joined to anyone other than himself. I start to explain this, but my husband stops me. "Don' try an' disagree, love. Ya' know in yar' heart what I'm sayin' is true. If it weren't far' me, ya 'would no havin' ta' be leavin' this home in the Mundane world ya' love so much."

I look at the Merlin standing outside the circle. "Can you give us a minute, please."

The faintest smile dresses his usually composed expression. "As you wish, Lady *Mac Nuada*. Take all the time you need." Then he politely steps back, though I'm pretty sure not out of hearing range.

I push Dylan, who is now making his feelings known rather vocally, towards my husband. "Here…hold your son for a minute." Declan takes possession of the baby, who notes that he's been passed off to his father, and instantly quiets down in curiosity. I place each of my hands on both sides of my husband's cheeks. "Listen up, Tax Man…and listen good."

His Jr. Lordship makes a face at the pressure I'm using with my hands. "Ouch! Ya' don' have ta' press so hard, Love."

"I want to be sure I have your full attention, Mr. Fitzpatrick. I understand that we haven't had the smoothest of journeys so far. In fact, we've probably been tested more than the average couple…Fae or otherwise. However, not in the least do I ever regret having the Universe send you as my *Mo Shiorghra*…and I know unequivocally that you feel the same exact way." I put a hand to my heart. "I feel it here," and then point to my head, "and here as well. The whole time you were in

North Korea, I felt your presence. It's how I kept going day after day."

"I felt you as well, Love," he admits. " 'twas all that kept me from given' up."

"Then how can you say that the Universe didn't make the perfect choice for us both? Look at that baby in your arms. He's living proof this is our right path."

"Aye, but look what it's all come ta', Lass? Ya' said so yourself…this home is where yar' happiest. Now because of me ya' have ta' take your wee *bairn* and leave it at a time when here is right where ya' wanna' be…just ta' end up spendin' time with ma' own unhappy family."

By now I'm getting tired of standing in this circle, and if we don't get to *I Idir* soon, I'll have to stop this whole party, nurse Dylan, and take care of my postpartum, lady necessities before we can prepare to leave again. A way for me to have the last word, something my husband always insists on having, comes to mind. I roll my tongue and do my best Declan impersonation. "A vera wise man once said ta' me, 'Home is whar' ya' are, Lass. The bricks, the stones, the location don' mean a feckin' thing without the one true desire of yar' heart.'"

"Don' be coy, Lass. Ya' know vera well I said that ta' ya'," his Jr. Lordship admits.

"Of course you did, Tax Man! Do you honestly think that I would feel any different? My home is anywhere you and Dylan are. Your family is my family, in all the good and bad this situation will undoubtedly cover."

"'Tis probably more bad than good waitin' at *Dun Siorai*, dearest Lady. My House tends ta' be a bit on the…

ornery side. I hope time there won't trample on yar' lovin' spirit."

"I've seen the 'ornery' of House *Nuada* up close and personal, your Lordship. Good grief...your own sister tried to murder me. Rest assured, I'm well aware of what's waiting for me at your ancestral home. You have to know, after all that's happened since we've met, that I'm just the right girl for those many challenges," I reply.

"Aye. There's no doubt that ya are, *Beag Tiogair* (Little Tiger). I love you, Sweet Rosie Lass."

I wrap my arms around my husband's waist, our son tucked between us. "I love you too, Tax Man." I call out to Lord Merlin, whom I'm sure has heard every word of our not-so-private conversation. "You can take us home now, Lord Merlin. We have everything we need."

Find out what happens to Rosie, Declan and their new
baby boy in
Wisdom Tooth And The Awful Truth

About the Author

Victoria Rocus is a retired educator, accomplished miniaturist, and full-time author living near the home of country music, Nashville, Tennessee, USA. When she's not writing new adventures for her imaginary friends, catering beach parties for mermaids, or finding homes for orphaned dragons, she's building and rehabbing one-of-a-kind dollhouses and accessories, just like her favorite character, Dr. Rosie Parker. Many of her multiple miniature buildings are 1/12 scale replicas of settings from her unique fantasy stories.

Victoria started her writing career as a weekly blogger while still teaching middle school language arts. Now retired from the educational field, she's been able to make writing a full-time adventure, penning several fantasy and romance stories she hopes readers will enjoy with both a sigh and a smile.

Find out more at: victoriarocusauthor.com

instagram.com/victoriarocusauthor
tiktok.com/@victoriarocusauthor

Acknowledgments

As I hold each finished book in my hands, it still humbles me to know how many talented, helpful, and generous souls are involved in its creation. Every tome is surely a community effort for which I am eternally grateful. As always, thanks to Sarah Williams, Tim Coulson and the team at Serenade Publishing for making sure Rosie and Declan always look and sound their best. No one does it better.

I am forever grateful to my regular Beta team; Carol Peden Fuller, Donna Gentile-Ruth, Michele S. Kaspar, Daniel Caddigan, and Kaia Vinney, along with fellow authors, Arla Jones and K.C. Nord, who always "tell me like it is."

A special shout-out to Marcia Joy Wurmbrand Crabtree for helping me name "bad girl Marcy," a character we all love to hate. Also, much thanks to Shannon Greene for your constant support all the way back to my blogging days. So glad to have you both on this journey with me.

To my husband Victor, for calling me an "author" long before I felt like one, and to my children, Steven, Michael and and Allison. I am forever grateful for your unshakeable confidence in me and what I could someday accomplish. Special hugs and kisses to my beautiful, new granddaughter, Valerie James, who was only a dream at the time this story was being drafted, and is now a precious, living treasure in our family arms.

Most importantly, a huge and exuberant note of appreciation to my readers for sharing your precious reading time with Rosie and Declan. Your support and loyalty mean the world to me. Sending a big thank you from the bottom of my story-telling heart, now and always.